Praise for P. C. Hodgell's
Dark of the Gods omnibus and *Seeker's Mask*

God Stalk

"Out of the Haunted Lands to the city of Tai-tastigon comes Jame, one of the few remaining Kencyr left to carry on their millennium-long battle against Perimal Darkling, an entity of primal evil. Establishing herself in the city, Jame becomes an apprentice in the Thieves' Guild, make friends and enemies, and begins to develop her magical abilities. Hodgell has crafted an excellent and intricate fantasy, with humor and tragedy, and a capable and charming female hero. Highly recommended."—*Library Journal*, September 15, 1985

"*God Stalk* by P.C. Hodgell takes some familiar elements of fantasy—a city of many gods, a Thieves' Guild, a heroine with the strange powers of an ancient race—and blends them into a delightful concoction bubbling with originality. The heroine, Jame, stumbles into the city of Tai-tastigon suffering from amnesia and the strain of headlong flight from her enemies. She finds herself in an apparently uninhabited maze, a chaos of weird supernatural effects. When the inhabitants finally appear, they're a quirky, lively, and (most of them) down-to-earth group who draw Jame into the network of their lives and concerns.

With this novel, [Hodgell] makes a promising debut, and its sequels could turn out to be major contributions to the fields."—*Locus*, September, 1982

"It's become increasingly hard to do anything new in the high-fantasy field, but there's still a big difference between those who can only reheat the same old stew and those who can take full advantage of all that's been done before to brew up a fresh mix. Hodgell proves with this debut novel to be in the latter group.

Jame is a fully fleshed character in a rich fantasy milieu influenced by the likes of C.L. Moore and Elizabeth Lynn. Like their work, this novel and the series it begins should prove popular."—*Publishers' Weekly*, September 21, 1982

"Those who regard fantasy as an insignificant branch of the literary tree lack understanding of the many ways in which all people approach that mystic realm we call 'reality.' Reading *God Stalk* might allow them to confront a few of their own demons. For the rest of us, whether because we are seeking ways of looking at our lives through fiction or because we simply want to explore someone else's vision, Hodgell's book is a dramatic introduction to a new world that both embodies and transcends our own."—*The Minnesota Daily*, September 28, 1982

Dark of the Moon

"In *God Stalk*, P.C. Hodgell set in motion a convoluted plot involving such standard elements of fantasy as dark lords, thieves' guilds, and homey inns, and she transcended convention through sheer force of imagination. The sequel, *Dark of the Moon*, takes all these tendencies even further, with more convolutions, more familiar themes, and—again—a redeeming, delightful originality of vision.

Already she brings a welcome freshness and flair to a field where creativity often seems more the exception than the rule."—*Locus*, September, 1985

"P.C. Hodgell is one of the best young fantasy writers we have and yet her work is not all that well known. This is partly due to her low productivity (two novels and a handful of short stories in the last ten years) and partly due to the difficulty and darkness of her work. Where so much of contemporary fantasy seems to consist of little more than a mindless reworking of Tolkien and Howard, Hodgell's affinities lie with the complex plotting of Mervyn Peake, the dark humor of Fritz Leiber, and the gruesomely poetic detail work of Clark Ashton Smith."—*Fantasy Magazine*, October 1985

Seeker's Mask

"You come away from one of Pat's books with your mind and heart humming. The reverberations of what you've read carry through into the world beyond the book's pages and you see things differently. Connections that originated in the novels link with our own lives, offering insights and questions, both of which are important as we make our way through the confusing morass of the world. The insights show us established paths we can take that we might not have seen before. The questions make us look a little harder so that we can forge our own routes.

"Like many of us, Pat has cast her net into the pool of what went before, but unlike most, she replenishes those waters with more than what she took. You can't ask much more of an artist and for Pat's unwavering commitment to give us so much, she deserves not only our support, but our admiration and respect as well.

"Pat Hodgell is one of the original voices and great talents of our field and I couldn't be happier to see her work back in print once more, with at least a fourth novel scheduled to appear in the future. If you're new to her work, get comfortable and allow a master storyteller to take you in hand."—Charles de Lint

BLOOD AND IVORY: A TAPESTRY

A COLLECTION OF SHORT STORIES AND ART

BY

P. C. HODGELL

Meisha Merlin Publishing, Inc
Atlanta, GA

This is a work of fiction. All the characters and events portrayed in this book are fictitious. Any resemblance to real people or events is purely coincidental.

All rights reserved by the publisher. This book may not be reproduced, in whole or in part, without the written permission of the publisher, except for the purpose of reviews.

Hearts of Woven Shadow Copyright © 2002 by P. C. Hodgell,
(Original to this collection.)
Lost Knots Copyright © 2002 by P. C. Hodgell,
(Original to this collection.)
Among the Dead Copyright © 2002 by P. C. Hodgell,
(Original to this collection.)
Child of Darkness Copyright © 1980 by P. C. Hodgell,
(Originally appeard in *Berkley Showcase Number II.*)
A Matter of Honor Copyright © 1977 by P. C. Hodgell,
(Originally appeared in *Clarion SF.*)
Bones Copyright © 1984 by P. C. Hodgell,
(Originally appeared in *Elsewhere Volume III.*)
Stranger Blood Copyright © 1985 by P. C. Hodgell,
(Originally appeared in *Imaginary Lands.*)
A Ballad of the White Plague Copyright © 2002 by P. C. Hodgell
(Originally appeared in *The Confidential Casebook of Sherlock Holms*)
All interior art work done by, and copyrighted by P. C. Hodgell
Blood and Ivory: A Taperstry Copyright © 2002 by P. C. Hodgell

PLEASE HELP FIGHT INTERNET PIRACY. Scanning and uploading this novel to the internet without the author's permission is not an act of flattery. It is an act of ***theft***. It is not only disrespectful to the author; it violates the author's copyright and takes money from the author's pocket by disseminating copies for which no royalties are paid.

BLOOD AND IVORY: A TAPESTRY

Published by Meisha Merlin Publishing, Inc.
PO Box 7
Decatur, GA 30031

Editing & interior layout by Stephen Pagel
Copyediting & proofreading by Josh Mitchell
Cover art by Christian McGrath
Interior art by P. C. Hodgell
Cover design by Kevin Murphy

ISBN: Hard cover   1-892065-72-X
        Soft cover   1-892065-73-8

http//www.MeishaMerlin.com

First MM Publishing edition: September 2002

Printed in the United States of America
0 9 8 7 6 5 4 3 2 1

Table of Contents

Hearts of Woven Shadow	13
Lost Knots	51
Among the Dead	59
Child of Darkness	85
A Matter of Honor	115
Bones	139
Stranger Blood	169
Maps	231
Art	241

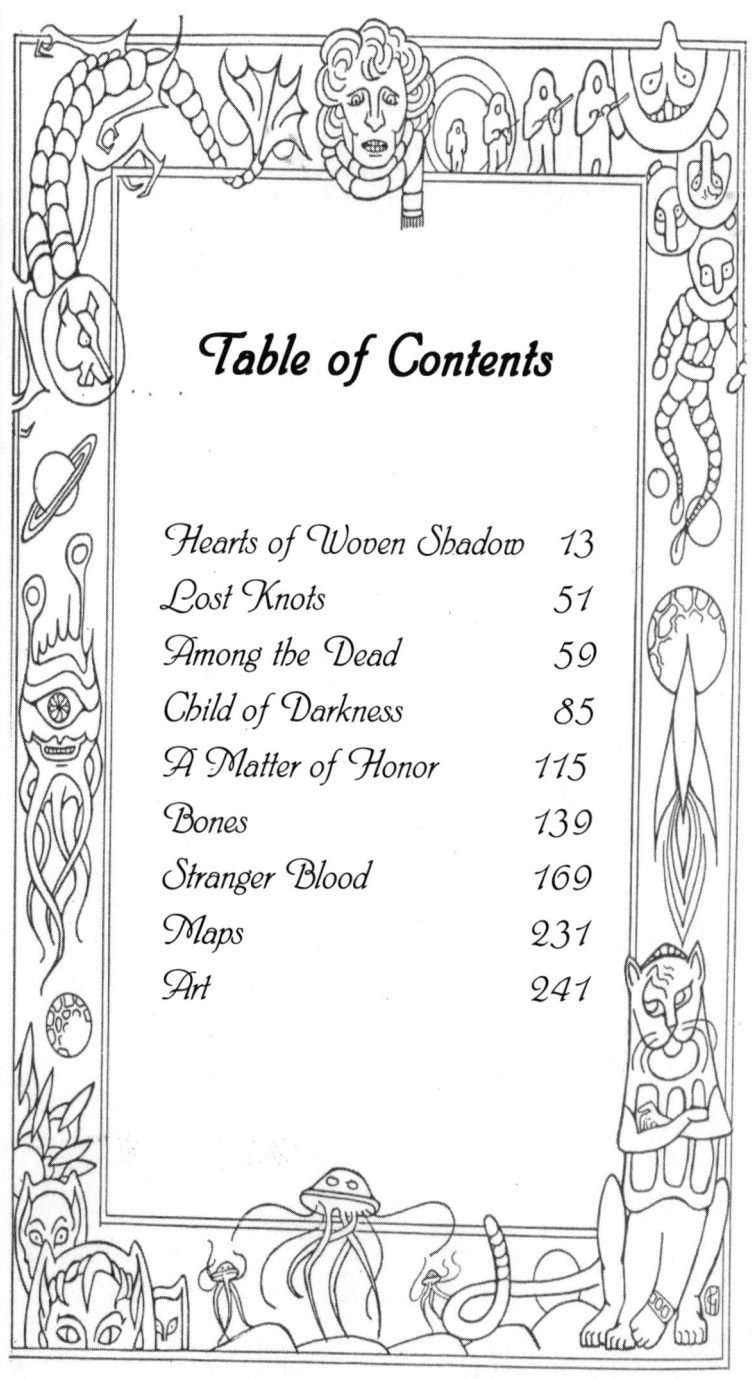

BLOOD AND IVORY: A TAPESTRY

An introduction to "Hearts of Woven Shadow," "Lost Knots," and "Among the Dead"

Epic fantasies usually begin *in medias res*, in the middle of things. Consider, for example, how much history comes before we meet Frodo Baggins in *The Lord of the Rings*, and I'm not just talking about its prequel, *The Hobbit*. *The Silmarillion* will give you a better idea. In this eon-long context, the One Ring can be seen as merely a loose end that must be tidied up before it and its master can destroy all of Middle-earth, smashing sundry lives in the process including those of various innocent hobbits.

This pattern runs through much of modern fantasy. The past is a looming shadow that shapes the present and threatens the future. Characters thus totter between light and dark, between simple, everyday life and cosmic destruction, on a scale that sometimes boggles the mind even of their creator.

To lower our discourse a notch, I have always been aware that certain events in the past shape my heroine Jame's life and world. Gerridon's fall is perhaps the most dramatic instance—all the more so because, like Sauron, Gerridon is still active behind the scenes some three thousand years later. In fact, he is Jame's uncle because his sister-consort, Jamethiel Dream-Weaver, is Jame's mother. How (and why) that happened is central to Jame's story. It also matters, of course, to her twin brother Torisen. They and one other are the innocents in my story, at least so far.

I knew many of the details before I sat down to write the following three stories, which appear here for the first time anywhere. However, I hadn't thought out all the ramifications. The time-line came as a surprise. So did Ganth Gray Lord, Jame and Tori's father. Is he also an innocent?

You decide.

P.C.

The Riverland

- HIGH KEEP (MIN-DREAR)
- MERIKIT VILLAGE
- KITHORN (RUINS)
- TAGMETH (RUINS)
- RESTORMIR (CAINERON)
- RIVER ROAD
- SNOWTHORNS
- VALANTIR (JARAN)
- MOUNT ALBAN (SCROLLSMEN'S COLLEGE)
- TENTIR (RANDON COLLEGE)
- WILDEN (RANDIR AND PRIESTS' COLLEGE)
- SHADOW ROCK (DANIOR)
- FALKIRR (BRANDON)
- CHANTRIE (RUINS)
- GOTHREGOR (KNORTH)
- OMIROTH (ARDETH)
- NEW ROAD
- KRAGGEN (COMAN)
- KESTRIE (EDIRR)
- THE SILVER
- OSEEN HILLS
- 0 25 50 MILES
- THE WHITE HILLS
- WYRDEN

P.C. HODGELL

HEARTS OF WOVEN SHADOW

Gothregor
2983

It was the sixth night of summer, and the moon was dark. High over the Riverland, wisps of cloud blew confusedly this way and that, making the stars flicker. Mountains blotted out the sky to east and west, but the hunched, gathering darkness to the north was far more profound, and ominous.

Gothregor's forecourt lay in deep shadow. Across it, however, the gallery windows of the Women's Halls flared briefly with wary light and flickered with shadows. No one slept. The fortress waited and watched as it had night after night after night.

"Dead!" cried a muffled voice. Stone ground on stone as if the very walls shrank from that terrible cry. "Dead, dead, dead!"

Between the forecourt and the inner ward of Gothregor rose the keep, ancient, fragile heart of House Knorth on Rathillien. Its door opening into darkness. The low-beamed hall within seemed to exhale—*haaaaa*—its chill breath rank with a hideous stench and the buzz of flies. Inside, footsteps paced the stone floor, their echo instantly smothered. On and on they went, around and around, and a low, hoarse voice went with them, muttering.

"How l-long?" asked one of the people standing in the doorway. He spoke in a husky whisper, as if the smell had taken him by the throat.

A large shape moved uneasily behind him. Furtive light from the windows opposite caught the glint of a randon captain's silver collar. "Five days, lord. Ever since we brought the body back from the college at Tentir. He won't let the priests have it."

"Sweet Trinity. A soul trapped for f-five days in a rotting carcass...I don't understand." The Highborn ran distraught fingers through dark hair flecked with gray. He was young, barely eighteen, but life had already raked him with its claws. "What h-happened, Sere? How did my brother die? And why wasn't I told sooner? God's claws, I was only upriver at Wilden on house business! You m-must have passed right by me on the River Road, without a word. If this lady hadn't somehow learned of it..."

"I'd like to know how," muttered the tall Kendar named Sere.

He shot a hard look at the slender young woman standing back a pace, listening, motionless except for where the fretful wind teased her traveling cloak. Under hood and mask, her expression was unreadable.

Behind her, her attendant smirked. The lower half of his face seemed briefly to distort, the lip's corner hitching up into the shadow of his cowl, then snapping solemn-straight again.

Sere blinked, then rubbed tired eyes and turned his back on them both.

"The Randon College at Tentir has been sealed to prevent spread of the news," he said to the Highborn in a low voice. "The Commandant was to have come with us to explain what happened, but he preferred the White Knife. So have many here."

Behind him, another burst of flame bloomed above a courtyard hidden within Gothregor's crouching darkness. A gust of wind breathed the stench of pyres into the forecourt, and stray ashes drifted down, silent calamity riding the air.

"I have seen war, and death, and madness, but this...The Highlord's grief is...terrible. And contagious." A tremor, frightening in itself, shook his strong voice. "I think it could almost unmake our world. We randon are trained, after a fashion, to protect ourselves; but our children aren't. Lord, *do* something. After all, *you* are the Knorth Heir now."

The young Highborn flinched. "Trinity. I'd forgotten that. What a m-mess, and how like my dear brother to have caused it, even in death." He swallowed, and his thin face sharpened. "All right. Wait here. You too, lady."

Skirts rustled impatiently. "But..."

He rounded on her with a suppressed violence that sent her gliding backward several steps into the windy forecourt. Her attendant skipped out of the way.

"I said, *wait!*"

It was almost a berserker flare. The big randon tensed.

The hooded attendant put his hand on the young woman's shoulder and leaned forward to whisper in her ear. Her lips twitched into a brief smile.

"I had forgotten," she said in a low, pleasant voice, the purr of a cat to a mouse. "You were expelled from Tentir last fall, were you not, dear Ganth, for your...er...temper, as well as for that other thing which we Randir will never forget."

"M'lord Grayling left by choice," said the Kendar sharply. "You know very well, lady, that no blood price can be demanded for any...um...accident at the college. Even a fatal one. We wish he had stayed."

"To learn s-s-self—" Ganth clenched his fists, fighting the nervous stammer. "Control. There. As you see, I am neither berserker nor god-cursed S-s-shanir. I am *not.*"

"So you say," murmured the lady, "and so, of course, you are. Or not."

Ganth Grayling took a deep breath. It was hard to remember how irresistible he had found this girl when they had first met, he a shy boy of thirteen, she a fine young lady at least three years his senior.

It had been Autumn's Eve, five years ago. His father was in the keep's low hall, chanting the names of the dead to keep their memory alive as he did every year on this night. The only better immortality was to win one's way into a singer's song or a scrollsman's scroll. Ganth's brother Greshan should have been with him, but had gone hunting instead. Time enough later, he had said, to learn who was who in that moldy gallery and Father, laughing, had let him go. There had been no question of his younger brother taking his place. After all, Ganth would never be highlord—or anything else worthwhile, according to Greshan. So he had walked among the white flowers of his grandmother's garden, wanted nowhere, feeling lonely and restless. Then, suddenly, there she was, black and silver in the starlight.

She shouldn't have been in the Moon Garden at all, of course: Highborn girls were usually confined to the Women's Halls of Gothregor where they were taught to become proper ladies. Then too, she had been trespassing on Knorth ground, avid to see how the Highlord's family lived; and he had been charmed into showing her.

"Lady Rawneth of the Randir," he said now with brittle courtesy. "I am s-sorry for your loss in this most recent tragedy, if one can be said to lose what one has never actually possessed, but this business concerns only my h-house."

As he turned back to the dark hall, the Kendar touched his arm. "Lord, be careful. He drove us out with Kin-Slayer, unsheathed."

The Highborn hesitated. That ill-omened blade had never yet been drawn without shedding blood.

He wished suddenly, intensely, that the randon would go in with him, and not for fear of any sword. Last fall, it was Sere who had welcomed him to Tentir, to the start of a new life as a randon cadet. He had thought, surrounded by so many other students, it would not matter that Greshan was also at the college, starting his final year. It had mattered. Now he must face his brother again...and his father. Alone.

Ganth stepped over the threshold and began to pull the door shut after him. Its lower edge grated loudly on the uneven floor.

The footsteps stopped. "Who's there?"

"I, Highlord." He fumbled for steel and flint on a ledge beside the door. "Your son."

The answer came in a hoarse howl, raw with pain. "My son is dead!" The hall seemed to rock. Ganth caught the doorpost to steady himself.

"Your other s-son, lord. Ganth Grayling."

He found the first wall torch by touch, struck fire, and kindled it, then the next, and the next. Between them, faces moved uneasily in the flaring light. Men and women, young and old, portrait tapestries woven out of threads teased from the clothes in which each had died—all had the distinctive Knorth faces: high cheekbones, large silver-gray eyes, thin mouths often twisted in pain, or arrogance, or cruelty. Kendar weavers had the right to portray their Highborn masters as they had been in life.

They had been kind (thank Trinity!) to his mother, Telarien, dead less than a year with the birth of her last child—Tieri, a daughter. She hung in shadow on the far wall, her death still a wound too raw to face.

These banners, however, were far more ancient, layered, many dating back to the Fall nearly three millennia ago. Unbidden, the ancient lament echoed in his mind:

Gerridon Highlord, Master of Knorth, a proud man was he. The Three People held he in his hands—Arrin-ken, Highborn, and Kendar. Wealth and power had he and knowledge deeper than the Sea of Stars. But he feared death. "Dread Lord," said Gerridon to the Shadow that Crawls, even to Perimal Darkling, ancient of enemies, "my god regards me not. If I serve thee, wilt thou preserve me, even to the end of time?" Night bowed over him. Words they spoke. Then went my lord Gerridon to his sister and consort, Jamethiel Dream-Weaver, and said, "Dance out the souls of the faithful, that darkness may enter in." And she danced.

Two-thirds of the Kencyrath had fallen that night and stayed in the shadows to serve their dire master until, one by one, he devoured their souls, reaped for him by the Dream-Weaver. That was the price of his immortality, paid by others.

But these Kencyr had escaped, following their new Highlord, Glendar, into this new world, Rathillien. *"A watch we will keep,"* they had said, *"and our honor someday avenge. Alas for the greed of a man and the deceit of a woman, that we should come to this!"*

Three thousand years ago. One hundred and fifty generations. Now here they hung moldering in a dark hall, as long as thread clung to thread and their names were remembered.

Ganth flinched. Starting out of the shadows in front of him was a tapestry that had given him and many another of his house nightmares since childhood. Perhaps that was its purpose. Although one of the oldest banners in the hall, it was always hung outermost, "to warn."

"Of w-what?" Ganth had once asked his grandmother, Kinzi.

"Of heart's desire," she had said. "Of passions strong enough to break the soul. We are a passionate house, and not always wise."

Most of the dead were portrayed with hands lowered in benediction. This woman, however, had raised them to cover her face. Blood ran down between her long fingers, each one tipped with an ivory claw, over gaunt cheeks, into a mouth that gaped in a silent scream.

Everyone knew that insanity ran in the Highlord's house. Most blamed it on the Shanir taint, the curse of the Old Blood, that carried with it both power and madness. This lady had been Shanir, allied by her traits to That-Which-Destroys, the Third Face of God. Power and madness, madness and...

Stop it, Ganth thought. Defiantly, he touched the woman's frayed cheek.

His fingers came away wet. The tapestry *was* bleeding. As he backed away, he saw that many more were as well. Blood trickled down their sodden threads and dripped, stealthily, onto the floor. The room brimmed with its furtive patter.

"Ancestors preserve me," he murmured, and turned.

Kin-Slayer's point wavered inches from the hollow of his throat. Down its flame-lit length, he met the pale, mad eyes of his father, Gerraint Highlord.

"Your brother was worth a dozen of you! Why is he dead and you still alive?"

The words fell like a sharp blow on thin ice. Beneath, Ganth sensed black waters, colder than death. Gerraint might say anything now. So might he. *Control,* he thought desperately, fighting to breathe. *Keep control. He is old, and sick with grief, and very, very dangerous.*

Skirts rustled behind them. Rawneth had followed Ganth into the hall and now stood by the pall-draped catafalque, her attendant hovering dusty black in her torch-cast shadow. She pushed back her hood. Firelight shone off sleek ebon hair, intricately braided.

"So it is true," she said, her voice muffled through the cloth that she held to her face against the stench. "I thought the rumor was a trick to put me off."

Gerraint stared at her. "You fool!" he spat at his son. "Why did you bring that woman here?"

Ganth stood still. Despite Kin-Slayer at his throat, he refused to back into that bleeding banner, within reach of those claw-tipped fingers. "You s-sent me to Wilden to make a contract with 'that woman,' Lord Randir's daughter, to heal the breach between our houses. Remember? However, Lady Rawneth preferred my brother Greshan to m-me, or perhaps only the next highlord to a second son."

"Ha. Not such a fool, then, as you."

"Oh!" Her exclamation made them both turn again sharply. "He moved!"

In a moment, Gerraint was beside the bier. He dropped Kin-Slayer, seized a cold, flaccid hand and chaffed it between his own scarcely warmer ones. "My son, my son, wake up! You can't be dead! I know you aren't!"

So far, death had scarcely touched Greshan's handsome face. In life, good looks and charm had always gotten him whatever he wanted—that, and being the long-desired, half-despaired of heir to a house desperately short on sons. Five years later, Ganth had come as such a surprise that Telarien had nearly died giving birth to him. She had never been well again. It was hard to tell whom Gerraint blamed most for her death: Ganth, the infant Tieri, or himself.

Now here lay Greshan, his only other son, like an effigy of the perfect hero, clothed in gilded leather armor whose gleam was only slightly dimmed by five days of dust. Beyond that, all that betrayed him was the dark fluid leaking from his mouth and nose and, like bloody tears, from under the long fringe of his eyelashes. That, and the flies.

His chest rose again slightly as if with a secret, in-drawn breath.

Aahhh...! breathed the death banners on the walls.

Neither they nor he exhaled. Leather armor strained taut, creaking, over Greshan's stomach.

"Gas," said Rawneth, with interest, drawing closer again. "The body is bloating. Do you suppose it will eventually explode?"

Ganth gingerly picked up Kin-Slayer. "Lady, for Perimal's s-s-sake!" And this was the man whom she had wanted for a consort?

Greshan had found them in Grandmother Kinzi's quarters. While going through the Matriarch's clothing chests, Rawneth had unearthed an intricate piece of needlework, ivory with age. She was fingering it while Ganth looked on, increasingly nervous and anxious that she should leave. What if Gran came back? She was only across Gothregor in the Women's Halls, visiting the blind Ardeth Matriarch, Adiraina.

"Well, well, well." Greshan lounged in the doorway. He reeked of the hunt, of sweat, blood, and offal; a filthy, gorgeously embroidered coat was draped over one shoulder. Tunic laces hung loose, half undone, at his throat. "What have you brought me, Gander? Will I enjoy it?"

He and Rawneth talked. Afterward, Ganth couldn't remember exactly what they had said, only the tone, first wary on her part, then bantering on both.

They circled each other beside Kinzi's bed. Her long, black hair stirred and rose about her as if in an updraft, although the room was close and still. Her fingertips brushed against his bare chest, leaving faint red lines. He slid his hand (the nails dirty, Ganth noted with revulsion, dried blood caked under them) through her shining hair, then suddenly gripped it and jerked her face up to his. She stifled a cry, but tears of pain glittered on her cheeks. He bent his head, licked them off, and shuddered.

"Bitter," he said thickly. "And potent. Is the magic in your blood as strong?"

"Taste it and see."

The tendrils of black hair that had wound about his hand slowly relaxed into a caress. She gave a husky laugh.

"You should meet my cousin Roane. He likes to play games too."

"Later. Gangray, get out."

She eyed Ganth askance over Greshan's shoulder, black eyes glittering half in mockery, half in challenge. "Oh, let the little boy watch...unless he wishes to join us and become a man."

Let him watch.

Greshan had watched him at Tentir. Ganth hadn't noticed at first. There was so much to do, so much to learn. For the first time in his life, he had felt he might amount to something. He even had friends, after a fashion, with whom to swim after the dust and heat of the day. Then he had seen Greshan and the Randir Roane watching him from the bank. No one ever wore clothes in that mountain pool, but of them all only Ganth had felt suddenly, terribly, naked.

Now, beside his brother's bier, he looked down at Gerraint's wild, white hair, haloed by carrion flies, and his face twisted. "Father, please, let him go. Besides, h-he wasn't the hero you think. He could be petty, and vicious, and..."

Gerraint lunged. Ganth found himself trying to level Kin-Slayer at his father's throat to hold him off. The blade fell from his nerveless hand, ringing, onto the stone floor.

"A lesson for you, boy. Only those prepared to use that sword can wield it. What are you but an empty gesture? Petty? Vicious? *Greshan*?" He laughed, a bark of searing scorn. "Don't think I've forgotten the vile lies you told about him when you were both children. Oh, I knew then how little to value you!"

"What lies?" asked Rawneth.

Ganth shot her a harassed look. Lies were the death of honor. True or not, one did not speak of such things in front of an enemy, and that she clearly was, now and forever.

Gerraint had bent again over the body and cradled its face between his hands. Gelid blood oozed over his long, thin fingers and emerald signet ring, down the pall and onto the floor. Drip, drip, drip. "Oh, my son, my son. You should have come home in triumph, with full randon honors. Instead, your welcome feast rots in the hall and the dogs fight over it. I don't understand. I don't understand."

"Oh, but surely the Knorth Heir goes to Tentir for more than a pretty collar," said Rawneth. Her spy whispered in her ear again. "Ah. I see! The randon decide if he is worthy to become the next highlord. If not, well, unfit lordan have died at Tentir before, one way or another, have they not? Unavenged, too. As you keep telling me, Tentir will allow no blood price."

Ganth remembered how little attention Greshan had paid to his duties at Tentir, assuming that no one would dare deny the Knorth Lordan his collar in the end. Surely that hadn't been enough to get him killed, though. Besides, this past season the college had been under the command of the Knorth war-leader—until he had committed suicide rather than explain the Heir's death to his father.

We have enemies, Ganth thought, fully realizing it for the first time. *Perhaps even within our own halls.*

Gerraint was shaking his head, harder and harder. White hair whipped. "No, no, *no*! Greshan, unworthy? Madness. You!" He seized Ganth by the jacket. "Somehow, this is all your fault. You were always jealous of him!"

"No! Yes. S-sometimes. I had no cause to love him, but I never wished him dead. Trinity! D'you think I *want* to be the next highlord?"

"Over my dead body!"

"Of course," murmured Rawneth. "How else? And, of course, over Greshan's too."

Gerraint ignored her. "It goes back to last autumn and the death of that wretched Randir, doesn't it? *Doesn't it?* Damn you, boy, what did you *do?*"

"You know what I did." Ganth felt himself growing cold with anger and alarm. His stammer had disappeared. *Control*, he thought desperately. *Control. Remember only so much, nothing more.* "I killed Roane. At Tentir. In my brother's quarters. At three in the morning."

The dormitory in the Knorth barracks, the row of cots full of soft breathing. How many slept, exhausted by the day? How many lay awake, as he did, listening to his brother's nightly carousal in his chambers overhead?

(*Don't remember. Don't!* But he did.)

Greshan's drunken shout of laughter. Roane laughed too, but more softly. Ganth knew, instinctively, that the Randir was drinking one cup to every three of the Knorth Lordan, while seeming to keep pace. Roane had been the Heir's shadow ever since Ganth had come to Tentir, and probably before that. Together, they concocted the various cruel "jokes" for which Greshan was becoming famous. What were they plotting tonight?

A hand on his shoulder, making him jump. The voice of Roane's servant in his ear: "The Lordan wants you. In his quarters. Now."

Ganth wrenched his mind back to the present. He met Rawneth's eyes over his father's shoulder. "D-do you know what your cousin and my dear brother tried to do to me that night, lady?"

She shrugged, dismissing it. "Boys will be boys."

For the first time, the old man looked almost frightened. He clung to Ganth. "What is she saying? What does she mean?"

"If I told you, f-father, you would only call me a liar. Again."

"No." His grip tightened. "I won't listen. No, *no, NO!*"

Ganth cried out in pain as Gerraint's power surged through him, reaching out, ruthlessly pulling in strength from everyone, everything, bound to the Highlord's will, down to the very stones of Gothregor. Distant voices screamed. The whole fabric of the Knorth was being wrenched out of shape, about to tear. Through his father, Ganth felt minds shatter and spirits crack. His own heart lurched in his chest. He wondered if he was dying. He had often wanted to, but not now, not now. So this too was the power of a highlord, to break as well as to bind.

"I think it could unmake our world," the randon captain had said.

Ganth could sense him now, standing outside the door of the keep like a rock, all his training at full stretch to anchor the Knorth's reeling soulscape. Other wills scattered throughout the fortress joined his, most randon but one above all others so strong that Ganth could see her standing small and gallant at her window overlooking the Moon Garden—his grandmother Kinzi, the Knorth Matriarch. Behind her, a lesser presence but still there, adding her strength, was his young cousin Aerulan, and in her arms his infant sister Tieri.

Kinzi was staring across the dark roofs at the tower keep.

"Gerraint!" she cried. Her high, clear voice rang through the troubled air, piercing bone and stone. Dull thunder from the north rumbled under it. "What are you doing? Stop it, at once!"

Her cry flung father and son apart. Gerraint staggered against the bier, shaking it; Ganth reeled into the eastern wall and slid down its pad of banners to the floor.

"Not...strong...enough," Gerraint panted.

Rawneth stood rigid with anger. "Kinzi. Always Kinzi."

Just so, she had bared her teeth at the Knorth Matriarch on that distant night when Kinzi had found Rawneth and Greshan in her quarters. Perhaps Kinzi had even heard the Randir's last, taunting words flung at a young Ganth: "*Let him watch...unless he wishes to join us and become a man.*"

Ganth had always thought of his grandmother as a fine-boned sparrow. True, she was remarkably trim and unusually small for a Highborn. When he hugged her, he could rest his chin on the top of her neatly groomed head. That seemed so strange since all his life, growing up, he had only felt safe in her shadow. Greshan had jeered at him for that, but never in front of Grandmother herself. No one laughed at Kinzi Keen-Eyed.

Before, Ganth had never quite understood. She was his dear, tiny Gran, who sang at dawn as sweet as any bird and loved riddles. He had smiled at rumors that the Highlord did nothing without her advice and had dismissed whispered stories of her fabled rage, which he had never seen.

He saw it now.

Greshan's sneer froze. Slack-jawed, for once he looked every inch the stupid man that he was. He gasped. His breath smoked on the suddenly chill air.

Kinzi stood in the doorway, motionless. "Leave," she said to her grandson, in a tone to freeze the blood. "Now." Greshan goggled at her, made a choking sound, and reeled past, out of the room.

Knorth and Randir faced each other.

"So. You would bind the Highlord's heir if you could."

"Do you think it beyond me, Matriarch?"

"I think you believe that very little is."

They were circling each other now, gliding, the tall, elegant girl and the tiny old woman. Ganth backed into the corner, as far away as he could get. It seemed to him as if the room was tilting this way and that, twisted by the clash of their wills; but there was no question who was the stronger.

Kinzi held out her small hand. "Give me that."

Ganth realized that all this time Rawneth had been clutching the embroidery with its fine pattern of knotwork. Now she tried instinctively to hide it behind her back, but Kinzi's hand was still out. Step by grudging step, she drew the younger woman to her and took the cloth from her grasp.

"If I were to tell the Highlord what those knots say..." Rawneth began defiantly.

"Would you indeed, and betray the very heart of the Women's World? What Adiraina writes in the love-knots of this old letter is meant for me alone."

"If I told..."

"You would be excluded forever from the solace of sisterkin-ship—if, indeed, anyone should ever want you. As it is, I cast you out from the Women's Halls. Never come back. And leave my grandson alone. He may be a fool, but he is not for the likes of you, nor do you want him for anything but his bloodlines. I smell your ambition, girl, rank as a whore's lust."

The Randir drew herself up, trembling with rage.

"Do you think you Knorth will rule the Kencyrath forever," she spat, "you, who are already so few? And who will come next, when your oh-so-pure blood is finally spent? Do you think about that, old woman, in the long nights? You should. Change is coming. I have foreseen it. I am part of it."

"Not today. Not while I live. Go, snake-heart. Now."

And Rawneth went, out of the room, out of the Knorth quarters, out of Gothregor.

Kinzi sank onto her bed and dropped her head into her trembling hands. She looked suddenly smaller and more vulnerable than Ganth had ever seen her. It frightened him.

She looked up. "Ah, child. You shouldn't have seen that. Forget."

And he had, until now.

"Kinzi," Rawneth was saying through clenched teeth. "Always Kinzi. She is stronger than you, Highlord, and perhaps always has been. I see that now. Still, there may be another way." She frowned, thinking.

Her servant drew silently back, as if to give her mind room to work. His shadow, separated from hers, sprawled grotesquely at his feet, twitching, ever changing.

A slow smile crossed her face. "There are older powers on Rathillien than ours, and other gods. If I call them, perhaps they will come. But first...Highlord, if I bring Greshan back, do you swear on your honor that he will take me for his consort, with the option for children? One legitimate son would suffice."

"Father, no!" Ganth struggled to rise. "You c-can't! She means a half-Randir heir to the Highlord's seat. In thirty millennia, only pure Knorth have held that honor!"

Gerraint drew himself up. "Be quiet, boy! Look around you. There are far more of us here, dead, than alive in our halls. We have been a dying, failed house ever since Gerridon betrayed us to the shadows. I, too, am dying, and I foresee what misery you would bring to the Kencyrath if you were ever to become highlord after me. Trinity, another god-cursed Knorth berserker..."

"I am not!"

The surge of anger braced Ganth, and Gerraint stumbled but recovered quickly. He was older at such games than his son, and far more ruthless. Ganth collapsed back to the floor, clutching his chest.

He realized dimly that this tearing pain belonged to his father, not to him, and that the old man was using his son's strength to sustain himself. He would drain it all if not stopped. Did Ganth want to fight for his life? Did he even want to live—or was that thought, too, his father's? Gerraint would sacrifice them both to bring back Greshan. Perhaps Ganth should let him. What good had he ever been to anyone, before this?

Gerraint regarded him with scorn. "Berserker I said, berserker I meant. The Old Blood, the old power—but you will never recognize what you are, boy, and because of that it will eat you alive. Truly, Greshan is our last hope." He turned to Rawneth with bitter courtesy. "Restore him, and I bless your union. No doubt Lord Randir will do likewise. Beget whatever offspring you will, or can."

Rawneth flung wide her arms with a cry of triumph: "Ha, Kinzi!"

Then she unfastened her cloak and let it fall. Beneath it she wore a tight, black bodice and a full skirt spangled with stars that glinted as she began slowly to turn, arms out again, long fingers winnowing the air. She had let her nails grow almost into talons, Ganth noted with a spasm of nausea. Behind her mask, her eyes were closed. Her braid tumbled down and swung wide, darting, probing, as if with a mind of its own. When she stopped in a swirl of stars, it coiled around her neck.

"This is an old place," she said, as if to herself, "full of deep power. This keep is built on the ruins of a Merikit hill fort, as is Wilden, as are all our strongholds up and down the Riverland. Trinity knows on what the Merikit built except that it was…no, *is*…strong. But sleeping. Muffled. The House Knorth is still reeling. You almost shattered it tonight, Highlord, all by yourself, and so nearly brought down the bounds between the worlds but there are so many Kencyr dead here, still on guard. These banners…they must be destroyed."

She was facing Ganth and the oldest, eastern wall where the torches flared. Between them hung the ancient dead, rank on serried rank.

Gerraint made a choking sound. All the names that he had learned year after year at his father's side, all the Autumn's Eves since that he had chanted them himself, honoring the dead, keeping whole the fabric of his house…

"Well?" Rawneth was enjoying this. "Will you let your son molder with these other lost souls? Will you give him to the pyre?"

"No." He rubbed his left arm as if it hurt and shivered. No!" With a sob, he threw himself at the wall, clutched a banner, and ripped it down, crying, "For my son! For my son!"

Behind it was another and another. Many disintegrated at a touch, their woof of old cloth hanging in rotten tufts on the rougher warp threads. Cords snapped. Faces distorted in silent shrieks and slumped down in a cloud of dust. As each fell, the Highlord sobbed out its name.

Ganth huddled beneath this storm of destruction, too weak to escape. His heart fought in his chest. Fragments of burial cloth clung to the cold sweat on his face. He gagged, tasting, breathing the dead.

Through the billowing dust, he saw Rawneth standing by the bier. She was softly clapping her hands in delight.

"Go down, go down, old house," she crooned. "Fall to ruin—go!—so that others may rise."

Behind her stood the one who had come with her in the guise of servant and spy. She couldn't see his face, but Ganth did. It was twitching from one cast of features to another, over and over, with each name that Gerraint cried, with each falling banner. Cruel as the portraits often were, the caricatures mirrored on that shifting face were obscene in their gleeful malice. What in Perimal's name had Rawneth brought into the heart of the Knorth? Did she even know herself? A creature out of legend, out of childhood nightmare, one of Gerridon's fallen, a darkling changer...

"Gran!" Ganth cried, and hid his face from it in the crook of his arm, "Gran, help!"

For a moment, he saw her tiny form sitting hunched on her bed, head in hands, supported by Aerulan. She seemed to hear, tried to rise, but fell back. "Oh, my strength is spent! I am too old. Child, fight him! Feel your anger. Draw power from it, as I do!"

But his heart was clawing at his chest like a trapped animal and he...couldn't...breathe...

Harsh panting echoed his own. Gerraint stood motionless in front of him, gripping the banner that hung over Ganth's head. The changer had raised his own hands and was cowering behind them in mock terror. Ganth knew suddenly beneath which tapestry he had taken shelter.

Gerraint braced himself and jerked downward. There was a tearing sound. Rawneth stared. So did the changer, with lowered hands and a blank countenance probably as close to his own as he still possessed. The banner fell, folding on top of Ganth as if bending over him. A terrible face rushed toward his. Gerraint had wrenched down those concealing fingers, tearing them clean out of the tapestry. Beneath were empty sockets streaming with blood: she had clawed out her own eyes.

Power and madness...

Ganth tried to thrust the banner away, but it clung, its threads wrapped tightly around him. The stench of moldering cloth half-choked him. He could feel the weight and dying writhe of the body that they had clothed—Trinity, dead how many centuries?

Madness and...

"*Let me not see,*" keened a threadbare voice in his ear, in his mind. "*Let me not see. Oh, Jamethiel!*"

Ganth gasped for air, struggling to free himself. His thoughts swirled like birds flung up into a storm-torn sky, the dark earth reeling under their wings. Death was nothing, or should be. The pyre freed the soul from its cage of flesh. To be trapped, while even a bone remained unburnt...horrible, horrible.

But what of blood? Sweet Trinity, how many here had died violent deaths and still carried the stains of their passing on their banners, long after they themselves were nothing but ashes on the wind? This lady whose name he didn't even know...

"*Oh, Dream-weaver! Why did you do it?*"

...how long had she hung here in agony and mute despair?

His own mother, Telarien, had bled to death in childbirth. If he were to look into her eyes now...

"No." Ganth lurched to his feet, still trapped and blind in the other's death throes, her memories like bleeding wounds in his mind.

"'*Then went my lord Gerridon to his sister and consort, Jamethiel Dream-Weaver, and said, 'Dance out the souls of the faithful, that darkness may enter in. And she danced...'* Oh, sister-kin, let me not see! But I have seen."

Ganth staggered into someone—Gerraint, he thought—but his own terror had already broken the Highlord's grip on his mind, and if he had hurt his father, he neither knew nor, for the moment, cared.

Then he fetched up against something else hard enough to double over it. Finally, he managed to claw the rotten shroud away from his face. He was leaning over the catafalque, over his brother's corpse. Greshan's lips parted as if to speak. What moved them, however, was only the white seethe of maggots that bred in his mouth.

"NO!"

Ganth shoved his brother away. The corpse fell off the other side of the bier, trailing flies, and hit the floor with a meaty thud. The pall, dislodged, slid down over him. From where he sprawled by the northern wall, Gerraint cried out in horror. Turning, Ganth tripped over the banner that had slid down to entangle his feet, and fell hard on something that knocked the breath out of him.

Looking up, dazed, he saw Rawneth laughing down at him: "Little man, I could watch you all night."

"Oh, sh-shut up!"

Someone must have opened the door, Ganth thought as he groped for the thing that had nearly broken his ribs. Certainly, there was a powerful draft, almost a wind, whipping his hair into his eyes. Thunder rumbled, muffled to a tremor in the stones. Something above fell with a clatter. Banners rustled uneasily as air rushed down the spiral stairs at each corner of the lower hall. Maybe the keep's roof had blown off. Maybe the old walls would tumble in on them all. Best, perhaps, if they did.

"A dying, failed house," his father had said, and what had Rawneth chanted? *"Fall to ruin...go!"*

Something jerked at Ganth's foot. He looked down to see threads wrapped around his ankle like fingers, clutching. The wind was tugging at the tapestry. That was all. Then a face lifted out of the tangle of flying cords, eyes ragged bleeding holes, blanched lips mouthing words he tried not to hear:

"My soul and honor I ransomed with my eyes. I have seen, I have seen, but oh, kinsman, let me not fall!"

His hand closed on Kin-Slayer's hilt. He wrenched free the blade and hacked at that terrible face, at those desperate, clutching fingers. "Filthy Shanir, let go of me!"

She...it...the banner tumbled away, driven by the wind toward the guttering torches and between them, through a stone wall that was no longer there.

A vast space opened up beyond, and the wind poured through into it as if into a gaping mouth, fringed with unraveling banners. Ganth stared. This was hardly what he had meant when he had wished that the keep would fall in on them all. Instead, it seemed to have opened outward—into what? The flaring torches dazzled his eyes. He regained his feet, holding Kin-Slayer.

"Did you expect this?" he demanded of Rawneth.

She shook her head, staring. "No. Oh, no."

The void drew him. He moved toward it, shielding his eyes from the torchlight. The wind faltered, then turned, sluggishly, to breathe in his face: *Haaahhh...* It stank of old, old death, of ancient sickness and despair. *Aaaahhh...* a slow, deep inhalation, as of a sleeping monster, and the banners clung, shivering, to the keep walls. *Haaahhh...*

At first, it was like looking into deep, black water, a darkness thick enough to move with its own slow respiration. Then Ganth began to make out a floor, dark marble shot with glowing veins of green that seemed, faintly, to pulse. It stretched far, far back to a wall of still, white faces. Like the chamber in which he stood, the monstrous hall beyond was lined with death banners, but thousands upon thousands of them, a mighty host of the dead, watching.

Under their eyes, two figures revolved around each other, the one in black only visible when it eclipsed the one clad in white. They appeared to be...dancing.

Ganth edged closer to the wall that wasn't there, drawn by that second figure. He was almost sure that it was a woman.

Let me not see...

Something brushed against his face. Jumping back, startled, he saw what he had previously been looking straight through: the merest wraith of a banner stretched across the void's mouth. Like flies caught in a long abandoned web, old blood held tufts of rotting cloth to frayed threads. The whole shivered and seemed to gather itself. For a moment, Ganth looked into the ghost of a face known to him only from legend.

"G-glendar?" he stammered.

Question answered question, in a wisp of breath: *"Have you seen?"* The specter shuddered. *"I have seen."* And it fell to dust.

"Rise up, Highlord of the Kencyrath," the Arrin-ken had said to Gerridon's younger brother on that terrible night— Glendar, whom his family had counted as worthless, who had been taught to think of himself as little better. *"Your brother has forfeited all. Flee, man, flee, and we will follow."* And so he fled into the new world. Barriers he raised, and his people consecrated them...

But those people were gone, their banners torn down by a grief-mad father, and the way that they had guarded in life, in death, lay open. Huddled against the northern wall, Gerraint hid his face in his hands and wept at what he had done.

The changer laughed. "Ah, Glendar. Who will remember you now, you who could have lived forever? Knorth, you should rejoice. See? There in the shadows walks your own true lord and master. The Arrin-ken can't change that, not in three millennia, not in a thousand."

As Rawneth turned on him, his face immediately reassumed the aspect it had worn in the courtyard, the only one, apparently, that she knew. She slapped him, hard. "My spy. My creature. Who are you to say such things?"

The blow twisted his smile, and his eyes glittered before he cast them down in mock abasement. "Why, mistress, how could I be your...creature and not know your mind? Have I said anything that you have not already considered? Then consider this also: to whom do you owe loyalty? Where does your honor lie?"

Ganth backed away, toward his father. He felt the other's words twist like a knife in his soul. What if Glendar and all who had followed him were the truly fallen, for having abandoned their rightful lord? Where lay honor then? Perhaps the emptiness he had always felt came from living a lie.

The darkling eyed him askance. *Little man. Hollow-heart. My master could make you whole.*

Rawneth drew herself up. "Change is coming, and we Kencyr must change or perish. My honor follows my interest. What can this shadow lord do for me?"

"Ask, and see."

She laughed, but behind the mask her black eyes shifted to the beckoning darkness and she bit her lip. She would kill the man who played her for a fool, but if this offer was real...She approached the breach, swaying willow-supple. Her voice, mock coy at first, sharpened with an ambition as keen as hunger, as strong as madness:

"Master, master, will you grant me my heart's desire? Will you raise the dead to love me? Will you give me an heir to power?"

A long pause. The darkness breathed in...and out, in...and out. Ganth swayed, dizzy, unconsciously trying to match that vast respiration. Then, out of the shadows, a voice spoke. It was slow, deep, and distorted as if heard under water. Ganth couldn't distinguish the words, but Rawneth listened, rigid, her mouth partly open.

"Yes," she breathed. "Oh, yes!"

Gerraint made an inarticulate sound and struggled to rise. Ganth put a hand on his father's shoulder to restrain him. They both stared at Greshan as he stood in dusty black beside his bier, smiling.

Rawneth gave a crack of laughter edged with hysteria. To stifle it, she jammed her knuckles into her mouth and bit them until they bled. Then she glided toward the man whom she had chosen as her mate. Her hair unbraided by itself as she went and floated up as if she were descending into deep water. They began to circle each other, two figures of darkness, hands down at first, then weaving in the kantirs of the Senetha, almost but not quite touching. Skin tingled with the nearness. Breath wove with breath on flushed lips. Ambition was there, but also thwarted lust sharper than famine, so that even Ganth ached with it where he stood, watching.

"I *will* have my will," murmured the Randir, "now and forever. It has been promised to me." And she gave Greshan her bloody hand to kiss.

Gerraint tried again to rise. Again, Ganth pressed him down, not taking his eyes off the two by the bier.

Greshan looked at him askance and raised an eyebrow. *What, will you allow your brother to be blood-bound by your mortal foe?* He gripped Rawneth's hand so that her bones ground together. She shuddered in luxurious pain.

"Here?" he said, with a glance at the bier.

"No. I have a more...fitting place in mind. Come with me, my love, my consort. Come to Kinzi's precious Moon Garden, and let her watch."

"Go on ahead, my lover, my mate. I will join you there."

"Soon, then."

They kissed as if they would devour each other, and parted.

"Remember your word, Highlord," she said over her shoulder, "if that still counts. My son will be your true heir." With that, she departed in a swirl of her starry skirt.

Gerraint beat his fist against the floor. The emerald signet cracked stone. "Why didn't you stop them?" he cried at Ganth. "He is confused, seduced by that...that...but you—you were always weak and jealous. Always! And so you stood aside. Greshan, my son..."

"He isn't G-greshan," said Ganth. "Forget the face. Look at the clothes."

The changer grinned, his features shifting almost at random. He pulled up his hood to over-shadow them.

"So I fooled you too, old man, but not you, boy. And you did nothing. You must truly hate that woman. Ah, but she is clever. I told my master that if I brought her here, now, she would find her way to him. Darkness seeks its own level."

"Then seek yours." Ganth stood between the changer and his father. "In the shadows or in the garden, I don't care. Just g-go."

The changer eyed the sword in his hand. "That blade and I will meet someday, but not tonight. As for going..." He craned around Ganth to address Gerraint. "Do you really want that, old man, with our business unfinished?" He stepped back and flipped aside a corner of the pall. The flies that had gathered, thwarted, on the cloth, rose in a swarm and settled again on Greshan's sprawling corpse. "He isn't getting any fresher, you know."

"Oh, for Trinity's s-sake," said Ganth. "If you won't call a priest, father, I will. Here. I'll s-start the damned pyre myself."

Stepping to the wall, he took down one of the torches. Before he could turn, however, something smashed into the back of his head. Stunned and bleeding on the floor, he looked up to see Gerraint standing over him with a fragment of paving stone in his hand.

"F-father!"

"Greshan is my son. I have no other." He turned, panting, to the changer. "I've come this far, broken oaths and betrayed my house—all for its own sake, I swear! Do you swear your lord can do this thing?"

"Gerridon is your lord too, old man, whatever the Arrinken say. Ask, and see."

Gerraint made a choking sound, then lurched around to face that breach into eternal night.

"Master, master!" he cried. "Will you grant me my heart's desire? Will you restore my son to me?"

Ganth struggled up on an elbow. His head was splitting and his vision blurred, or perhaps the latter came from trying to focus on that vast, shadowy hall beyond the keep's chamber. The void breathed in...and out, in...and out. Then it spoke, in the distorted rumble of a voice in an empty room, buried fathoms deep.

Ganth was vaguely aware of the dark figure who had come almost to the threshold. Like his servant, he was cowled and muffled, but somehow gave the impression of a leanness bordering on famine. That, Ganth dimly supposed, was Gerridon, the Master of Knorth, who had betrayed all for this meager, immortal life. So many death banners, rank on rank...had he devoured all his followers, to come to this? His hall, Perimal Darkling itself, surrounded him like the belly of a beast that has swallowed everything, even itself, and still hungers for more.

But it was not at Gerridon that Ganth looked. Behind him, in the middle of that cold hall, Jamethiel Dream-Weaver danced. A slim, graceful figure in white with flowing black hair, she seemed untouched by shadow or age, innocent beyond evil, beautiful enough to stop the heart.

Wraiths danced with her, tattered souls shivering in the threads of their death banners, torn loose from the keep and swept in this maw of darkness. There was Glendar, hardly a wisp. With a sigh, he melted into his sister's white arms and was gone. One by one, the others followed, their empty threads tumbling to the cold, dark floor. Only a ragged specter with bloody eyes remained. She and the Dream-Weaver circled each other, one dance mirroring the other in water-flowing kantirs, drawing ever closer.

"...*sisterkin*..."

One, or both, breathed that word, and they came together. Jamethiel stroked the other's wild hair, murmuring words Ganth could not hear, as hard as he tried. Then, very gently, she kissed those ruined eyes. With a shudder, the gaunt ghost folded into the Dream-Weaver's embrace and gave up her tortured soul, lip to lip.

Ganth shivered.

"*Beware,*" his grandmother had said. *"We are a passionate house, and not always wise."*

But Kinzi hadn't grown up starved for acceptance, for any scrap of love, so he would not accept her judgment. At last the emptiness within him had a shape, now and forever, that only one being could fill. He would die for the Dream-Weaver. He would kill. He would foreswear any oath he had ever sworn, if only she would look at him. And she did, dreamily, with the smallest of smiles. Silver eyes, mirrors to trap the soul —was he reflected in them?

Mistress, mistress, will you grant me my heart's desire? Will you leave the dead to love me?

Too late. The dance turned her and her gaze slid away. What did she see now? It didn't matter. He had seen her.

His father was speaking. "That is your price? A contract for a pure-bred Knorth lady?"

Ganth scrambled to remember what he must have half-heard. What lady? Not Rawneth; she was Randir. Not the Dream-Weaver, surely, unless…unless…His heart leaped. A contract with whom?

His father sounded equally bewildered.

"But, Master, you already have a consort." He and Ganth both looked at the pale shimmer where Jamethiel danced, the opaque air a halo around her. She bent, graceful beyond a lover's dream, to gather up the tangled threads of the dead. The darkness rumbled. "Oh," said Gerraint, blankly. "You want a child, a…daughter? But why?"

The cowled head turned as the Dream-Weaver drifted toward him. Absently, smiling, she kissed him, and the ghost of souls glimmered from her lips to his within the hood's shadow. He reached out as if to return her caress, but stopped himself. Her hair slid through his fingers like black silken water as she turned and drifted away. His hand clenched and fell.

"Such power comes at a cost," said the changer. He smiled crookedly at Ganth, as if he had read the young man's heart. "She is already dangerous to touch. Soon it will be worse."

"I don't believe you," said Ganth.

The smile became a grimace. "Of course you don't."

Gerraint was frowning. "We are so few, and fewer still of our women are free to make new contracts." He crossed his arms, hugging himself. It was both a sign of pain, for his gray face shone with sweat, and his unconscious gesture when he meant to shave the truth. "However, there is my daughter Tieri..."

"Who is only a year old!" Ganth burst out. "You haven't even asked to s-see her since Mother died. Do you really hate the child that much?"

"What is she compared to my son? What is any female but a potential asset to her house?"

The shadows spoke.

"Age doesn't matter," translated the changer. "Only bloodlines. There are rooms in the Master's House where time barely crawls. He will retreat into one of them and await his...pleasure. As for the Mistress, she will do his biding, as she does now."

Dancing, humming to herself, the Dream-Weaver wove the threads of the death banners into a new fabric picked out with flecks of ancient blood. The flecks were words; the whole, a document that she presented to her lord.

Ganth floundered to his feet, using Kin-Slayer as a crutch. From the throbbing in his head, he wondered if Gerraint really had cracked his skull. He knew beyond question that this contract would be his sister's death, but Gerraint had already reached into the shadows to seal it with his emerald ring.

"How cold!" he murmured, withdrawing his hand. "My fingers are numb."

They were worse than that. As Gerraint stared, blanched skin split open across his knuckles and the meager flesh beneath drew back on tendon and bone. Then the bones themselves began to crumble. Ganth caught the signet ring as it fell and threw an arm around his father to steady him. Cold rage unfolded in his mind like black wings spreading. He could feel them flex.

"Bastard," he said to the changer. "You knew this would happen."

"No. How the shadows enter each man's soul is his own affair."

"Nonetheless, I will kill you someday, darkling."

"Perhaps, unless I kill you first. Such dear enemies should know each other's names. Mine is Keral." He stood by the door, again wearing Greshan's face, and bowed. "I go now to make a lady happy—for a time. Alas for the greed of a woman and the grief of a man, that you should come to this! Farewell, Ganth Grayling."

Then he stepped out into the boisterous night. The door scraped shut after him, cutting short the startled exclamation of the Kendar captain still on guard outside, locking.

Gerraint swayed, clutching his arm. "So cold," he moaned.

It *was* cold. Ganth looked down. Thick, murky air was flowing out of Perimal Darkling, close to the floor. *Haaaahhhhh*...breathed the darkness, exhaling. Ganth drew his father back.

They retreated slowly almost to the western wall, trailing chalky dust on the floor. Gerraint began to stumble with shock. His hand had crumbled entirely away, and the flesh of his forearm was withering fast. Ganth held him insecurely in the circle of an arm, his own right hand clutching the signet ring; his left, Kin-Slayer's hilt.

Thick air settled around the bier, sluggishly rose, and piled up over it. Torchlight flared through sullen, slowly writhing coils of shadow. Shapes moved within them, crawling over and under each other, over and under, like half-digested souls or lovers impossibly entwined. One had no eyes. Its mouth gaped as if, silently, to scream.

Aaaaaahhh...breathed the darkness, inhaling, and sucked the clotted air back into its maw. Firelight flared—on a naked stonewall. The gate had closed.

A scraping sound came from the far side of the bier, then a heavy grunt. A hand rose and fumbled at the bier's edge. A figure clad in gilded leather dragged itself upright. It hawked, spat out a mouthful of maggots, and slowly turned. Greshan squinted at his father and brother with death-clouded eyes.

"'m hungry," he muttered, chewing and swallowing.

Gerraint had cried out with joy at his son's first movement and tried, weakly, to break away from Ganth. "Your welcome feast awaits. Oh, my dear son, won't you come with me into the hall of the living to eat?"

"'m hungry," said Greshan again, thickly, swaying. There was a terrible stench as he voided the gas of decay from both ends and somewhere in between. "'s better. 's of bitches at Tentir. Challenged me. Tricked me. Hurt me. Thought I was dead. Joke's on them, eh? All the time in t'world to make 'm pay when I am highlord. All t' time. I will give 'm blood to drink, an' more, an' more, an' more..."

He sniffed and shambled forward. "I smell death on you, father. Time you were gone. Ring and sword. Give me. My time. 'm hungry. Dear, dear father, feed me..."

Gerraint seemed to melt out of his son's grasp. Perhaps he had fainted. Ganth, perforce, let him slide down to rest against the wall and turned to face his brother.

Greshan gave a thick gurgle and hawked up more maggots. "Well, well, well. Dear little G-g-g-g-ganoid. M' childhood playmate. Remember what fun we used t' have? Our midnight games? You din't enjoy them much—that was half the fun—but I did. An' then you tried to tell father!" He grinned through broken teeth. "Oh, that was funny! Remember?"

"I remember," said Ganth, and he did. Everything.

The slow walk up the stairs to Greshan's quarters, knowing that every step was watched by fellow cadets no longer even feigning sleep. The wash of heat and light rolling over him as the door opened, the closeness as it shut behind him…

At first, dazzled, he could see nothing but the fire roaring in the grate. The room was hot and airless, sour with the stench of sweat and spilt wine. Roane's servant shoved him from behind. He stumbled forward, tripping over a welter of beautiful, filthy clothes, the soiled, spoiled wealth of his house. Someone laughed. Now he could make out two figures sitting on either side of the hearth, watching, waiting.

"Well, well, well. Dear little Gangrene." Greshan's voice slurred only a bit, a sign that he was very drunk but nowhere near passing out. "All grown up and come to Tentir to play soldier. So you still like games. Shall we show my dear friend Roane how we used to play? Now, be a good boy and take off your clothes."

Slowly, with numb fingers, Ganth removed his tunic. They laughed at his lean build. Not much muscle there. No wonder he was doing so poorly at Tentir.

He wanted to say, "How can I do well, when you always watch me?" but he couldn't speak.

"Now the pants," said Greshan.

When he didn't move, his arms were seized. Roane had two servants with him, not just one. Roane also had a knife. A long, narrow one, double-edged. Ganth saw it as the Randir stood and sauntered toward him, turning it over in his hands so that the firelight played off of it.

Now Roane was behind him. "Little boys should do as they are told," he said.

The knife's cold kiss made Ganth flinch as it slid down first one leg, then the other, cutting away his clothes.

Greshan leaned forward, licking his lips.

"Your house is soft, rotting from within," Roane breathed in Ganth's ear, too low for the Lordan to hear. "We will mold it to our liking until it falls apart in our hands. Now be a good little Knorth, like your drunken lout of a brother, and submit."

Ganth stared into the heart of the fire, willing himself far away as he had as a child so that whatever happened, happened to someone else.

But he was no longer a child, and this was wrong.

Sudden pain, and sudden rage—black, cold, powerful.

His hands twisted in the others' grasps and gripped them in turn. The next moment, he had sent one floundering into his brother and the other headfirst into the fire. The knife's point skittered across his hip. He grabbed Roane's wrist, pulled, and bent. They were on the floor now, he on top, the knife between them. Firelight shifted across their faces as the servant lurched out of the fireplace and staggered, wrapped in flames, about the room, futilely pursued by his mate.

Ganth looked down into the Randir's astonished eyes. "Let's see how you like it," he said softly.

Then he drove the blade into the other's stomach and leaned on it. Down it went, through muscle walls, scrapping against the spine, into the floor. There, slowly, Ganth screwed it home.

Someone had been hammering for some time on the door. Now the lock broke and it burst open. Sere stood on the threshold, dark shapes behind him.

Ganth ignored them. He saw only his brother, staring at him slack-jawed with amazement, beginning to back away. Ganth rose and followed him. Somehow, he had acquired a sword, and there was an emerald signet ring on his finger. Greshan held out hands as blotched and swollen as bad sausages. He backed into the catafalque, knocking it over.

"No, no...brother, dear brother, I'm y'r lord. I want to live..."

"But you are dead. You died a long, long time ago."

The randon in the doorway reached behind him and hauled forward someone in a priest's robe. "Say it," he demanded, giving the man a shake that rattled his teeth. "Say it now."

The priest gulped, and spoke the pyric rune.

Greshan burst into flame. So did many of the banners lining the walls that had been woven of bloodied thread.

More kindled as the Lordan blundered into them. Ganth, following, hewed him down. Kin-Slayer felt light in his hand, eager. He struck again and again, to kill memories of weakness and shame, to obliterate them forever so that, finally, he might live.

The randon called him back to his father's side.

Gerraint sprawled against the wall. His right sleeve and the whole right side of his coat hung limp, empty. Half of his face began to sink and wither on the bone even as they watched. He reached out and gripped Ganth. "Tell me it isn't true," he said with difficulty, able to use only the left side of his mouth. "Tell me, as children, he didn't...didn't..."

Ganth considered the child he had been, soft and weak, who might have forgiven this dying man and found a way to show him mercy. That was the boy who had stumbled out of Tentir that autumn night wearing clothes picked at random from his brother's filthy floor, leaving all his hopes in tatters behind him, forswearing forever (or so he had thought) the black rage that had made him do such terrible things.

"Another god-cursed Knorth berserker..."

No. Anger was power, nothing more, nothing less.

The Knorth Matriarch had known that when she bade him draw on it, and so he had, and so he would continue to do, for now he needed strength as never before.

"Father," he said evenly, meeting that desperate gaze, "I didn't lie."

Gerraint's hand fell away from his son's sleeve and he turned his ruined face to the wall. His clothes began to smolder.

"Leave him," said Ganth to the randon as the latter bent pick him up. "His pyre is laid and he is ready for it. Let him burn with his son."

Sere looked sharply at him, then inclined his head in submission and rose. "Yes, Highlord."

On the threshold, Ganth looked back. Gerraint's body was already burning. So was the banner above it, Telarien's sweet features melting into flame. He tried to carry his mother's image out into the night, where his new household anxiously waited, but only one face went with him.

Let me not see... but he had seen.

Secretive and smiling, Jamethiel danced on and on, weaving dreams and desire in a corner of his soul.

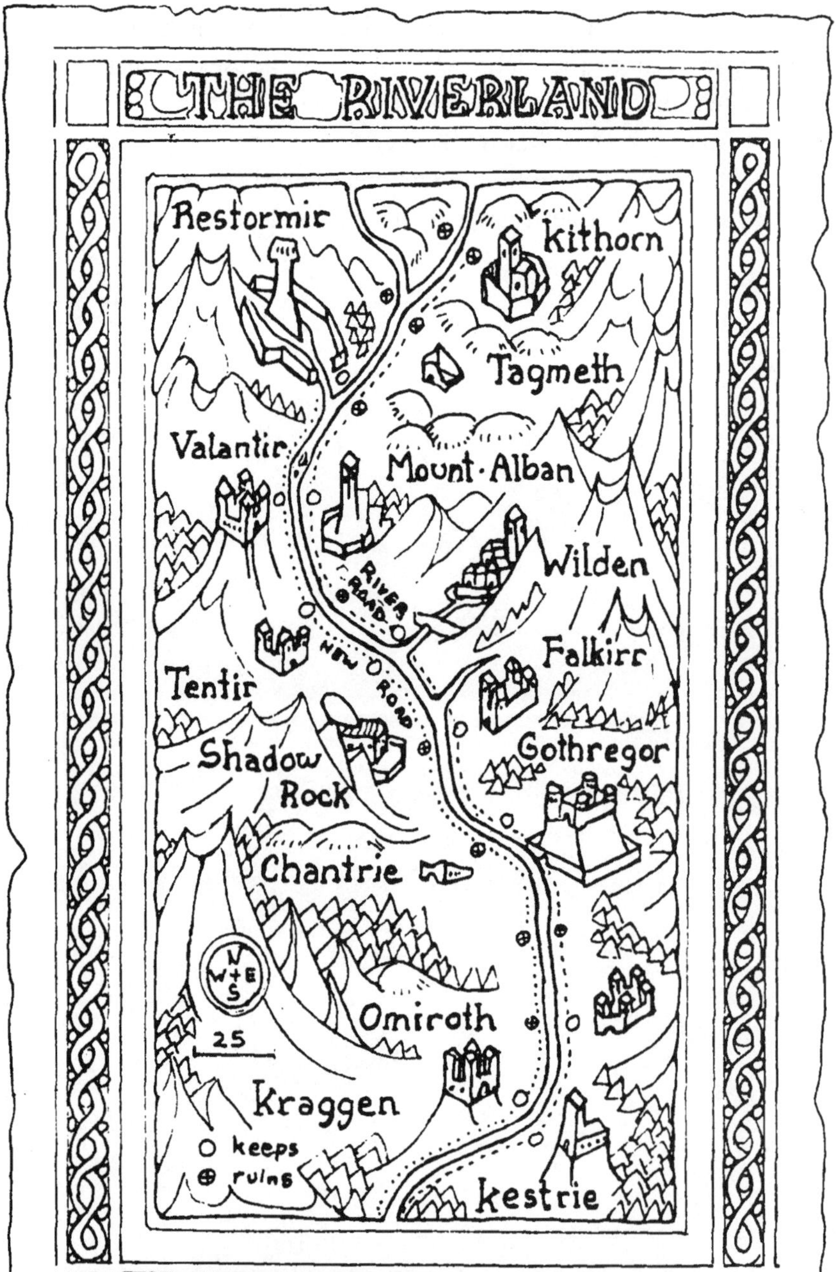
THE RIVERLAND
Restormir
kithorn
Tagmeth
Valantir
Mount·Alban
Wilden
RIVER ROAD
NEW ROAD
Falkirr
Tentir
Shadow Rock
Gothregor
Chantrie
N
W E
S
Omiroth
25
Kraggen
keeps
ruins
kestrie
THE RIVER SILVER

F

LOST KNOTS

Gothregor
2993

[A cloth letter, unfinished, undelivered, found in the quarters of the Knorth Matriarch Kinzi Keen-Eyed on the night that Shadow Assassins massacred the Knorth ladies]

...and so, dear sisterkin, I will spend some time stitching this note to you while I wait for my grandson Ganth and the others to return from the hunt, being too on edge to do anything else.

How the Tishooo howls! Does it also shake your tower in the Women's Halls?

Odd, to think of you so close, and yet so far. We could have been together tonight if not for this stupid hunt—for a rathorn, no less. I asked Ganth not to go, but you know how restless and unmanageable he has been of late. I tell him he should take a consort, but he only gives that bitter laugh of his. He has someone in mind, though, I swear, but whom? Oh, my dear, I used to know him so well. It hurts me to see him turned so hard, as if afraid to show any softness, and as for his temper...! If only he would recognize its Shanir source, I could help him master it. Instead, I fear that some day it will master him.

Speaking of berserker tendencies, yes, you should send your granddaughter-kin Brenwyr to me. You have done wonders with her since her mother's death, but an untrained Shanir maledight is so very, very dangerous. Worse, I fear that she and Aerulan have quarreled—over little Tieri! Sometimes I wonder if we of the Women's World are any wiser than our squabbling men-folk, but at least we rarely draw blood.

And so, circling, I near the heart of my unease.

Can it really be ten years since Gerraint died? You have been impatient with me for not having told you more about that night. In truth, Ganth has told me virtually nothing of what happened in the death banner hall before so much of it burned, and you have laughed at rumors that Greshan was seen walking the halls of Gothregor when he was five days dead.

Well, I saw him too. In my precious Moon Garden. With that bitch of Wilden, Rawneth. She led him in by the secret door behind the tapestry and there, under my very window, made love to him.

Except it wasn't Greshan.

I knew that the moment I saw him, and I didn't warn her. Oh, Adiraina, I was tired and angry, and so I let her damn herself. Then he changed—into whom, I don't know. I couldn't see his face, but Rawneth did. She gaped like a trout, then burst out laughing, half in hysteria, half, I swear, in triumph. What face could he have shown her to cause that?

I have since bricked up my window, but that question continues to haunt me. Especially now.

It has been three months since Lord Randir died and four since the Randir Lordan disappeared. My spies tell me that Rawneth contracted the Shadow Guild to assassinate him—much luck they seem to have had against a randon weapons-master, as strange as he may be in other respects. Now she insists that Ganth confirm her own son, Kenan, as the new lord of Wilden.

And here we come to the heart of the matter.

Rawneth went back to Wilden that same night, contracted with a highborn of her own house, and some nine months gave birth to Kenan. But who is Kenan's father—the Randir noble or the thing in the garden? Without knowing, how can I advise Ganth to accept or reject his claim? And so I have summoned Rawneth and her son to Gothregor while you are also here, since your Shanir talent lies in determining blood-lines at a touch. You will tell me, dear heart, and then I will know how to act. I must admit, I do hope our dear Rawneth has mated with a monster.

But if so, why did she laugh so triumphantly?

How the wind howls! Now something has fallen over below. I hear many feet on the stair. Perhaps it is Ganth, come home at last...

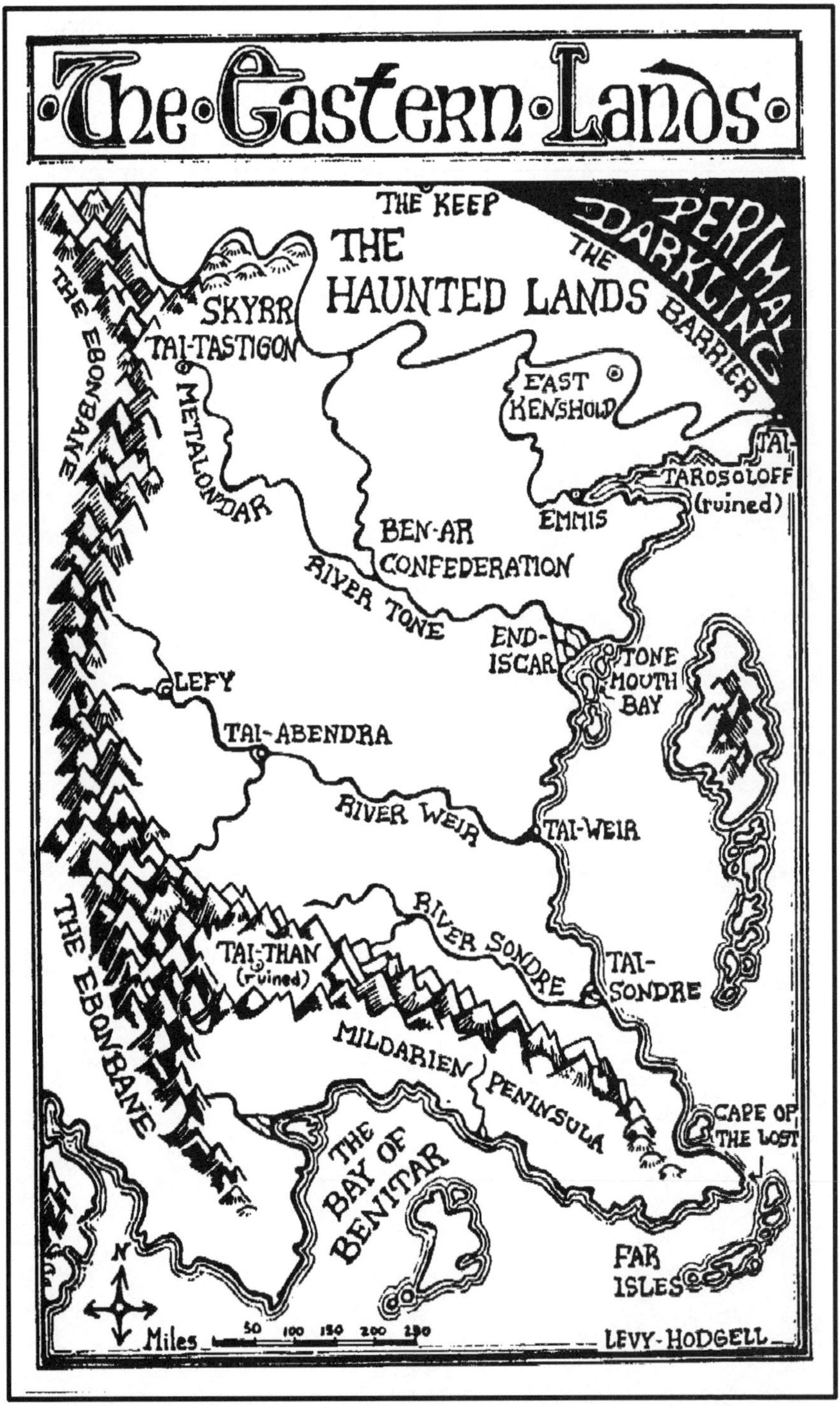
The Eastern Lands
THE KEEP
THE HAUNTED LANDS
PERIMAX
THE DARKLING BARRIER
SKYRR
TAI-TASTIGON
METALONDAR
THE EBONBANE
EAST KENSHOLD
TAI-TAROSOLOFF (ruined)
EMMIS
BEN-AR CONFEDERATION
RIVER TONE
END-ISCAR
TONE MOUTH BAY
LEFY
TAI-ABENDRA
RIVER WEIR
TAI-WEIR
RIVER SONDRE
TAI-THAN (ruined)
TAI-SONDRE
THE EBONBANE
MILDARIEN PENINSULA
CAPE OF THE LOST
THE BAY OF BENITAR
FAR ISLES
N
Miles 50 100 150 200 250
LEVY-HODGELL

# AMONG THE DEAD

3004

"Tell me a story," said one of the twins.

Anar clawed his way out of the past like someone scrambling up a rubble-strewn slope. Here were bits of his childhood at the scrollsmen's college, where he had been happy. Hard to remember, now, how that had felt. Here were the ruins of a beautiful, embroidered coat—Greshan's, probably, that cruel swine. Anar had often wondered about m'lord's childhood with such a brother, how much it might have influenced the man he had become. Here was a scrap of memory, charred at the edges, that still seared: a pyre and at its heart, a small, indomitable woman wrapped in flame.

Oh, Kinzi, and all the women of my house, burning, burning, the taste of their ashes bitter on my lips...

He scrubbed a dirty hand across his mouth and blinked up at the child on the hillcrest above him, dark against the slow, opalescent seethe of the Barrier.

Was it the boy or the girl? When not together, they were hard to tell apart. The same wild black hair, cropped short; the same eyes, storm-gray or silver as light or mood caught them; at seven years old even still much the same build, thin and wiry...there was even some confusion as to which had been born first. But one had fingernails and the other, this one, usually hid her hands because she didn't.

The girl Jame perched above the keep's straggly kitchen garden, watching him, waiting.

"A story," she prompted. "Something true."

"Not all stories are," he said absently. "You ask the singers about their precious Lawful Lie." Not that she could: the only singer to go into exile with his lord had been among the first to die.

He stared at the roil behind her of the Barrier that separated this world from the next. Beyond it, shadow folding into shadow, Perimal Darkling waited. That was true enough, ancestors preserve them. So was the Master's House, that nightmare looming out of a fallen past. He could almost distinguish the crooked lines of its many roofs, shifting in the shadows of countless moonless nights, its windows without number opening to the soulless dark within.

Trinity, but it was close. Only once before had it been closer. The garrison had been some three years into its exile then, long enough to see that it would only end in death. The sooner the better, they had thought, and so again followed their lord headlong into hopeless battle, this time against primordial darkness itself.

Death, at last, with honor...

Anar shuddered, remembering the slow churn of mist under that cliff of shadow that had confounded and dragged them apart. Only he and two score others had stumbled out. Some, gaunt with hunger, mad with thirst, said that they had been trapped for days, for weeks, in that murky limbo. Some only stared with hollow eyes, mouthing the same words over and over again:

"'m hungry, 'm hungry..."

That had been the garrison's first experience with the haunts that gave this accursed land its name.

It was also when they discovered that their priest, Ishtier, had run off, taking his lord's Kendar mistress and his own priestly powers with him, just when they had most needed a pyric rune to deal with their own walking dead.

Of them all, only the Gray Lord had penetrated the shadows and come at last to the Master's Hall, or so Anar guessed. Where else could he have found that beautiful, nameless lady whom he had brought out with him to grace his bed and bear these children, brother and sister, with so much of her strange magic in the silver shadow of their eyes?

Words whispered in his mind, silken fingers meant to tease out memory like a snarl:

Let no one see...

See what? Of whom had he been thinking?

Anar floundered for a moment before the subtle sinews of his patchwork priest-craft steadied him.

He had come to this twisting of the way before—every time, in fact, that he thought or spoke of the twins' mother. Others looked puzzled if he mentioned her, as if she were a fading dream, half or wholly forgotten, a thread of sweet song, a movement of heart-breaking grace limned in moonlight, a fleeting glimpse of glamour.

Let no one see...

Only the children remembered, and the randon Winter, who had her own reasons, and the Gray Lord.

Anar felt his breath catch. Somehow, he had forgotten: there was the House, looming, and Lord Grayling had gone again, alone, to storm it, to reclaim the fey bride whom he had somehow lost or perhaps just misplaced. How long had he been gone? Days? Weeks? If he didn't return, what would happen to his people, who had gone into this bitter exile for his sake? Did he even care?

Pushing aside the thought, the scrollsman pulled up something that should have been a carrot. It was the right color, at least, but its tip twitched like a rat's nose and its white rootlets stung his hand. Anar snapped the root in two, ignoring its thin, piping shriek.

"Dare you to dig up a potato," said the child. "All those eyes, blinking. Ugh."

"At least they don't scream," said Anar.

He blinked, remembering the pile of limp vegetables that already lay in the keep's kitchen, some of them still mewling weakly and trying to crawl away. Since m'lord had stormed out, no one had felt like cooking or eating. What a waste. It had taken long, hard work to make the soil of the Haunted Lands yield even this sorry crop. Only the collective will of the garrison continued to make it possible—that, and Anar's own makeshift attempts at priest-craft which, he knew, were slowly unraveling his mind.

"I don't think you're mad," said the child, judiciously, "or at least not as mad as Tigon. He keeps trying to eat his own toes."

Sweet Trinity, he must have been thinking out loud again.

"Yes," said the child, "you are, off and on. What does 'fey' mean?"

Don't think. Talk.

"A story," he gabbled. "You asked for a story."

But what story could he safely tell? M'lord had forbidden him even to teach these children their father's true name. Someday, he might inform his son and heir, Torisen, but never this fey, unwanted daughter, already too like her mother for comfort.

"That word again. 'Fey.' Is that why Father doesn't like me?"

Shut up and talk.

"Suppose," Anar said, desperately launching himself, "that there is a land where the animate and inanimate, the living and the dead, don't overlap."

"You can always tell them apart?"

"Yes. No. Most of the time. Suppose the lord of that land came home one day to find all the women of his family slaughtered."

"They didn't turn into haunts?"

"No. He had a priest speak the pyric rune and they all burned up. Crackle, crackle."

"Who killed them?"

"This lord had many enemies, but he thought he knew whom to blame and he set out to punish them."

Anar shivered, remembering the Highlord's rage as he turned from his grandmother Kinzi's pyre, his berserker madness that had infected them all.

"Did he make them pay?" asked Kinzi's great-granddaughter.

"No. He guessed wrong. I think. Anyway, there was a big fight and a lot of his own people got killed. After that, they didn't want him to lead them anymore, so they drove him away."

Why was he telling this of all stories? M'lord would kill him! Belatedly, Anar shoved half the carrot into his mouth to silence himself. The rootlets writhed and stung as he bit down.

Let me not speak...

"What happened to him? How does the story end?"

"I don't know." The words were slurred, his mouth already swelling. "So far, it hasn't."

The child waited to see if he would say anything more or, perhaps, fall over dead. When he did neither, only flapping a hand helplessly at her in dismissal, she jumped up and ran away.

The hills of the Haunted Lands seemed to roll on forever, under a rolling sky. Jame ran down through the coarse, clinging grass and up, down and up, jumping off the crests, trying to fly.

From a rise, she saw the squat tower of the keep, dark against the Barrier except where the crystal dome over the lord's solar caught the evening light. The sun was going down to the west; to the east, a gibbous moon slowly climbed the sky. A fitful, sour wind from the north ruffled her hair and combed the grass over her toes.

Turning southward, Jame plunged down again; then, more slowly, she climbed. Beyond, she could hear Winter grunting instructions:

"Here. Aim. The foot, so. Your shoulders...turn them into the strike. Better."

Jame dropped to her stomach and wriggled up to the hilltop. Through a fringe of grass she watched as their former wet-nurse taught her brother a fire-leaping move of the Senethar.

Winter, a big, raw-boned Kendar, towered over her young student, holding a large hand higher and higher to make him extend his kick. Scowling with concentration, Tori pivoted and struck. His bare foot slapped against her palm.

"Good," she grunted, and hooked his other foot out from under him. "Not so good."

Tori had landed on his back without adequately breaking his fall. The rock-hard ground smacked the air out of him and for a moment he lay there gasping.

"Up," said Winter. "Again."

Jame watched, idly plucking stems of grass and letting them snake through her hair. They wriggled and tickled as they tried to take root in her scalp. She thought they camouflaged her nicely, until Winter turned her long, horse-face up toward her.

"Come down," she said; and then, to Tori, "Enough for today. Practice that."

Jame clambered to her feet and skidded down the hill. Half way to the bottom, she launched herself at Winter, but the Kendar simply caught her in mid-air. The randon's hands completely encircled the girl's waist.

"Too thin," she grunted, swinging Jame around and setting her down beside her brother. "Eat more."

"Oh, Winnie, please teach me how to fight too!"

"She can't," said Tori, brushing dust off his much-patched backside. "You're a girl."

"So is Winnie."

"Was," said the Kendar, and knelt to put away the practice weapons. "A long time ago. You," she glanced at Jame, "are not a girl. You are a lady. It shames us all that m'lord will not let us treat you accordingly. Still, I would teach you too, if your father had not forbidden it."

"That's unfair!"

"Much is. Accept it."

"Anyway," Jame said to Tori, "while you were busy falling on your butt, I got Anar to tell me a story, all about a lord who got kicked out by his own people. So there."

Winter glanced over a shoulder at her. "So. The scrollsman has told you about the White Hills. Interesting. And about time."

Anar hadn't mentioned the White Hills. "Were you there?" Jame asked, probing for more.

Winter bound up the sword case. "Yes," she said, without turning. "Sere was too. He came at me in battle with the Highlord's madness in his eyes, and I killed him for the sake of our unborn child."

"You had a baby?" Tori asked. "What happened to it?"

"He was born here in the Haunted Lands, and here he died."

"How?"

Winter sat back on her heels, still not facing them. "Your mother had no milk. I was still nursing Tob, there being nothing fit in this accursed land to feed a child. Besides, he was...slow. Even then, two nurslings I could have managed. Not three."

The twins waited. They both knew which two Father would have chosen.

"Your mother was so beautiful. Tob ran to her, and I let her hold him. In her arms, his soul left him. I...dealt with what was left. It was the only time I ever saw her cry except for once more, when she gave you into my charge."

The twins looked at each other. Jame asked for them both: "Do you still love us?"

At last the Kendar turned. "Of course," she said. "You were my nurslings."

Jame collared her by the leg. Winter ruffled her hair, plucked out the wriggling grass, and tossed it into a patch of snap-weed where it was immediately torn to pieces.

"Now go." She tipped up the child's chin to regard a fading bruise. "Stay close to the keep, but away from m'lord if...when he returns."

The twins ran off, chasing each other turn and turn about over the swooping hills. Jame pounced her brother, catching him off guard and in the face with her elbow. He yelped in pain. They rolled down the slope, scrabbling like puppies. At the bottom, she broke free, dashed up, and threw herself down on the crest. Tori joined her, wiping a bloody nose on his sleeve.

"Why did you do that?"

Winnie told you to Practice. Besides, I wanted to see how you would block the blow. You didn't. I was trying to learn something."

"Father says it's dangerous to teach you anything. Will the things you learn always hurt people?"

She considered this. "Maybe. As long as I learn, does it matter?"

He snuffled loudly and wiped his nose again. "It does to me. I'm always the one who gets hurt. Father says you're dangerous. He says you'll destroy me."

"That's silly. I love you."

"Father says destruction begins with love. Anyway, you did hurt me."

"Crybaby."

"Little girl."

"Daddy's favorite."

"Freak."

She hid her hands in her armpits but drew them out again almost immediately to gnaw on her nail-less fingertips. "They itch," she said, defensively. "I hate them. When I grow up, I'm going to have a different pair of gloves for every day in the week. Winnie's child...d'you think he was the third? Remember? We used to dream that there were three of us. We used," she added wistfully, "to have the same dreams."

"We were children then," he said, not meeting her eyes. "I don't dream anymore. Much."

Father beat him when he did. Somehow father always knew.

"Shanirs dream, boy. Are you a filthy Shanir?"

After that, Tori had begun to sleep less and less, often keeping his sister awake with him. For the last two nights, neither of them had slept at all.

They rested now, watching the Barrier. The setting sun cast rays of light slantwise across it, veiling what lay within, but a low, continuous rumble betrayed its presence. Snake-tongues of lightning flickered back in the dark.

"Father is still out there, looking for Mother," said Tori, "but two nights ago she left footprints in the dust beside our bed. That's proof. She *is* still here."

"I know. Last night she must have been dancing through the death banners in the hall. You know the one with the man with the wart on his nose? Well, you can't see it now, the wart or the nose. He turned around to watch her."

"She shouldn't hide from us," said Tori, tearing grass with his fingers, ignoring a tiny chorus of cries. "Father has a right to her. So do we. She belongs to us, doesn't she?" When his sister didn't reply, he repeated fiercely, "Well, *doesn't* she?"

"I...don't know where she belongs." Jame gave him a sudden push and sprang to her feet, away from his angry eyes and bewildered pain. "I know: hide-and-seek. You be Father, I'll be Mother. Catch me if you can!"

And she was off, plunging down the hillside in a swirl of flying hair, thin legs, and tattered rags, running headlong toward the keep.

The grey horse stumbled, its gaunt sides foam-flecked and heaving, black with sweat. The grass of the Haunted Lands had proved treacherous fodder and this, Ganth's war-horse, was the last of the garrison's mounts. He gouged its flanks again with cruel spurs, ignoring the rattle of its breath and his own parched, aching throat. He *would* win through these shifting veils of light and shadow. The House loomed before him, no closer than it had been an hour, a day, a lifetime ago, but he would lay his white bones on this endless bleak moor before he gave up.

"Gerridon!" he howled at that bleak filmy facade. "I have come for my lady. Return her to me!"

The stallion shied, stumbled, and fell. Ganth Gray Lord rolled to his feet. Wavering shafts of light fell through the Barrier as if through dark water onto the matted turf, a world in shifting shades of gray.

A black-clad figure had emerged from the long shadow of the House. Under its hood, its face shifted. One corner of the mouth hitched up nearly to a hidden eyebrow in a lopsided smile, then quivered nearly straight again.

"Believe me, Grayling, my blood wouldn't agree with that blade."

Ganth's hand dropped from Kin-Slayer's hilt. "No, not Gerridon. Keral, his faithful dog. Where is your master?"

The changer glanced over his shoulder at the House. A continual rumble came from it, stone on stone, as if, at a glacial pace, it was grinding forward. Silent lightning played across its many angles. "He is coming, room by room, out of the depths of the House, but not to meet you. Dead or alive, you will never stand in my lord's hall again."

"Where is my lady? Where is the Dream-Weaver?"

The mask of rage cracked. A desperate boy stared through the ruins of a disastrous middle age.

"P-please! Ever since that night in the death-banner hall at Gothregor, awake or asleep, no one else has seemed real to me and nothing else has mattered. If I had ever dreamed that she was here, waiting…"

"She wasn't. Not for you." The other's face changed again, settling into Greshan's handsome, heavy lines. "Gander, Gangoid, Gangray, you silly little man. Twenty years ago, you were nothing. So you became highlord. So what? All you accomplished was to get your womenfolk slaughtered while you were out hunting—yes, even your precious Gran Kinzi. Whose name d'you suppose she cried before the knife cut it short?"

"Don't!" Ganth covered his ears. "I didn't hear then; I won't listen now!"

"Evidently."

Greshan's face warped back into the changer's feral grin. "Still, it was the massacre of the Knorth women that brought your need in line with my master's: his sister-consort for you, a child of her blood for him. He would have reclaimed both her and her get sooner except that time in the House passes so oddly, now fast, now slow, that even Gerridon sometimes misjudges it."

"Her 'get.'" Ganth made an impatient gesture, sweeping his children aside. "Compared to her, what are they, ?"

Keral blinked. "What, more than one? Not...twins? Damn. I warned my lord that he should be more specific in his contract, but he brushed me off. 'My lady knows my will.' Huh. Perhaps he didn't know hers."

The changer began to pace back and forth in the shadow of the House, thinking out-loud.

"twind. But then so were Gerridon and Jamethiel, incomplete, unbalanced by the missing third. Surely, by now, the time for the Tyr-ridan has passed and the three faces of God will never meet. From the start, it was a false promise, made by a false god. What my lord began with his so-called Fall, he will finish, and all of us who chose the winning side will have our reward. But first..." He stopped. "At least one of the twins *is* a girl, yes?"

"Yes. She bears her mother's name. From the first, I saw Jamethiel in her eyes, but the way she looks at me now..." Ganth shuddered and cradled his bandaged hand. Dried blood stained the cloth over his knuckles.

"What did you do?"

"N-nothing!"

"Oh, but you wanted to, didn't you? The taint is in the blood, and the attraction. Remember your brother Greshan? What he did to you...admit: some part of you enjoyed it. You Knorth. You come together like sparks in a holocaust and consume each other. And now you also have a son. Tell me, Gangrene, have you taught him yet how to play the midnight game?"

He slipped out of the way as Ganth lunged for him, tripping the Knorth as he passed "Now, now, temper. Or was Gerraint right?" His face shifted. Ganth's father drew himself up and glared down at his son. "Trinity," he said in that well-remembered voice, with freezing scorn. "Another god-cursed Knorth berserker."

"I am n-n-not!"

"Then control yourself, boy. These aren't the White Hills, and you have a son to consider. Ah, that poor, little tyke. Thanks to you, what is left for him to inherit?"

Ganth rose. His eyes smoldered silver in a white, haggard face. The shadows of the land rose with him, drawn up by the strength of his sudden, cold rage.

"What will Torisen inherit? My vengeance against those who brought me to this end and our house to such ruins. Trinity, why didn't I see it before?"

In his turn, he began to pace. The changer matched him step for step, up and down in the long shadow of the House, his half-hidden face slyly mocking the other's rage and despair.

"The slaughter of my kinswomen at Gothregor, the debacle in the White Hills, both were conceived within the Kencyrath itself, and by whom but the filthy Shanir?"

"Tsk, tsk, jumping to conclusions again, but then we all did regarding your womenfolk. As it turns out, one survived."

Ganth stopped short, staring. "What?"

"Oh yes. A child. *The* child, in fact, for whom my master holds a contract duly sealed by your father, for your sister Tieri."

"Liar!"

The darkling's eyes glinted dangerously. "Ah, be careful whom you insult. The reckoning between us may be slow in coming, yet it will come."

"I would have known if any of my blood still lived!"

"Would you? How? In the White Hills you threw down your name as well as your title and stormed off into a self-imposed exile. You say they forced you? Did you fight them? No. You had to make your grand gesture. They must love you, obey you without question, or Perimal take them all. Such is the Highlord's due. My master felt much the same. What did the Kencyrath, your house, or your blood matter to you then?

"To be fair, I only just learned about Tieri myself." Keral laughed in rueful admiration. "That clever Ardeth matriarch, hiding the brat for all these years, right there at Gothregor in the Ghost Walks. That's what they call your former quarters, you know."

"Ardeth. A house rotten with Shanir. I should have known."

"Then know this too. You have come for 'your' lady? She was barely yours even when you held her in your arms. Do you think she loved you? Do you think you were even real to her? The tighter you tried to hold her, the more she slipped away, into dreams and nightmares, into the layers of that rotting keep where you choose to fester in the ruins of your life. Let her go."

"I can't!"

"I know. Poor, lost, little boy. Then go back, Grayling, as fast as you can. Though you couldn't find her before, she is still there, waiting for her master's call; and here you are, hunting again in the wrong place."

Ganth stared at him aghast, his rage forgotten. "Still there?"

"Oh yes, but not for long. A day, an hour, a minute before you arrive...then gone, forever. Think about it."

The Gray Lord looked wildly about for his mount. It had regained its feet and stood watching him, unblinking. If it no longer breathed, he didn't notice. He sprang onto the haunt that had been his war-horse and set spurs to it.

Keral watched him go, smiling to himself. Then he turned. The doors of the House swung open to admit him.

Following her sunset shadow, Jame trotted across the stone bridge, through the gatehouse, into the keep's circular courtyard. She hoped that Tori would follow, that he was only giving her a fair head start. Playing hide-and-seek alone wasn't much fun. Recently, a lot of other things hadn't been either, but she kept hoping. Sooner or later, something interesting was bound to happen.

Now, where should she hide?

Small, stone chambers lined the courtyard, their backs to the outer wall. Some were domestic offices—a forge, an armory, a kitchen full of raw, wilting vegetables, a bakehouse, its oven days cold, a privy...

No, all too obvious.

Then there were the garrison's barracks.

Kendar sat listlessly outside on benches or lay out of sight within on their narrow pallets. They still looked and acted as if Father had cracked them on the head with a board on his stormy way out. Only Anar and randon like Winter seemed to have kept their wits. Jame wasn't quite sure about Tigon. The common Kendar were usually kind to her—when Father wasn't in a rage. Then they couldn't seem to help themselves. She slowed, feeling their leaden eyes on her. As she passed, some muttered words in a hoarse, familiar voice not their own:

"Another god-cursed berserker...filthy, filthy, rotten Shanir..."

But she wasn't Shanir, Jame told herself, balling up her fists in the pockets of her cut-down but still too-large shirt. She was only a freak with no nails and itching fingertips that drove her half crazy. Surely there were worse things than that.

Like hunger.

Right now, even a raw, near-sighted potato sounded good. It was another smell, though, that made the child's stomach growl, even though she couldn't identify it. The garrison, perforce, ate only overcooked vegetables, boiled grains, and stewed grass. This was something different. Jame followed her nose up the stairs to the tower's first-story entrance.

Tigon crouched over a small fire set between the inner and outer doors, cooking something. He tilted his broad, scarred face to grin up at the child as she stopped beside him. "I finally caught the little buggers." He plucked a nugget-shaped object out of the fire and popped it into his mouth. "D'you want one, lass?" he asked indistinctly as he chewed. An ecstatic expression lit up his battered face. "I have three left."

"No thank you, Tig." She regarded the randon's bloody, nearly toeless feet dubiously. "Will they grow back?"

"I hope so. All those damned, stewed weeds..." He spat out a small bone and smacked his lips. "Ah, you poor younglings. You don't know what you're missing."

A mutter rose from the courtyard, the words disjointed at first but each speaker slowly picking up the cadence:

"He is coming. He is coming. He is coming..."

"About bloody time," said Tigon. He wiped greasy hands on his jacket, rose, and lurched against the wall with a grunt of pain. Jame grabbed his belt to steady him. "Thank ye, lass. Not to worry. It only hurts when I stand, and worth every damned toenail." He glanced down at her bruised face. "Here now, you'd better make yourself scarce."

With his shovel of a hand, he scooped her into the hall and closed the door firmly behind her.

Well, she thought, standing in the sudden gloom, *that was interesting, but not especially pleasant.*

She began to wander about the circular hall, absently gnawing on her fingertips, feeling lonely and cut off from the growing commotion outside as the Kendar woke from their daze. Tori hadn't followed her, either. *Father says, Father says...*the more Father said, the farther Tori drifted away from her. It was like slowly losing sensation in an arm or a leg, except this was in her mind. The same thing had happened with Mother.

She paused in front of the worn death banner where the man with the warty nose had glowered out at the hall for as long as she could remember. Yesterday, he had shown only his back. Today, he was gone, leaving bare warp threads. The same thing had happened to banners all around the hall. Was she the only one who noticed? Well, they had been very, very old, nameless and dead long before her time. Her family must have lived here forever, although, oddly, none of the worn, woven faces in the hall had looked anything like Father, Mother, or anyone else she had ever known.

Another mystery.

Like Mother.

She was fading away too, only it had taken years, and she wasn't quite gone yet. Jame considered this. She didn't exactly miss her mother, since she hardly knew her. Besides, there was Winter. Tori seemed to feel her absence more strongly than Jame did—unless, again, that was Father's influence. Jame wished she could help Father. She had tried, but the very sight of her seemed to enrage him. Her hand stole up to her bruised cheek.

She knew she shouldn't have gone into the master chamber under the cracked, crystal dome, where her parents had lived in the brief time they had been together. She and Tori had been conceived and born in that big, ramshackle bed—the only one, in fact, in the entire keep.

Other bits of unique furniture included a small table heaped with bottles of dried up cosmetics and a large, dim mirror. Tapestries lined the windowless walls. In repairing them, the Kendar had added their own faces to the host of people who marched across their threadbare plains, as if to say *Consider us, too, among the dead.* Anar was there, and Tigon, and Winter, holding an empty-eyed child whom Jame now realized must be Tob.

Mother had seldom left this room, and Father still kept it ready for her return. He had forbidden anyone else to enter it.

Hard, though, to keep out a curious child.

When Jame had found the garland of flowers on the bed, it hadn't occurred to her that they were another present from Father to Mother, trying to win her back. True, they stank somewhat as all blossoms did in the Haunted Lands and twitched when she picked them up, but he must have searched long and hard to find them. Jame had only thought that they were pretty and had put them on over her own wild, black locks. Peering into the mirror, she had wondered *Is this what a lady looks like?* and pulled a face at her reflection. Then it had seemed only natural to go down to the hall and dance for the warty man who must, surely, have a very dull time of it hanging there on the wall, what with his ugly warts and all.

At first, she hadn't seen Father watching her. Then his husky voice had stopped her in mid-step.

"You've come back to me," he said. He looked half dazed with a relief so intense that it wiped twenty years off his face. "Oh, I knew you would. I knew..." But as he stepped hastily forward and saw her more clearly, the softness ran out of his expression like melting wax. "You."

Before she could move, he struck her hard across the face, slammed her back against the wall and pinned her there. She could feel his whole body shake. Before, she had been wary of him. Now she was terrified. "You changeling, you impostor, how dare you be so much like her? How dare you! And yet, and yet, you are...so like."

His hands rose as if by themselves to cup her bruised face. She stared up at him, hardly knowing what frightened her but very much afraid.

"So like..." he breathed, and kissed her, hard, on the mouth.

"My lord!" Winter stood in the hall doorway.

He drew back with a gasp. "No. *No!* I am *n o t* my brother!" And he smashed his fist into the stonewall next to Jame's head.

Now she touched the dry spatter of his blood, remembering how he had stormed out that day, shouting for his horse and his sword. He was going to reclaim his love, alone, and he would kill anyone who got in his way.

Winter had knelt beside her. "All right, child?" Jame remembered nodding, and not being able to stop until the randon touched her shoulder. Then Winter had risen but paused, briefly, looking down at her. "It isn't entirely his fault," she had said, and gone out to ready her lord's gaunt gray stallion before someone got killed.

If not his fault, Jame wondered now, *then whose?* Perhaps she was to blame for having taken those flowers. She sensed, however, that it also had something to do with love.

That was where destruction began, according to Father. Was this how it ended, with speckles of dried blood on a stone wall? If so, she would do without it, except for Winter. And

Tori. Whether he liked it or not, she would go on loving her brother—even if, right now, she felt more like hitting him.

"If I want, I will love," she told the empty hall. Her words became a chant, her small, bare feet stomping in time to it:

"If I want, I will learn.

"If I want, I will fight.

"If I want, I will live.

"And I want.

"And I will."

She was dancing now, a scarecrow of a girl, but with a grace and strength of which she was barely aware bred into her very bones. She followed the movements she had seen Winter teach Tori, the fighting kantirs of the Senethar, shaped to the defiance of her mood. Bend, turn, strike...ha!

Someone danced with her.

At first, Jame didn't notice. Then, out of the corner of her eye, she caught a pale glimmer, gone when directly faced, or rather shifting again to the side, just out of sight. It moved with her or she with it, mirroring each other in reverse. Her own movements grew more fluid and sure. Wonderful. Intoxicating. She lost herself in them, and found that she was dancing with her mother.

They circled, the fey child and the lovely woman with her dream-lost smile. Jamethiel's white gown and long black hair flowed around them. Her slender hands caressed the air so close that Jame felt their warmth on her face. She wanted to lean into them, to feel a mother's touch that she only remembered in dreams, but they glided away.

Dangerous, dangerous, murmured the air.

But why?

The hall shifted subtly around them, and shifted again. The faces were back against the walls, watching from their banners. No. They were drifting ghost-like in and out of the webs of their own deaths, sometimes turning to look, puzzled, sometimes turning away with a frown. This had all happened long ago, Jame realized. The years eddied and flowed while

Mother sang softly to herself, to her daughter, unaware that her very presence frayed the souls around her. This was where she had been all this time, wreaking ruin in the keep's past without even noticing. No wonder Father couldn't find her.

Outside, hooves rang on the flagstone amid warning cries: "Haunt!" "Catch it!" "Shut the gate!" "Too late."

Then Father hammered on the hall door, demanding to be let in.

Silly, thought Jame. *It isn't even locked.*

But that all seemed far away and unimportant. She danced on, lost in her mother's smile.

Somehow, they were upstairs now, in the forbidden chamber under the crystal dome. Jame couldn't see her own reflection in the big mirror, but she could see Jamethiel within its clouded surface, dancing in a dark, vast hall over a floor veined with glowing green. A shrouded figure waited for her. They circled each other, almost but not quite touching, in the ghost of an embrace. Then she danced on, deeper into the mirror, farther and farther away.

Only then did Jame realize that she was alone, in an empty room, in a bleak keep, in the heart of a haunted, hopeless wasteland. Amoung the dead.

The shadowy man held out his hand to her. She understood that he was offering her everything that she had been denied by Father: knowledge, power, and perhaps even love. And there was Mother—lost, found, and now about to be lost again forever. Jame touched the mirror. Her hand passed through it into cold air. He reached for her.

"Found you!" Tori bounded into the room. "That was the best game of 'seek' ever. If Father finds you in here again, though, he'll kill you."

Then he saw the mirror, and his jaw dropped.

Jame snatched back her hand.

"Don't!" she said sharply to her brother, grabbing his arm. Instinct told her that it would be fatal for him, the wrong twin, to enter that dark hall.

He stared past her into the shadowy, silvered depths. "But it's Mother! She's come back to us! I knew she would, I knew..." His voice faltered. "No, she's slipping away again. Let me go! I have to stop her!"

He reached for the mirror.

Jame hit him.

He turned on her, more astonished than hurt, and then furious. "Don't you understand? If Mother comes back, Father will leave us alone. If she doesn't, sooner or later he's going to kill us!"

"'Destruction begins with love'?"

"Yes! Now let me go!"

She wouldn't. In a moment, they were fighting in earnest, back and forth across the room. Tori's nose began to bleed again. So did Jame's lip when he split it against her teeth with a fire-leaping kick. In doing so, however, he over-extended. She caught his foot and tipped him backward onto the bed. Its worm-eaten legs collapsed. With a soft explosion of dust and feathers from an ancient mattress, the whole structure fell in on itself.

An inhaled feather set Jame to coughing helplessly. This wouldn't do; she had to rescue Tori. She was groping forward when a hand closed on her collar and jerked her back.

"What in Perimal's Name d'you think you're doing?" growled her father.

Then through the settling cloud he saw the ruined bed, with his son's legs sticking out of it. He tossed Jame aside, waded into the sea of feathers, and heaved the footboard off Tori. It had fallen on the boy's head, stunning him and further bloodying his face. He looked terrible.

Ganth turned on his daughter. "You little bitch! What have you done?"

Then, looking past her, he saw the mirror. Dust had dulled its surface, but something moved within it like a distant star. Hastily wiping the glass with his sleeve, he saw a blurred image of the Master's hall. A pale figure danced in it. His breath condensed on the cold surface and again, frantically, he wiped it away.

"Give her back!" he shouted, and struck the mirror with his fist.

"Now, now. Don't break the glass." The words, as distorted as the image, came from within. The figure had minced closer. Draped, loose skin instead of the white gown, flesh that shifted uncertainly between male and female—the changer Keral grinned and preened, naked, inside the mirror.

"Too late, Grayling. The Mistress is back where she belongs, with us, and here she will stay. You missed her by about ten minutes."

Ganth made a strangling sound. Then he grabbed Jame by the arm and jerked her forward, ignoring her stifled cry of pain. "You want the girl? Here. An exchange."

"Too late. My master has reconsidered. This child is too…unmanageable. Look at her! Can you see her ever taking the Dream-Weaver's place? Besides, she has shown none of the Shanir traits that my master requires. His gifts would be wasted on her. And now he has an alternative: a pureblooded Knorth child by your sister Tieri."

"Tieri has no child!"

"Not yet, but soon."

The scene in the mirror changed to a blur of white flowers and a sad young woman walking among them. A shadow fell across her and she turned.

"Tonight, in the Moon Garden, the contract that your father made so long ago with my lord Gerridon will at last be fulfilled."

With a terrible cry, Ganth shattered the mirror and ground its pieces to dust beneath his feet. Then he turned on Jame.

"You! This is all your fault!"

She recoiled, sure that he meant to kill her. She couldn't fight him; he was too strong, and beyond reason with frustrated rage. She had to escape, but where was the door? Tapestries covered every wall, all those mute, familiar faces, watching.

She bent over her brother and shook him. "Tori, wake up! Help me!"

The boy groaned but didn't open his eyes. Maybe the falling board had cracked his skull. "This is all your fault," he muttered, almost in his father's voice. Then a singular smile lifted one corner of his mouth. "Why, child," he said, and this time Keral spoke through him. "Didn't you know? Daddy is a monster."

She had paused too long: Ganth's powerful arm circled her throat from behind and jerked her up, off her feet. She kicked backward, without effect, and tore at his arm. Cloth ripped. He swore and dropped her. She scuttled out of reach, stopped, and stared, first at his shredded, bloody sleeve, then at her own no longer nail-less fingers. The itching tips had split open and peeled back. As she flexed them, appalled, sharp ivory claws slick with her own blood slid in and out, in and out.

"Shanir," he breathed, and the word was a curse. "A filthy, god-cursed Shanir. I should have known."

"No!" she said, holding out her hands as if to disown them. "I can't be!" She would chop off her fingers, she thought wildly, as Tigon had his toes, or trim them back to the quick. Anything...but too late: Father had seen.

He came after her, with Kin-Slayer unsheathed.

Jame retreated, crying, "Anar, Tig, Winter, help!" But none of them were here, except in their woven images.

She ripped down a tapestry, looking frantically for the door. The weaving fell over her pursuer in a cloud of dust. Swathed and stumbling in its heavy folds, clutched as if by hands of knotted thread, he hacked at the familiar faces.

"Traitors! How dare you try to shield her?"

Jame had her hands on the panel that depicted Winter, Tob, and a big man behind them whom she supposed must be Sere, Winter's long-dead mate. There behind it, at last, was the open door. Through it came Winter herself.

"Traitor!" screamed Ganth again, and cut her down.

Jame tried to support the randon as she sagged, but she was too heavy. "Winnie! Are you all right?"

Clearly, Winter was not. Ashen-faced, she clutched her lower abdomen, but even such strong hands as hers could not stem the tide of blood. Already, the floor was black with it.

Ganth lurched against the wall as if his own legs had failed him. He looked almost as stricken as the randon. "Oh my God. First Sere, then Tob, and now you. Oh, Winter. Ancestors forgive me."

He refocused on Jame who crouched before her mentor, trying futilely to staunch that terrible wound. She turned, nails out, prepared like some small wild creature to defend a loved one to the death, and would have gone for her father's throat if Winter hadn't gripped her arm.

"Run," she said to Jame. "D'you hear me, child? Run." Then, "My lord, you are still…not your brother…"

Her voice faded. She slumped sideways, hands dropping limply to the floor, coils of intestines spilling over them. Kin-Slayer had cut her nearly in half.

"You!"

Ganth's berserker flare seemed to pick Jame up and throw her out of the room. She ran with no thought except to escape—down the stairs, through the hall, out of the keep, into the Haunted Lands. Collapsing on a hillside, gasping for breath, she still heard echoes of the raging curse that had driven her out:

"*Shanir, god-spawn, unclean, unclean…*"

She stared at her…nails? Claws? Her hands were still covered with Winter's blood, as was her face with her own from the lip that Tori had split. At some point, it had begun to throb. Her fingertips hurt too. She clenched her fists to hide the nails, driving them into her palms. The more they hurt, perhaps, the less empty she would feel.

Unclean, unclean…

Tori had let this happen. No. What could he have done, even if he had been conscious? But would he try to follow her this time? Not against Father's will. No one would.

Night had fallen, and a cold wind blew. The grasses sang or moaned or sobbed, according to their kind. Haunts would soon be abroad. She couldn't stay here, and she couldn't go home. She had no home, not anymore.

Something large, pale, and ungainly sailed across the face of the moon. That was odd: nothing flew this deep in the Haunted Lands unless, perhaps, it had come from beyond the Barrier.

Watching it, Jame didn't at first notice the vibration in the earth. Then the moon vanished, eclipsed by Ganth's war-horse as it roared over the hill's crest, over her head, nearly clipping her with its steel-shod feet. Its saddle was empty. It swerved, red-rimmed nostrils flaring as it caught her scent. Jame had seen haunts before. They were always hungry, but not for grass.

Something pallid swooped down onto its back. It shrieked with rage and bolted. They plunged past, first one way, then the other, the haunt bucking, the rider groping for reins and flying stirrups. They disappeared over a rise. Jame waited, crouched close to the ground. No good trying to run or hide: with the haunt's keen senses, this was one game of "seek" she couldn't win.

And here they came, trotting back, the stallion in sullen acceptance, the rider tucking in the loose flaps of skin that had previously allowed him to fly. He grinned down at her.

"Well, well. I come to fetch my master one prize and find, perhaps, another. So you are Shanir after all, girl. I smell it on you. Perhaps my master cast you aside too quickly. In any event, it would be wise to make provisions in case his plan tonight fails. Would you like to come back with me to his House?"

Jame stood up, fighting the urge either to hide her nails or to use them.

"You said he didn't want me, that his gifts would be wasted on me."

"Maybe. In that case, we can always feed you to his new war-horse."

"Otherwise, he will teach me?"

"Oh, all manner of wonderful things." He extended his hand. "Well?"

As Jame hesitated, into her mind came the defiant words she had chanted to the keep's blank walls which even the dead had abandoned:

"If I want, I will learn.

"If I want, I will fight.

"If I want, I will live.

"And I want.

"And I will."

She took the changer's hand.

"Home, then," he said, pulling her up behind him.

Changer, haunt, and child cantered off together toward the Barrier, into the shadow of Perimal Darkling.

An introduction to "Child of Darkness"

This is the first complete story I ever wrote. You should know that, although I've fantasized about Jame and her world ever since childhood, I only got up the courage to commit said stories to paper after college. That was when I decided that I either had to realize my life-long ambition to be a writer or I had to do something else with my life. So I started writing, rather like someone throwing herself head first over a cliff.

If I had waited to know everything about this epic, I would never have written about it at all.

As it was, I tackled Jame as best I could, putting her in a familiar context—college, during the Vietnam protests, which in science fiction terms translated into a post-WWIII dystopian world. The rationale for this was that there must be more worlds down the Chain of Creation and that Jame, in fleeing Perimal Darkling, had over-shot Rathillien and crash-landed in the next world down the Chain—a world created by the Kencyrath's failure to stop Perimal Darkling in Rathillien. It was, if you like, an alternate history. I don¹t know if it will ever come to exist.

P. C.

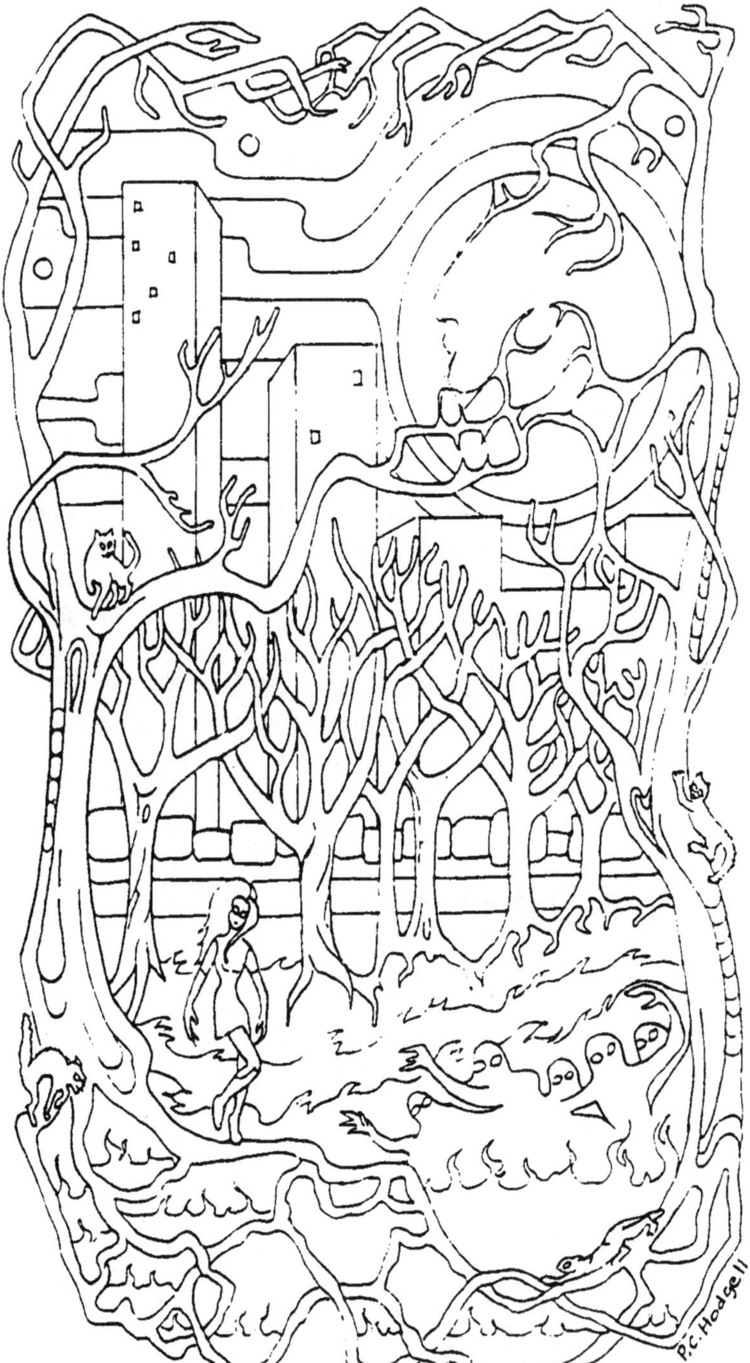
P.C. Hodgell

CHILD OF DARKNESS

"The moon is blue, Sam," said Tania's voice on the 'phone.

"Oh God," I said. "Tonight? D'you know what it's like outside—or in here, for that matter? There are uncracked text tapes stacked to the ceiling, I have a decade of post-holocaust pounce and counter-pounce to get straight, my lecture notes up to the midquarter have disappeared and the farking exam is in two days! Complications I don't need!"

"It's still blue. Please, Sam."

I threw the recorder at the bed, missed, hit the wall. Sounds of chaos in a plastic shell. So much for the rest of the notes.

"Awright, awright...hey! Who says?"

"Jame," she said, and clicked off.

Samuel, I thought to myself, *what the hell? First St. John tells us to sit snug for the night, which makes sense on finals' eve, and now Jame is calling the pack out via Tania, who's using the emergency code for the first time since—when? The cafeteria riots? What gives?*

Only one way to find out.

Next-of-kin updated with dorm security, I set off at a trot on the rim walk, bound for St. John's apartment on the other side of the central forest, staying close to the security posts.

Hard to b'lieve there used to be a stu b'hind each of those visored stone faces. Get boxed once too often and the brain goes like mashed pseudo-spuds. Admin loves veggies. Just re-psych 'em a bit, pump in loyalty to the government, and turn 'em loose to guard the buildings. Instant camp-cop. I could have been sliced n' diced in front of one and he wouldn't have lifted a paw to help me. But he would have reported the tom with the blade. Maybe only failing exams and wasting Admin property will get you boxed, but murder loses you credits. Therefore, killings on the walk are rare, even if pouncings aren't.

Not that it was any night to trust logic. Prefinal weeks are always hairy, and this one had been worse than any since that blue moon night six quarters ago when a whole norm pack had disappeared without a trace in the forest and Mang the Knifer, come to collect Jame Talissen for Sid Dillon's harem, made the mistake of trying to tomcat some for himself. That was when our Jame started their private war on a high note by somehow slashing him 'cross the face in four places at once and putting out his right eye. On a night just like this…

Sam, my boy, I said to myself, *these are fine thoughts for a lone tom out rim walking on finals' eve. Switch channels b'fore you go wobbly. Click back to the call.*

Ours wasn't so much a pack as "an interdependent defense unit" (St. John's term). If we were rallying, tonight of all nights, it was b'cause one of us had hit grief. Question was, who?

Ammie? Our weakest link, poor kit. Last finals, she came in a point too low on an exam—first time in her life—and the punishment box they stuffed her into turned out to be defective. Mishaps will evenuate, says Admin. Huh. St. John loved her b'fore the accident, still did afterward, so far as we could tell. As for Ammie, everything but St. John just sort of faded out of her world. Poor pretty kitten. Maybe poor St. John too.

But if it *was* Ammie, why didn't St. John call himself, and why pull in the entire pack?

Figured the other way, what emergency could Jame have that she'd want us involved in? She was of the pack, but didn't always run with it, if you get what I mean. If she was a tom's friend, she'd stand by him 'til the sky fell; but if she needed help herself, would she go to him for it? Not our Jame. A strange, wild kitten, that, even for a Kennie. Half-feral, St. John used to say. No one handed *her* grief for the fun of it.

So this was serious.

So what did you expect, microceph? And here you are tooling 'long the scenic route when a packmate—never mind which one—needs you.

So I cut off the pavement, down the slope, and into the trees. Like I said, it was no night for logic.

Spent the first mile dodging packs. This being exam eve, most of them were prowling the woods for game or holding circuses in their own territory. When one of those toms knows that, barring a miracle, he's in for a full tour in the box come next week for failing every exam on the sheet tomorrow, no way is he going to waste time cracking texts the night before the ceiling falls. All he wants is to forget, and friend, if he latches onto you as a diversion, you've had it.

The farther in I got, though, the quieter it b'came. First, the distant cry of packs faded out, then the wind, then even the insect hum. Dark, silent, spooky. Me, I'm a city-bred tom, used to prowling the levels from the top where most people live down to the haunted substrats and their piles of bones. Had never even seen a tree b'fore I hit campus. Was just deciding to take my chances back in pack territory when I stumbled into the clearing at the forest's center. Lordy, it felt good to be under open sky again. Over the treetops, the lights of the taller buildings ringed the forest. They were real to me, y'see; the clearing and woods weren't, what with their silence like a sponge and the ground littered with growing patches of mist.

Then I saw it, coming up between the horns of the science complex and by God, Tania was right: it was livid as a drowned man's skin and pocked with white mold. The clearing got brighter and brighter, 'til it seemed to glow. The moon, the blue moon.

Something cold touched my ankles. The mist was flowing sluggishly out of the tree shadows and into the clearing, and it glowed too. But there was no wind…

Next thing I knew, I was 'cross the open space and half way through the woods on the other side. Seems I ran straight through Duley's boo-juice loonies somewhere en route without even noticing, much less saying hello—something I'd normally do, they being 'bout the only decent norm pack on campus. Didn't stop at all 'til my knees gave out on the steps of St. John's dorm.

Two minutes later and fifteen stories up, Tania met me at the apartment door, stricken-eyed.

"What is it?" I said, hearing my voice skitter upward. "What's happened?"

Lancaster popped up b'hind her. "Quiet!" he hissed at me, loud enough to loosen plaster.

There was a thud in the other room and the sound of bare feet running. Tania shrank back against me as Ammie burst through the inner doorway. The smile on her face looked as if it were held up by poor tape, and in her hand was a med-kit needler with the three-inch hypo out, gleaming cold.

For a second, we just stared. Then Lancaster screeched and dove for cover b'hind the sofa, nearly colliding with Miri who'd been perched there and was now en route out the window, anti-grav pack whining. Ammie spun 'round once, lost world eyes skimming the room. Then she focused on the open hall door (with Tania and me still in it) and started for it, the needle in her hand tracing a silver arc b'fore her.

Jame appeared in the bedroom door, rubbing her elbow.

"Watch the door!" she called to me.

I took a deep breath and pushed Tania ahead of me into the room, keeping both hands on her shoulders in case I had to shove her clear. Wasn't necessary. Soon as the light hit my face, Ammie pulled up short, her smile crumbling. The needler hit the floor. A moment later she was down too, hands over her face, sobbing. Then Jame was on her knees beside her, arms 'round her shoulders. They stayed like that for a minute b'fore Jame picked up the instrument and got Ammie back on her feet.

I couldn't help b'cause of Tania. When Ammie folded, so did she, or would have if I hadn't caught her. Soon as the two kittens had disappeared into the bedroom, I put her in the room's only chair, liberated, like the sofa, from some stu lounge. She was shaking fit to fall apart. We were always afraid that campus life would kill her sooner or later. No empath, even one who only felt for half the population, had ever lasted through graduation. We might have lost her then and there if the crying in the other room hadn't suddenly died.

Jame came out of the bedroom, sheathing the needler.

"What kind of circus was that?" I asked her. "And who took the bite out of your elbow?"

"The floor," she said, glancing down at raw skin. "Ammie heard you at the door, pounced for the needler, and knocked me off the bed. You needn't laugh. Not now, anyway. St. John is dead."

"You don't know that!" It was Lancaster, up from b'hind the furniture and shriller than ever. "Two anonymous messages, and for that you call us out on finals' eve? Dammit, I have a final tomorrow afternoon!"

"And I have one in the morning," says Jame, cold as the Dean's heart. "The pack comes first. Sam, are you all right?" Guess I looked pretty green. "W-what happened?"

"He answered a call from the Under-Earth hours ago," said Miri from the window ledge, breathless as always, "and then someone 'phoned Jame and Ammie to say he was dead, so when Ammie heard you she must have thought he'd come home after all, and grabbed the needler to take to him like she always does with shiny things, and that's all we know...all!"

Jame had been leaning 'gainst the wall, gloved fingertips pressed 'gainst her eyes. Now she looked up. "Where are the rest of us?"

"Tsuma is in sanctuary at the library," said Tania's small, bleached-out voice from the bottom of the chair. "The Spider is on duty at the comp center. St. John is..."

"WE DON'T KNOW THAT!"

It was nearly a scream. Seeing that Jame had never learned to suffer nerps gladly, and looked ready to explode in this one's face, I jumped in fast: "So what do we do now?"

"First," glaring at Lancaster, "we don't panic. Second, we verify. Tsuma and the Spider are safe enough for now.

You two stay here until we get back. Miri, if you go out, keep to the air."

"And me?" I said, afraid I was going to get left parked under a table somewhere.

"If you're willing, you run with me. To verify." The half smile turned grim. "Alive or dead, St. John is coming home tonight."

Ten minutes later we were in the forest, traveling fast. We didn't meet any interference that trip, for a wonder: no hunting packs, and still no noise. Every time we came to one of those slow mist streams, Jame either detoured 'round or jumped over it. That made me feel better 'bout getting the fur up b'fore.

Watching how that kitten moved made me wonder how anyone could not know she was a Kennie, but then people didn't know much 'bout the Kencyrath in those days. Most folks thought it was just one of the mutie groups that popped up after the war. Me, I guessed different. Splintered as humanity had b'come, the Kencyrath was...something else again, with its own caste system, fight form, and even god. I'd run with enough Kennies in the city to know that much. Still, Jame Talissen threw me. Everything I'd come to expect in a Kennie she had: the lithe build, night-sighted eyes, and fine hands; the parallel streaks of honor and violence. But every trait was stronger or stranger in a way I couldn't quite nail down. It made me wonder if I really knew the Kennies at all.

I was thinking 'bout that and watching Jame when my foot sank into a patch of mist and I pitched forward flat on my face. Jame was crouching b'side me quick as a blink. Concern disappeared b'hind that solemn mask she usually wore to hide laughter, soon as she saw I was all right.

"Gotta watch that, Samuel," she said. "It's much too early for broken necks. Save that for later. C'mon."

She took my hand. We ran the rest of the way to the Pit.

The Pit. Just a gaping hole in the ground from the top. At night, just another big, black shadow. Easy enough to step right over the edge. Plenty of toms bought a straight ticket to the Under-Earth that way and arrived terminally zonkers. Not necessary. Not if you knew the footholds. Jame did, and so did St. John. They'd been drug runners to the Under-Earth for twelve quarters, altogether. Wasn't the sort of job they could do by daylight, either, what with all the rules 'gainst helping the Earthers in any way, most of all by smuggling in bootleg medicine swiped from the Center. Would have been a force ten box for sure if they'd ever been caught.

We sent down slow and easy that night, past the soil layer with its tree roots groping out like frozen snakes, past the plastisteel shell that supports the whole campus, down into the stagnant air of the Under-Earth.

Heights freak me, so I didn't rubberneck, much as I would have liked to. See, this was my first trip Earthside. The place used to be a living museum—y'know, a community preserved the way it had been back maybe two hundred years ago, b'fore the world went mad. Everything else like it had been razed to make way for new layers of the city. This town held out as long as it could. Then the 'versity made its proposition: the town would have its protection and patronage, plus access to the woods the 'versity meant to plant topside, if the locals would let their whole valley be roofed over and the new school built on top. Maybe greed got them; maybe they were just plain tired of fighting the zoning board. Anyway, they agreed. The dome was put up and an artificial sun was hung under it. Things went fine 'til the war. Then the school was knocked out of business, the access tube in the Pit destroyed, the sun extinguished, and the people Earthside died by the thousands, in the dark.

But not all of them. A few survived, and their descendants, warped by decades of darkness, radiation, and interbreeding, were the ones we called the Firsters. Weren't many of them left, and those weren't what you'd call the best of company.

I was running over that in my mind and wondering if I shouldn't be climbing up that pile of debris twice as fast as I was coming down it when my foot hit solid earth and I knew it was too late for second thoughts, however intelligent. We'd arrived.

All I could see at first was more debris and some big rectangular holes in the ground, each one with a faint, cold light gleaming up from its depths. We were standing 'mid the ruins left when the houses nearest the bottom of the Pit had been razed to make the huge mound down which we'd just climbed. Only the basements were left. Beyond, however, rose the phosphorescent outline of buildings.

Minutes later we were trekking down main street b'tween rows of black decaying houses and skeletons of trees straining up into the darkness. Dome was so far up, it couldn't be seen. Everywhere there were little streams of water like luminous slugs crawling through the dark weeds, and the death light of fungus, and the choking smell of rot. Everywhere, the mist bubbling up in the hollows slow and thick as pus, doors gaping black, glowing veins of mold on sagging walls, dust-dim windows showing items the peelings signs above never promised to sell, curtains held together with spider webs, eyes.

I saw the faces at the windows, white and still as the dead, watching us pass. They b'longed to the toms, yeah, and the kittens too, who had opted out. When they saw they didn't stand a chance of ever graduating free and clear and that the only alternatives left were a) to contract out to the government, thereby b'coming twenty year slaves, b) to hang on here 'til the box turned their brains to mush and the psych people got hold of them, or c) to die, and b'come med center property, they chose to drop out and down. Earthside, they never had to worry 'bout another exam, the box, the packs, or stuffing their kids under the bed every time there was a noise in the hall. It also meant they would never walk free in the topside world again. Since one of the 'versity's main purposes was to keep all the younglings under its thumb 'til they could be tied into the new society one way or another, isn't surprising that Admin didn't feel kindly to the ones that skipped out by going Under-Earth. The Earthers were nothing but vermin to it, and we all knew that sooner or later it would move 'gainst them. That was in those watching eyes, too: suspicion, hate, anger. The weight of it bit into my shoulders.

"Has it occurred to you that this isn't the safest place to be?" I asked Jame.

"Relax. No one's going to pounce us."

"Su-u-ure. I bet St. John told himself the same thing."

"St. John must not have had an escort. We do. Look."

I looked, and then, back b'hind the rows of houses, I saw them. Kids, dozens of Earther kids, white faces, huge eyes, skinny bare legs, skimming through the ruins of backyards, never making a sound, never taking their eyes off of us. They looked hungry. I tried to ignore them.

Then we came to the edge of town, with the rank, rolling fields freckled with corpse lights stretching out before us up to the mountain that ran into darkness to meet the horizon of the dome. Last house out was a big, brick one, nearly invisible under luminous mold. Its door stood open.

"We're expected," Jame told me. "Don't say a word once we're inside. He's been having one holy hell of a time lately, and there's no telling what he might do if you cross him."

Only one tom she could mean by that: Rimmon, lord of the Under-Earth. St. John had told me 'bout him. He'd been one of the brightest toms on campus with less than a quarter to go when he killed Sid Dillon's brother by accident in a pack clash. After that, it was either turn Earther or zonker, so he came b'low. Took up mushrooming, then organizing. Pretty soon, he had the whole territory under his paw. Drove out the Firsters, gave the place the first order it had had since the war. Then he caught the optic rot and went blind. He wasn't such a bad tom, according to Jame, but pain made him unpredictable, and sometimes vicious.

At first, it looked as if the house was empty. Just big rooms soft with dry rot, lit by murals of luminous lichen. Then there he was motionless in a corner, a tall skeleton of a man all in black, stretched out on a pile of silver grey rat skins. A scarf was wound tight 'round his eyes. Threads of mycelium crept out from under it and down over cheekbones near sharp enough to cut the paper white skins stretched over them. The minute I saw him, I guessed something St. John hadn't told me. Jame clinched it when she gave him a formal salute and said in Kens, "Honor to you, lord."

"And to you, Shanir," said the Highborn. Clipped words, the last one almost spat out. Jame went wary-eyed. "So, my runner found you."

"No runner, just a voice on the 'phone. Is it true, then?"

"Yes. I didn't know he was Earthside 'til one of my hunters found him. This was in his back." He reached into the furs, keeping his head still as a skull nailed on a post, and drew out a knife. Heavy blade, notched hilt, ugly.

Jame took it. Something in her face b'tween skin and bone seemed to twist. "And the body?" she asked, very softly.

"Gone. It was being held for you near the Pit, but the camp-cops staged a surprise raid and snatched it."

"He doesn't miss a twist," Jame said bitterly. "St. John dead, Ammie threatened, and now this. He's playing mouse with me. Well, we can play a game or two ourselves."

She bent over and whispered something in Rimmon's ear. The tom's head jerked back, anger or surprise, couldn't tell which, turning to a hiss of pain as his hands shot up to the bandage. Jame's gloved fingers were over his in a second. No emp could have reacted faster.

"It can't be done," he said, voice taut. "Not even by you, not even tonight, not even with the help of that filthy book. Don't try, Jame. You, of all people, know there are worse things than death.

That was too much for me. "Listen," I said to both of them, "will someone please tell me what's going on? I haven't scanned even half of all this."

The eyeless face lifted and turned on me.

"So...the little friend can talk."

Then he was speaking to me in Kens, so low I could hardly hear. Was as if the air 'round me was thickening, pressing in, and the darkness of the room b'gan to blur. Call it sorcery or high psi. All I know is that the words were in my ears, in my brain, and I was going blind.

Jame caught my arm. "Stop it!" I heard her say, sharp as bones breaking. "Is it his fault he can see and you can't? Leave him alone!"

Rimmon laughed, and the pressure was gone so suddenly that my knees almost buckled. Jame steadied me.

"Idiot," she hissed in my ear. "I told you to keep quiet." Then, to Rimmon, "Well? Will you do it?"

His mouth relaxed into a wry grimace. "If I can't hinder, I may as well help." The hands sketched a ritual gesture of submission, half mocking. "As you will, Shanir."

Again the salute, colder this time. "You honor me, lord. Honor be to you. C'mon, Sam."

She'd just turned to go when Rimmon's hand shot out and clamped on her elbow, and I nearly went for his throat, like a Pekinese after a cobra.

"If things go wrong tomorrow," he said to her in a low voice, "come back to me. Here you'll be welcome, and safe."

His whisper followed us out of the dark room, dry, rustling, almost gentle: "Be careful, Shanir."

"You know who killed St. John, don't you?" I said to Jame as we headed back through the dead city, again with our escort keeping pace.

No answer, to that or any other question I bounced off her, all the way to the Pit and up the mound of debris. Don't think she even heard me.

Then, topside, with the black woods leaning in on us and the full moon staring down, "Samuel," she says, "I have an errand for you. Go to my room and find the Book Bound in Pale Leather. Bring it to St. John's apartment. If I'm not back in two hours, try to burn it, then do what you can for Ammie."

She was almost under the trees b'fore I got back enough wits to shout after her.

"Hey! At least tell me what's going to happen tomorrow!"

For a second she hesitated, slim and white in the shadows. Then, "Dissection exams," she said, and was gone.

Sweet Trinity, of course. Where do zonkers go? To the morgue. Why? So that med students, like Jame, can cut them, like for a dissection exam. Jame had some bad enemies high up, those days, as well as some unlikely friends. They'd give her St. John to cut, and she wouldn't, and then it would be the box for sure. They'd make sure she never left it sane, like poor Ammie.

It took me maybe five minutes to reach Jame's dorm, and longer to find the book, which turned out to be tucked all nice and snug in her bed. When the room's cool air hit it, the little white hairs studding its pale binding bristled. I picked it up, and nearly dropped it again: the damn thing seemed to have a pulse. Not liking the feel of it at all, I found an old knapsack and gingerly poked the book into it.

I was headed back for St. John's by the rim path with that damned book heavy on my back when memory suddenly zapped me. Only one tom on campus sported a blade like the one that had killed St. John, notched for every cat he'd cut: Mang. Right then and there, I knew damn farking well where Jame had gone.

Guess I just stopped thinking then. In fact, guess I just plain panicked b'cause the next thing I knew, I was tearing through the forest, crashing into bushes, falling over roots, swearing with all the spare breath I had at Jame, Mang, myself, the whole farking campus—in short making one hell of a racket.

Oh, I paid for it, all right. You don't just go galloping through the central forest on finals' eve.

First thing I heard was the distant whine of anti-gravs. Then eyes of light blinked at my b'tween the trees. B'fore I could take cover, they were on top of me and I was on the ground fighting for breath in a circle of screaming plats and roars of laughter. Just when I thought I'd start screaming myself, something grabbed me by the collar, jerked me up on my toes. The plats skidded to a stop, all their lights on me, or rather, on us, b'cause I was dangling, half strangling, from the fist of a farking giantess.

Which figured. All Tungia women are huge, and Mama's platform racers seldom rode with anyone not of Tungia stock. Not did they have much use for any tom, there being no Tung males, unless he was at least as big as St. John.

"What're you doin' out so late, tomkin?" said a big, lazy voice. "Jame Talissen should keep her squire in on a night like this."

Then my eyes cleared and I saw that it was Mama herself who had hold of me. Mad as I was at being called "tomkin," much less anyone's squire, this was one Tung I didn't mind seeing. Like I said, our Jame had the damnest friends. So I spilled the whole story to this one, but fast. When I got to the solo raid I thought Jame was making on Sid Dillon's headquarters, Mama gave a rumbling chuckle.

"Trust little sister to go after the biggest game," she said.

"B-but she's going to get cooled!"

Mama cocked her head and stared at me, amused. "You got to learn 'bout Jame Talissen," she said. "Now there's one kitten with claws. But if that's Mang's blade, she may finally be takin' on too much, and if Jame don't help me cram for the English exam Tuesday morning, sure as Dillon's a one-balled tom I'll be boxed come Wednesday morning. So okay." She slapped me on the back, damn near knocking me off my feet. "We go see 'bout rescuing the hellcat...if she needs it."

Someone in the darkness let off a whoop, and the plats came on with a tooth-jarring whine. Mama jerked me up b'hind her on her machine. Wasn't much standing room, b'lieve me, or any power to spare. Somehow, though, we made it without bumping ground or breaking necks to the fire-gutted gym

Dillon's pack used as a rally point. The lower windows were boarded up, so we had to climb up a fire escape to the fourth level to get a good look-see inside.

Sure enough, there was Jame, standing alone in the circle of a spotlight, with the pack all 'round her in the shadows and Dillon himself lounging in his big chair up on the balcony. The notched knife was in his hands.

"Eh," said Mama in my ear. "That's big game, all right. Listen, tomkin, I'm gonna try something." She pulled an enormous knife out of her belt and shoved it into my hands. "You stay put," she said, and disappeared down the ladder. I used the thing's point to pry open the window.

Dillon was laughing, gently tilting the blade back and forth so that the light blazed off of it. A soft, almost pretty face that tom had, but the laughter made something nasty of it.

"Vicious, but not stupid," he said, still smiling at the knife. "Oh my, oh my. Your faith in my intelligence is touching, love, but vicious? You're half right, though: I didn't have anything to do with cooling St. John." Then, to the shadows below: "Mang, its your blade and your score. You want to say something?"

The pack made room for him. He stepped out into the circle of light and grinned at Jame. I could see the four parallel scars running down his face, and the drooping eyelid. She turned to meet him, moving smooth on her feet as silk on ice, into the first patterns of the Senethar fight form.

"Seems to me," she said in a low voice, "we've gone beyond the conference stage. Wouldn't you say so, Mang?"

"Could be, kitten, could be. But I still want to talk."

It was the slow drawl of a tom who has the whip hand and enjoys it. He was circling her now, thumbs hooked in his belt, head cocked sideways, still with that damn insolent grin on his ruined face.

"Haven't seen much of you lately. If I was the suspicious sort, I might think you didn't like me anymore, but I know better than that. You been waitin' just like me, waitin' for another nice moonlit night, waitin' to be free."

His hand stretched out, nails jagged and black, as though to stoke her face. She glided out of his reach, almost but not quite in a wind blowing move. His fingers slid through her hair as she turned. He laughed, a mean, oily, not quite sane sound.

"I must have been right, 'cause now that you're free, here you are. How's life been treatin' you, kitten? You got any griefs? 'Cause if things aren't just right, I want to fix them. This is our night, pretty eyes."

"It was St. John's night too, before some brave tom knifed him in the back, and Ammie's until a 'phone call caved in her world," said Jame, still turning with him, slow and easy in the patterns of the form. Her voice was steady, even pleasant, 'cept for an odd, throaty undertone getting stronger by the minute. "So many games, and it's still so long 'til dawn. Why do I get this feeling that we've barely begun?"

"'Cause you're smart, baby, just like I always said. This *is* just the start. How many in that pack you run with? Eight? Nine. One for each scar and four for the eye, and you know who goes first? Yeah, St. John's bonkers mouse. Only you won't be there to see it."

He snapped his fingers. Something flashed down to him, to be caught with the sharp slap of steel on flesh. From the balcony, a low, hungry laugh. The blade with the notched hilt burned bright in his hand.

All 'round them, there was a rustling in the shadows, a swaying forward as the eyes moved in. They thought they had her. They could almost taste the blood. Jame looked at Mang over the weaving point of the knife and b'gan to smile.

"Oh brave, brave tom," she said, and her voice was a deep rumbling purr that made my very bones shake. "I was going to save you for someone else, I really was, but not now. Come dance with me, lover. This is our night."

And she b'gan to take off her gloves.

It occurred to me then that I'd never seen her hands without them. When the first one came off, I understood at last how she'd scarred Mang so badly. By the time the second one had hit the floor, I knew that, whatever Jame Talissen was, she wasn't quite human, and it didn't matter at all.

They circled and circled while the pack strained forward and Dillon stared down, sharp, white teeth gleaming in the shadows, tongues licking dried lips. Death was a flicker of steel and ten long, curved fingers; a ragged leer and a half smile as thin and inhuman as the edge of any blade.

Then he lunged, and the lights went out.

For a second, there was silence. Then the big room turned into a madhouse. Could hear Mang shrieking "Get her! Get her!" in the dark. I jammed the point of Mama's knife under the window and wrenched it open. Wasn't thinking at all as I scrambled through and started down the wall. Window ledges are good as a ladder to a city bred tom. My heart was banging so hard I could hardly breathe. Then I was on the edge of the crowd. Something bumped 'gainst my arm and I slashed at it. It shrieked. Pushing my way toward the center of the room, I stumbled 'gainst someone else and raised the blade again in a dead panic. A hand caught my wrist in mid-air and Jame's voice hissed in my ear, "You idiot!"

She half dragged me through the pack and straight to the only door, something only a Kennie could have managed. It was locked. Jame swore under her breath, then suddenly stopped and gave a fierce little chuckle. I heard her scratch lightly 'gainst the wood panels. It swung open at once. She shoved me through. A Tung shut it after us and went back to leaning 'gainst it casual as if it were a tree trunk.

Jame turned on me. "You idiot!" she said again, really mad. "You could have gotten us both killed!"

That was when I saw the thin line of blood angling down her cheek just b'low the right eye to the edge of the chin.

"Hey, I didn't cut you, did I?"

"The way you were swinging," she said sourly, touching the red line with a fingertip, "it's a miracle you didn't decapitate me. But no, this isn't your work. The next time you pull the switch on me, don't do it in the middle of an attack, huh? It's damn distracting."

"Wasn't the tomkin's fault," said a voice behind us, and there was Mama. "Never mind the scratch—did you score?"

"Did you give me a chance to? Just the same, it was a pretty good try, considering that all the help was left footed. Sam, sorry I snapped at you, but these fits of heroism you've been having recently are beginning to scare the hell out of me."

"You should talk! What kind of bonkers idea was that anyway, taking on a whole pack single-handedly? Suicidal you've been b'fore, but never stupid."

"I know, I know," she said, looking disgusted. "I think we're all going crazy. Mang pounces St. John, I pounce a pack, and you, apparently, pounce anything that moves. Where is it all going to end?"

"Awright," said Mama. "Next play. Want us to step in on Dillon?" Her face lit up. "Be the biggest crash since Melba fell outta bed."

"Be spectacular, all right," Jame agreed. "Who am I to hinder great deeds? Fine time crash or not, Mang is going to want out. Keep the whole pack corked up here until the moon hits zenith, say, about three hours from now, then start the party. But make sure that he gets away."

I yelped. She hit me in the ribs with her elbow.

"I want to arrange for him to meet someone, and I need the extra time. How does that scan?"

"Rocky," Mama said, frowning, "but okay. Most of the time, you know what you're doin. Just don't get singed. And hang on to that squire of yours," she added, b'ginning to grin again. "He's small, but he's prime."

Jame wouldn't take the offered plat, wouldn't even let Mama send one of her people with us. She said she wanted to move fast, without the risk of cracking up on one or being held back by the other. Well, we moved all right. By then, I'd learned that the nastier things got, the quicker our kitten liked to tackle them. Just the same, by that time I'd been fed one more mystery than I could swallow. That was why, on top of a long slope with a pool of seething mist at the bottom, I caught her arm and made her stop.

"Does this seem like the right time or place for a conference?" she demanded.

"Right place or not, if I don't clear up some of these things now I may never get another chance. Maybe being used for target practice doesn't bother you, but me, I'm the sensitive type. I figure I've got a right to know b'fore someone gets lucky and cools me for good."

"They wouldn't take pot shots if you didn't bounce around begging for it," she said sourly. "All right, ask, and ask fast."

My chance at last. *Samuel*, I says to myself, *blow this and I'll never talk to you again.*

"So okay. Tonight I've seen your hands and Rimmon has called you 'Shanir.' That's a term I've run into before. Every time I asked 'bout it though, your people mumbled something 'bout children of darkness and changed the subject fast."

"'Name not the thing of power,'" said Jame, probably quoting from Book of the Law, "'lest it destroy you.'"

"Is that what you are, a 'thing of power?'"

"Tonight we find out. All right, this is how it goes: the norms have the muties; the Kencyrath have the Shanir, only the latter aren't something new. Just the opposite. To be one is to be of the Old Blood, to have certain traits that most Kencyr have lost, to be closer to certain forces."

"Ah ha," I said. "Then that would mean…"

But that was as far as I got, b'cause at that moment part of the sky fell on us with a shriek.

It was Miri. Her people may be light enough to lift off with an anti-grav pack, but their brains are 'bout as solid as their bones. Our pigeon had gotten her fields crossed and was flying more or less upside-down. Jame made a leap for her right leg, I for her left, and b'tween us we pulled them down. Beams realigned, Miri shot straight up in the air.

"Firsters," she shrieked down at us. "Firsters!"

"You and your damn tea parties," said Jame to me. "Where?" she shouted up as the Arian mutie cartwheeled out of control high 'bove us.

"Everywhere! Everywhere!" the answer came tumbling down.

I looked 'bout, breath snagged in my throat, and saw that she was pretty near right: we were almost surrounded. On three sides, silent figures had appeared under the trees, like twisted shadows. Mama, Rimmon, Dillon, you could take your chances with any of them. Not with a Firster. Victims of something that wasn't their fault, hunted by everyone, you could almost feel sorry for them. But not on a moonlit slope in the deep woods with the odds seven to one at best. No way.

"The senethar," Jame said in my ear. "Let's see how much you remember." I didn't know much to remember. So far, Jame had only taught me the first six figures of the water flowing form, and I'd never used any of them 'cept in practice.

No time to panic. Here came a Firster swinging a jagged piece of metal. I slipped out of the upward arc, caught his hand as it shot past me, and made him continue the swing up over his own shoulder. For a second he was down flat, staring up at me with eyes as pale and dead as the moon. Then he was scrambling to his feet again, making a whoofing noise. I'd forgotten that none of the first six figures are designed to take a tom out for good. So I kicked him b'tween the eyes. Jame had just finished with another two, and b'lieve me, they weren't 'bout to get up again.

More were coming, a good dozen.

"Too many, Samuel," I heard her say through her teeth. "Jump for it!" She was pointing down the slope toward the pool of mist.

I turned and started to run. Didn't think my feet could keep up with me at first. And the pool. You got any idea how ungodly wide something like that looks when you've got legs the length of mine? Well, I couldn't stop, and Jame had said jump, so I did.

Of course, I didn't make it. Not all the way, at least. My feet hit the mist and the next thing I knew I'd whopped belly down on the rim of land on the far side, with my legs thrashing 'round in what felt like a complete void. And cold? Friend, it was like the edge of outer space. Jame shot over me, diving headfirst into a rolling fall. The next second she was hauling on my jacket. A real quick kitten, that, but not very strong. I wasn't coming free half fast enough, and my legs were getting too numb with the cold to help.

A Firster came at us down the hill at a lurching gallop. One uneven stride took him from the far rim of the pool to nearly dead center. He sank in up to the waist, then, with a squeal, dropped out of sight like someone had pulled the ground out from under him. The scream seemed to go on and on, rapidly fading away into the whiteness.

Right then and there, I knew I wanted to get my legs out of that pool.

"C'mon, c'mon," Jame hissed as she tugged at me. "Can't count on them all to fall in…"

Bare feet pounded down the grassy incline b'hind us.

More than that there was the sound of heavier feet crashing through the forest toward us and of shouts. If it was more Firsters, we'd had it.

Then, just as the mist finally let go of my feet and the two of us went down in a heap, Duley staggered out of the trees above with a whoop. The rest of his pack wasn't far b'hind. Soon as I was sure that while others' grief was just b'ginning, ours had been postponed indefinitely, I turned to Jame, pointed to the mist pool, and said, "What's down there?"

It came out in a squeak.

She rolled over on the grass and looked at me. "You're getting hysterical, Sam."

"St. John is dead, you turn out to be a Kennie's nightmare," I said, hearing my voice go up like a slide whistle, "my legs are frozen, and I've just seen a tom fall through what ought to be solid ground into what certainly isn't the Under-Earth. Of course I'm hysterical! I repeat: '*What is down there?*'"

"If I tell you, will you stop screaming?"

"YES!"

So she told me, lying there in the long grass with the massacre of what turned out to be the last Firsters on campus going on up-slope, and me fighting the cold and the jeebies, lying b'side her. She told me that our Earth was only one in a series of overlapping threshold worlds that held together the multi-dimensional Chain of Creation. That thing down there, b'low the mist, b'low the frost, was what had destroyed the Kencyrath's home world. They called it Perimal Darkling.

"P-p-perimal w-what?"

"Darkling. Not that it is, exactly. Everything in it is mixed up: light and dark, heat and cold, life and death. Nasty, but fascinating…Anyway, the Shanir drew it to the surface so that it could be fought, but when it came it was too strong for them. The barriers fell, and everyone had to run. Where we ran to was here. What we arrived in the middle of was war. What triggered the madness that triggered the war was Perimal Darkling moving one world closer. Of course, all my people blamed the Shanir. They still do, perhaps with reason."

"T-that was decades ago," I said, glad to find that my teeth had almost stopped rattling. "Seems to m-me, we had a touch of that same madness six quarters ago, and again tonight. Why?"

She shot me a side-long look, both rueful and bleak. "Clever, Sam. Because twice now, that bastard Mang has stirred up all the Shanir darkness in me, and that in turn has called up the ancient enemy. I'm to blame for everything that's happened tonight—and I will pay, darkness against darkness, the only way a Shanir can. Any more questions? Then let's get on with it."

Half an hour later, I was sitting on the floor in St. John's apartment with Mama's big knife 'cross my knees and my back to the wall next to the bedroom door. The numbness in my legs had 'bout worn off. Was alone 'cept for Ammie, asleep in the next room, and Tania ditto, locked in the closet.

Had been a pretty grim scene when we got back. Ammie had fought clear of the sedative twice since we'd left and was coming up again as Jame helped me through the door. While she was in the bedroom putting the kitten under again and Lancaster stalked back and forth muttering, I folded myself into a corner and tried to put my head back together. All I could think of was the time I'd found Ammie sitting on the bed b'side a sleeping St. John with all those bright, useless bits of scrap metal spread out 'round her on the blanket like broken keys to the past. She was playing with them and chattering happily at him. Didn't bother her a bit that he was too zoned out to pay attention. She just wanted him to be there. Always.

Then Lancaster said *my god now what* and I realized that the moaning I'd been hearing was coming from the chair b'side me, not from the bedroom. There was Tania, looking like an out-patient from the morgue, carrying on the way Ammie had been when we came in. Psychic shock, said Jame, and put her down fast. Seems the poor kitten had been locked into Ammie's grief so long that she couldn't tell it from her own anymore. So we made her as comfortable as possible in the closet and locked her in. Not even sleep could ease those lines out of her face.

Turn 'em both over to the psych people, said Lancaster.

Be damned if she would, Jame said, what with psych finals starting the next morning. She picked up the knapsack with the Book Bound in Pale Leather still inside. I tried to stand up.

"You stay put this time," she said, pushing me back down. "Keep watch Lancaster will run with me—worse luck. We'll be back soon; before Mang, anyway, if Mama can only manage to hold him a bit longer."

"What're you going to do?" I demanded.

"Take advantage of the night's qualities," she says, one gloved hand on that weird, warm book. "Life and death overlap tonight, remember? And I made a promise: one way or the other, St. John is coming home."

Then she swung the knapsack over her shoulder and herded Lancaster out the door, bound for the morgue. Twenty minutes to get there, I thought. Twenty minutes to get back. And in b'tween, what? No idea, or at least none that I wanted to think through. Anyway, all I could do was wait and hope, like Mama, that Jame knew what she was doing.

A pale bar of moonlight was creeping toward me 'cross the floor. I watched it thinking 'bout all that had happened that night, 'bout St. John, Ammie, Jame and all the rest. It had been a good pack, but now it was bound to change, maybe even to fall apart. Without St. John, we were nothing but a bunch of strays again, misfits with nothing to hold us together but some scraps of friendship and the will to survive. Only Jame was fit to take over, but she never would on a permanent basis. Which was probably a good thing. Our unit was only set up for self-defense, and Jame, near as I could tell, lived in an atmosphere of perpetual violence. Running with her even for one night had pulled my muscles and nerves to pieces. Jame as a pack leader would have run us all to bloody tatters in a week.

'Til I started thinking 'bout that, I didn't realize how tired I'd become. Was so peaceful there and felt so good to be sitting down that I thought I'd close my eyes for a second, just to rest them.

I woke with a jolt in a pool of radiance. The moon was glaring at me over the window ledge, decaying mountains flecked with jade, valleys in suffocated blue. The room was humming with light. I lay on my side listening. Something had jerked me out of a deep six sleep. The whoosh of the tube? Had Jame come back? Was she standing there in the hall? Why didn't she come in? Then the sound, a weak scratching at the door. I scrambled to my feet and stood there swaying, Mama's knife clenched in my hand.

Silence.

Then it began again: scree...scree...screeee...

A shadow fell 'cross me and I heard plastiglass shatter.

"Well, well," said Mang, opening the broken window and stepping in from the outside ledge. "If it ain't the dwarf."

The door lock snapped with a sharp click. Another of Dillon's toms grabbed my knife hand b'fore I could turn 'round and twisted 'til the blade dropped.

"Think I wasn't smart enough to give the slip to a buncha Tungs, or to go out one window b'low and climb up?" Mang grinned at me, broken-toothed. "We were expectin' a warmer welcome, though. Where's the hellcat?" He grabbed my wrist and bent it. I think I screamed when it snapped. "You, wait outside," he said to the other tom, "I got some business here." Then he pulled the metal bands over his knuckles.

I stumbled back a step. The sudden pain had driven the shock out of my mind with a fire wind, and I knew damn farking well, as soon as I saw those bands, that if I didn't do something I was going to be beaten to death in the next few minutes.

The first swing, a rush of air breaking on the gleam of steel. I tried to use the fourth figure of the water flowing form, and found out fast it couldn't be done one-handed. The initial side step got me out of the way, but set me up like a picture for the reverse blow. The band caught me 'cross the mouth and almost lifted me off my feet. I staggered back, tasting blood. He came at me again, with that mad fixed grin on his face and a thread of saliva hanging from the corner of his mouth.

Think, dammit, I said to myself, backpedaling like mad. *It's your growth that's retarded, not your head. You can't use a water flowing technique b'cause the only ones you know take two hands. Fire leaping you don't know from a hole in the wall. Wind blowing...*

And there it was. The toughest form on the sheet, one not even Jame had mastered yet, but I did know this 'bout it: there was no contact. You found the lines of force and flowed 'round them. Like moonlight. Like a shadow. A long shot, lord, yes, but I knew my only chance when I saw it. So I took a deep breath and tried to relax.

For the first few minutes, it actually worked. That tom was a mass of mean muscle, all right, but he counted on scoring with every punch. The more he missed, the wilder he got. I was no master, though, and my legs had the strength of wet cardboard to start with. I knew my luck had 'bout run out.

Then I heard the sound in the other room, the squeak of bedsprings. Ammie was surfacing. I'd slept through the time when she should have been doped again.

The noise snapped my concentration. Next thing I knew, Mang had tagged me fit to cave in my chest, and my legs had turned to pulp. I was down flat b'side the bedroom door, fighting to breathe, when it opened. Didn't need to look up to know that Ammie was standing there.

Mang chuckled. The notch blade was in his hand, burning cold as death. He was coming toward...us? No. To get at me, he would have to bend; he wasn't. It was Ammie he wanted.

I was trying to get up and failing when something soft hit the hall door. It slid down the length of the outer surface. Wasn't even sure I'd heard it 'til I saw Mang swing 'round, the knife weaving in front of him. The door opened. Dillon's other tom fell into the room. His hands were over his face and blood was streaming out b'tween his fingers B'hind him I saw boots spattered red, the hem of a med tunic, a pair of hands with scythe-curved fingers dripping scarlet, and finally Jame Talissen's slow smile like a bittersharp edge of a blade.

Then she stepped aside. Someone stood b'hind her, too big to be Lancaster, not Mama either...who? Couldn't see the face, but Mang must have. The knife with the notched hilt slipped out of his hand and clattered on the tiles. He started to back up, slowly, making a gurgling noise. The square of the broken window framed his shoulders, moonlight flooding in 'bout them.

The knife was burning silver on the floor. I wanted that piece of honed steel. Now, b'fore Mang recovered and made a move for it. My good hand groped for it through the mist gathering b'hind my eyes.

Ammie got there first. She slipped past me on bare feet and scooped up that blade so fast that for a moment I thought I'd dreamed it; but there she was with it balanced on her palms, moving fast toward Mang. To this day, I don't know if she meant to pounce him with it or simply to return the damned thing. Mang didn't wait to find out. He jerked back another step as the kitten swept down on him. The back of his knees caught the edge of the window frame. For a second he was there, bending backward in a slow arc. Then he was gone. Not a sound. Nothing but hands circling in the air and plunging away. Ammie watched 'til the body must have hit bottom. Then she threw the knife out after him.

Was as if everything was b'ginning to move away from me. I saw Ammie turn, spot the large, shadowy figure in the doorway, and run toward it with a cry of joy. Then the darkness came rushing in.

When I came to again, it was early morning. The blue moon had set at last and thin sunlight was pouring through the broken window. First thing I saw was Lancaster, sitting on the floor with his head on his knees, like a man who's been sick and expects to be sick again. Second thing was the open bedroom door. Ammie was gone. The closet door was open too, but Tania was still there, asleep in a tangle of blankets. For the first time since I'd known her, she was smiling.

A hand brushed 'cross my cheek and I saw that it was Jame who was supporting my head. She was leaning 'gainst the wall and looked half zonkers with exhaustion. When she saw I was awake, she gave me a tired smile.

"It's all right, Samuel," she said, brushing more hair off my face. "Everything's all right. Mang is dead. St. John and Ammie have gone down to the Under-Earth. Rimmon promised to find a place for them where they'll be safe, and together."

I stared at her. Hurt like hell to speak, but finally I got it out. "B-but St. John is dead!"

"Of course," she said, and smiled.

An introduction to "A Matter of Honor"

This was the story out of which *God Stalk* grew. My idea at the time was to put Jame in a Fritz Leiber-esque setting and see what happened. For the Gray Mouser, see Jame; for Fahrd, see Marc. For the gods, well, see them for themselves, whatever the hell they are. It was supposed to be a five-finger exercise, to see if I could write a novel. I wrote the first draft at Clarion, the workshop for would-be science fiction and/or fantasy writers, and Kate Wilhelm bought it. That was my first professional sale.

P. C.

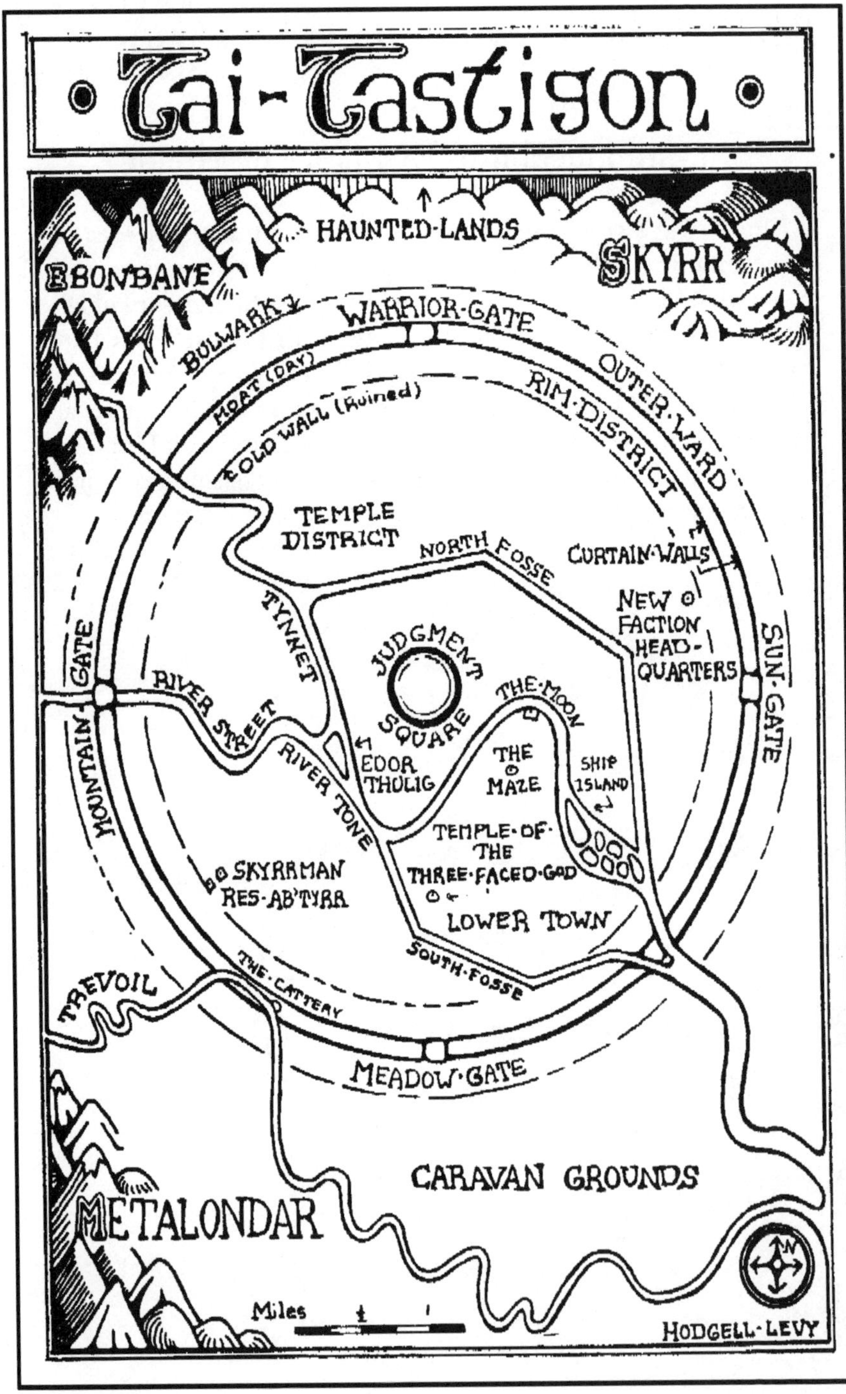
Tai-Tastigon
HAUNTED-LANDS
EBONBANE
SKYRR
BULWARK
WARRIOR-GATE
MOAT (DRY)
OLD WALL (Ruined)
RIM-DISTRICT
OUTER-WARD
TEMPLE DISTRICT
NORTH FOSSE
CURTAIN-WALLS
NEW FACTION HEAD-QUARTERS
TYNNET
JUDGMENT SQUARE
MOUNTAIN-GATE
RIVER STREET
THE-MOON
SUN-GATE
EDOR THULIG
THE MAZE
SHIP ISLAND
RIVER TONE
TEMPLE-OF-THE THREE-FACED-GOD
SKYRRMAN RES-AB'TYRR
LOWER TOWN
SOUTH-FOSSE
THE-CATTERY
TREVOIL
MEADOW-GATE
CARAVAN GROUNDS
METALONDAR
Miles
½
1
N
HODGELL-LEVY

A MATTER OF HONOR

It was sunset in the free city of Tai-tastigon. To the west, fire rimmed the Ebonbane Mountains, streaking their summits with veins of snow-kindled crimson. Far below, the last light was climbing the towers of the city's thousand temples. Shadows flowed into the labyrinthian streets.

In the southeast quarter the merchants were closing their shops. Strongroom doors swung shut, traps were set, guards emerged from the dusk to take their posts. Darkness settled there bit by bit, but to the north torches flared as the thieves' bazaar began its nightly trade. Those favored by the Master of the Brotherhood had set up their stalls within the protection of his great courtyard offering cream furs and emeralds, jacinth and blood velvet. Others, less fortunate, established themselves in nearby passageways, as wary now of the street merchants gathering up their wares for the night as the latter had been of them earlier. Meanwhile, everywhere the temples had begun to speak. Night came as always to Tai-tastigon with the murmur of chants and hawkers' cries, bells and barter.

This night, from somewhere in the maze of passages near the eastern gate, a sudden howl sliced through the twilight hum of the city.

"Ai, Baio-caina, Baio-caina, ai!"

The merchants on Half Moon Street who had not yet taken down their stalls paused, listening. Then they hurriedly gathered up all they could carry and ran.

Two figures rushed down the street. They were women, hardly, in fact, more than girls. Each held something out before her as though to keep it as far from her body as possible, something long, red, and dripping. Wailing, they raced on toward the Judgment Square where all roads met.

A low roar followed in their wake: many feet, many voices. Preceded by torches, a black mass surged. In another second, the tide of bodies swept Half Moon Street, crushing the abandoned stalls under foot. There were hundreds, thousands of them, young, beautiful, terrible. They ran hand in hand in five long chains.

The Talisman Jamethiel stopped at the mouth of the narrow lane, biting her lip in exasperation. In the excitement of her own chase, she had forgotten about the festival of the goddess Baio-caina, she had forgotten that certain roads would be inaccessible because of it. It was inexcusable for an apprentice of the Brotherhood, much less for a Kencyr. If they caught her here, by the third face of God, she deserved it.

The celebrants had seen her. They were calling to her.

"Talisman, Talisman! Join us! Dance with us!"

Jame glanced quickly over her shoulder. Two large forms had appeared at the other end of the alley. She jerked her cap down over her ears, took a deep breath, and plunged forward into the rushing mass. Hands closed eagerly on her hands. She was swept away. Baffled, the two guardsmen stopped just short of the spot where the girl had stood a moment before.

The celebrants moved swiftly, filling the street from side to side. As the way broadened, some hundred paces from the entrance to the central square, the five lines began to weave themselves into intricate patterns. Jame whirled with them. Despite precautions, her cap had been lost in the first few minutes and her long jet hair whipped in her eyes, half blinding her. She threw back her head, laughing out loud at the swift grace of the dance.

Then they were in the Judgment Square. Jame twisted free and slipped out of the crowd. A moment later she stood on the edge of the square. The celebrants were dancing around the Mercy Seat in the center of the area. So many flowers had been thrown on it that not a stone was visible. There was something sticking out near the top of the fragrant hill, something that looked at a distance like a large, dark red spider streaked with brown. It was a human hand, stripped of its skin. The rest of the body, as flayed as the single protruding member, was buried in white and amber blossoms. Up until the third hour of the afternoon it had still twitched at the touch of every fly. Not so now. The captured thief was at last dead.

Jame gave him and the worshippers a solemn salute, dodged two of the latter who wanted her to stay, broke the wrist of a third who was more persistent, and set off for home.

The inn where Jame lived and earned the honest part of her living as a senetha dancer was located on the north side of the Belching Kinka marketplace in the southwest quarter of the city. It was a popular place and did a roaring business from about the eleventh hour on, but this early in the evening it was usually deserted. It was a surprise, as she pushed open the heavy oak door, to see a wine goblet flying at her head. It was so much of a surprise that she almost forgot to duck.

"Whore...pervert...defiler of the one true temple! I saw you! I saw you dancing with them. I saw you honor that...that..."

The tirade turned into a sputter, and the sputter into a scream of rage as a Gorgo high priest rushed at her in a storm of whipping gray and silver fabric, brandishing a pudgy fist and continuing to shriek. Jame stared at him. The sheer ineptitude of the attack filled her with something very like awe. It would be almost a desecration not to let it fall apart of its own accord, she thought, but then, as the would-be assassin rushed toward her, she found herself instinctively slipping under the wild swing. The edge of her foot clipped the priest's left ankle, caught the right as it swung forward, and then, as the little man's momentum shot him forward over the threshold, swept up both sharply in a fine, high kick. It was a perfect demonstration of a senetha dance step altered into a movement of the lethal senethara fight form of the Kencyrath.

Tubain the inkeeper was waddling toward her across the room, wiping sausage fingers on his apron as he came.

"I don't think the honorable Loogan likes me very much," she said, closing the door. "Never play a joke on a priest. They have no sense of humor and they never forget."

"Priests," said Tubain with a fine rumble of contempt, "are not what you would call normal people. You should know that after all your trouble with M'lord Ishtier. Were you down in the square worshipping the goddess?"

"I was there," said Jame, making a face, "but hardly worshipping. It was a choice between dancing with the Baio-cainites and being taken and probably raped by the guards. They must have known that Marc has been hurt."

"Otherwise he would have been there to take them apart piece by piece, eh? They'll have their turn when his head heals, I'm sure. But Baio-caina...for a moment I thought you'd finally seen reason and given up the Three-Faced God. How you Kencyrs ever came to settle on such a grim master is beyond me."

"We didn't settle on him," said Jame sourly. "He settled on us. You have no idea what a curse it is to be a member of a chosen race. But I had better go see if Marc is all right."

"Remember," he bellowed after her as she started up the stairs, "you dance at midnight. You gave you word...and try *eating* something once in a while. No one's going to pay to see a skin full of bones, even if it *is* the only senetha dancer in town."

Jame stopped short on the steps. With the air of a street magician, she produced two overripe peaches from the wallet that hung with her belt.

Tubain broke into a roar of laughter. "The best apprentice thief in the Brotherhood, and she uses her talents to steal half rotten fruit! What would the Master say to that?"

Jame smile sweetly and pulled out a small leather bag. The innkeeper stared, slapped at his apron, and began to swear.

"He would probably say that practice perfects," said the Talisman, and tossed the bag of coins down to its owner.

Tubain knew his Kencyrs too well by half, Jame thought wryly as she bounded up the stairs two at a time. He knew it was safe to keep a thief child in his house because any Kencyr would rather lose a hand than break the laws of hospitality, and his life outright rather than break his sworn word. It was all a matter of honor, and honor, along with a fierce loyalty to each other, and a resentful but unquestioning belief in the god of the three faces, was an obsession among the people of the Kencyrath.

Jame shared their preoccupation with this concept of honor and the code called the Law that embodied it, but for reasons of her own. With neither strength nor friends to rely on, her survival in a violent world had always depended on wits, the same unquenchable desire to learn anything and everything that had led to her apprenticeship in the Brotherhood, and a moral flexibility that most of her kinsmen seemed to lack. She suspected that the latter was due to tainted blood. Her mother, after all, had been a priestess, and every Kencyr knew that prolonged contact with the Three-Faced God resulted in a certain contamination of mind and body. All her life Jame had fought the darkness in her, the sense of power and damnation moving together under the surface of her mind. Her loyalty to the letter of the Law, if not to its spirit, was her one grip on the normal world of the Kencyrath as she understood it. If the day ever came when she found she could lie under oath, do injury to a kinsman, or break her word, for any reason whatsoever, she would know that she was lost.

All such thoughts faded as the girl emerged on the fourth floor. It wasn't much more than a loft, with many apertures of varying sizes and the promise on this autumn night of many cold nights to come. Beneath the irregular line of windows that overlooked the market place, Marc lay face up on his pallet, snoring loudly. The big Kencyr was still in his guard's uniform except for the boot that Jame had hauled off the evening before, only to find she couldn't budge the other one.

Beyond that, the only unusual thing about his appearance was the bandage wrapped around his temples. It hardly seemed enough to justify the fact that for a night and a day he had been lying as motionless as a corpse, although not as soundlessly. It had been his boast, when he came staggering home with his broken head, that he could sleep off anything short of total decapitation. Now he was proving it.

As she checked her friend's condition, Jame wondered what he would think if he ever found out what she had caused to happen to the man who had injured him. At the time it had seemed in keeping with the best traditions of the Kencyrath, but now she suspected that she had overdone it a bit.

Satisfied at last that all was well, she stood up. Her reflection rose to meet her on the polished surface of the buckler that hung from the support between the windows. She regarded it with raised eyebrows. Eyes too big, cheekbones too high, lips too thin. Tubain, damn him, was right: she looked like a winter famine colt. Jame grimaced at the mirrored features and turned her back on them.

That was when she saw it. Lying on her own pallet was a small folded square of parchment. Jame crossed the room and picked it up. She frowned when she turned it over and saw the emblem stamped on it in black wax. She broke it open and read. The frown deepened. The girl stood there for a long moment with the paper in her hands, biting her lip. Then she turned back to the sleeping guardsman.

She crouched beside him and shook his shoulder. The snoring continued without a break. Another harder shake and a light cuff were equally ineffective. Then she braced herself and began to pummel him on the chest, gently at first and then with force. The sleeper muttered and made a vague sweeping gesture with one hand as though to brush away an annoying insect.

The girl sat back on her heels, massaging her knuckles, and regarded him thoughtfully. Of course, it was to be expected. The first impulse of any wounded Kencyr was to sleep and sleep deeply. It could easily be another two days before he woke of his own accord. Was it worthwhile to keep trying? Under the circumstances, probably not, but Marc would be more upset later if she didn't try than if she succeeded.

Accordingly, Jame stood up, unhooked the buckler, and swung it with all her strength against the stone support. The resulting crash might not have been sufficient to wake the dead, but Marc, after all, was only asleep. His eyelids peeled back slowly.

"Huh? Whazzamatter?" he said.

Jame knelt beside him and took his gray head in her hands.

"Marc, listen a minute. I've been summoned to the temple by Ishtier, Trinity only knows why. If I'm not back by the time you wake up again, I suppose you'll have to come after me. Do you understand?"

"Issshtier...?" Marc struggled up on one elbow. "You can't do that...he hates you."

"That's no distinction. He hates everyone. Now go back to sleep."

Marc gave his head a fierce shake as though to clear it, and immediately began to swear, one hand groping for the bandage. "God's claws," he muttered. "When I get my hands on the lad with the club..."

"No need to worry about him now," said Jame, suddenly expressionless. "He...uh...had an accident early this morning. His grapnel line snapped as he was climbing out of Merchant Dazda's compound with a few borrowed gems. Your brother guards caught him. Now he, or at least what's left of him, is in the Judgement Square on the Mercy Seat. Put down that boot. You aren't fit to do anything but sleep."

"Ha!" said Marc with a cheerful but somewhat blurry grin, climbing unsteadily to his feet and stomping to force his foot down into the heel of the boot. "You've raised the beast right and proper, and now you'll have to put up with him. I'm going with you."

Jame swore luridly under her breath. Of course he would say that. For the first time in her life she had a genuine protector even if, at the ripe middle age of eighty-three, he was old enough to be her great grandfather, and she was worse at coping with him than with her bitterest enemy. With a sigh, she helped the guardsman find and buckle on his old cross-hilted broadsword.

They went by way of the twisting streets that linked the southwest quarter of Tai-tastigon with the south. The passageways were full of life that night. Hawkers cried their wares. Merchants' sons strutted their finery. Men with bold, quick eyes slipped through the crowd. They passed the end of the incense sellers' street where clouds of myrrh, lavender and allentine waged war in the air and made the torches burn blue. Jame wrinkled her nose at the confusion of odors and jerked the trailing hem of her cloak out from under the hooves of a carthorse. Twice already someone had nearly stepped on it. It was of the sort favored by most thieves, voluminous and loosely fastened at the throat to tear off easily in the hands of a pursuer, but this particular garment was a hand-me-down from a much larger colleague. Jame swore to herself again to take up the hem as soon as she could, and promptly forgot all about it as a troupe of ophiolaters rushed past carrying the longest, limpest snake she had ever seen.

All activity and noise died away behind them as they neared their destination. The streets were completely deserted by the time the two reached the area of the temple. All was darkness and silence and slow decay there. No one asked what had happened to the buildings that lay in the shadow of the god of the Kencyrath; no one wanted to know the answer.

Jame and Marc paused on the steps. Above them, the front of the temple stretched up to the black sky as smooth and white as living bone. They crossed the threshold side by side, with Marc's great paw of a hand on Jame's shoulder.

Inside, there were floors of onyx, ivory walls, and the red, fitful winking of many torches. For Jame there was also the slow, suffocating pressure without and the growing core of darkness within that told her she was very near a source of the ancient power. The hereditary currents of her blood carried her to it unerringly through many stark rooms with Marc striding behind her. When she stopped, it was done so suddenly that the man nearly ran her down. They had come to the central chamber, and the great black granite image of the Three-Faced God loomed over them, three shrouded shapes melted into one another. Two of the dark figures were turned away. The third faced the room. It was overlaid with plates of pale marble carved so thin that they almost resembled a veil. The face and all the body except for certain sinuous curves and one hand were concealed in the stone shroud. The hand reached out and upward through a fissure in the masonry as though beckoning. Each long scythe-curved finger was tipped in ivory, honed and gleaming. Jame felt her own abnormally long fingers curl into fists at her side.

The presence of the statue was so overpowering that it was a full minute before either Jame or Marc realized that Ishtier was standing in front of it, watching them with unblinking yellow eyes. He was dressed all in white in honor of the image that towered above him, white for Regonereth, the most feared of the god's three aspects, white for That-Which-Destroys. His figure seemed sunken into the hieratic robes and the face in the shadow of the cowl was almost as fleshless as a skull's. Toward the end of most Kencyrs' lives, at some age between one hundred forty and one hundred fifty-five, it was natural for them to go into the sudden physical and mental decline that preceded death. Although Ishtier's body had been slowly collapsing in on itself longer than anyone could remember, his mind had never once been known to falter in its subtlety. Long contact with the god had been known to have even stranger effects than this.

"You wished to see me, My Lord?" said Jame.

"You, yes. Not him," he said brusquely. A curious humming murmur seemed to fill up the spaces between his words.

The strange noise made Jame frown, but she had no time to consider it. At that point Marc, despite a commendably brisk start half an hour before, suddenly began to sway. Jame slipped an arm around his waist to hold him steady and punched him in the ribs to forestall a rising snore.

"Pardon, My Lord," she said to Ishtier, getting her shoulder under Marc's armpit and heaving him upright. "We come as a set. If you try to put him out now, I shall tip him over on you."

Ishtier regarded the swaying giant sourly for a moment. Then, abruptly, something flickered through his expression. It was gone too quickly to be recognized. When his eyes turned back to Jame, they were as hard and unreadable as before.

"I have an assignment for you, thief," he said coldly.

Jame stared at him. "You want something stolen? For six months you do your best to make life impossible for me because I'm temporarily one of the Brotherhood, and now you want me to steal for you? Priest, you have a strange sense of humor."

"Hunzzaagg," said Marc.

"What?" snapped Ishtier.

"Never mind him," Jame said hastily. "He thinks he's awake. It's a common delusion."

"Humph!" the priest said. "Listen to me, wench. I said nothing of stealing. Look here." He stepped aside. There was a small altar behind him, with a fine silver chain lying shattered upon it. Jame caught her breath. "You see?" said that strange humming voice. "The Scroll of the Law is gone. Stolen. In this temple, until it is returned, only I the priest stand between the people of the Kencyrath and their god, all-dread be to him. I want you to retrieve it."

Jame struggled with an answer. The murmur was no longer only in her ears but in her mind as well. It had slipped between her thoughts, deadening as heavy folds of cloth. The air of the room had suddenly become too thick to breathe. There was nothing before her but the monstrous image of Regonereth. The ivory tipped fingers were reaching out...

Then Jame realized what was happening. She threw back her head and shouted with all the breath that was in her. Beside her, she felt Marc jerk awake and heard his startled snort, but her eyes were locked on Ishtier. At last she knew why the priest had been attacking her so long and so viciously over the past months. He had seen the darkness in her. He had suspected that she was closer to his god by right of blood than he could ever be. The test had come and gone before she was aware of it, and she had betrayed herself by breaking free from his will. The face that flared back at her was contorted with hatred and jealousy. Now it would be war between them to the end, for he would never again let her live in peace.

But there was something else at stake now, she remembered, still struggling with the fading wisps of mind mist. It was neither priest nor god that she was being asked to serve, but the Law. If she refused, the one link that she had chosen to acknowledge with her people would be broken. An abyss had opened; if she turned her back on that empty altar, it would be beneath her feet. There was only one way to go.

"Where is the scroll?" she asked in a low voice. "Do you know?"

"I know. It has been taken to the temple of Gorgo. Promise before our god that you will bring me the scroll that lies in the arms of the false image there. Your word on it, thief!"

"Priest," said Jame grimly, "death break me, darkness take me, the scroll will be in your hands within three hours. My word on it."

"What in the three worlds," said Marc as they left the temple, "was all of that shouting about?"

"He tried to whisper the power down on me," Jame said with a gesture of contempt, although she still felt rather shaken. "The old fool. If much more of it had come, he might have whispered the building down on us all. But you had better go home now. This next bit of work calls for my talents, such as they are, not yours."

Marc only snorted.

The one-sided argument continued street after street, past the subtle fire of the opal market, the crystal temple of Jacarth, and the Judgment Square, which Jame was careful to skirt by several blocks. Several times the girl considered slipping away. Even with his wits fully about him, Marc could never have caught her in the alleys and on the rooftops. But he knew where she was going. It would only mean that he was likely to come shambling in at some awkward moment, if he didn't fall asleep in some doorway first, and Tai-tastigon at night was no place for an unconscious man. It wasn't until they were crouching in the shadows outside the silver-streaked temple of Gorgo the Lugubrious God that she finally accepted the inevitable.

The sound of ritual mourning was rolling out of the wide gate and down the steps to them. Marc stared up at the bright entrance and the stream of celebrants passing through it. His eyes had a suspiciously unfocused look to them.

"How do we get in?" he asked.

Jame took a deep breath. "The most obvious way," she said. "Put your hood over your head like a proper worshipper, and try to wail a bit."

They went up the steps together and joined the crowd within. All were gathered in the outer chamber, waiting for the evening ceremony to begin and working themselves into the approved tearful state. There were seven tall pillars spaced around the edge of the room. Loogan was perched precariously on top of the one nearest the door to the inner chamber with his long silver gray robe flowing down to the floor on all sides of it. From below, one might have supposed him either to be a very tall man with a very small head or a street performer on stilts. The combination of his loud, simulated grief and the wild circling of his arms every few minutes to maintain balance added a good deal to the liveliness of the assembly.

The young thief began to edge her way across the packed floor. Behind her, she could hear a sound vaguely like the hoarse bellowing of a love-starved bull. Marc, who had never wept out loud in his life, was valiantly doing his best. Jame began to wonder if she was doing something profoundly foolish. There was an apprehension growing in the back of her mind that refused to take on a definite shape. Something about the expression on Ishtier's face...

A sudden pain in her hands brought her back to the present with a start. She had been holding her fists so tightly clenched at her side that the sharp nails had actually broken the skin. It was then that she realized she was not holding up her cloak. She made a quick grab for it a second too late. Marc's foot came down on the trailing hem. The clasp at the throat immediately let go, as it had been designed to do, and the whole garment fluttered down out of sight even as she twisted around to catch it.

From his high perch, Loogan gave a shrill yelp.

"The blasphemer, the Baio-cainite!" he screamed, pointing down at the slender, hated figure. "Take her, take her! A sacrifice, a sacrifice for the great Gorgo!"

Panic caught Jame by the throat. Scores of faces were turning toward her, contorted in rage; scores of hands were reaching out. The mass of humanity in the room rose about her like the crest of a tidal wave. The nightmare quality of the scene froze her where she stood.

"Sweet Trinity," she heard Marc say under his breath in a tone of self-disgust, and then she flinched as the full-throated war cry of the Kencyrath boomed out almost in her ear. The human wave froze. Up on his pedestal, Loogan did a passable imitation of an unbalanced statue. At that moment the inner chamber door opened and another priest, startled by the sudden roar, peered out. Marc reached past Jame with a muttered, "Excuse me," caught the man by the front of his robe, and threw him over his shoulder as easily as if he were a three-day-old pup. Instantly the room was bedlam. Loogan pitched head first off the column with a squeal. Roaring, the crowd of worshippers rushed forward. Marc grabbed Jame by the collar and threw her into the inner room. A stride carried him across the threshold after her. Pivoting, he slammed the door shut with his shoulder and dropped the bar into place across it.

"Well," said Jame, gingerly picking herself up off the floor, "here we are."

The inner sanctum of the temple was small but high-vaulted. The only thing in it, beside some long, heavy benches pushed back against the wall, was the stone image of Gorgo. The statue was of an obese, crouching man at least three times life size with unusually long legs; the bent knees rose a good two feet above the head. It had the most sorrow-stricken face imaginable. A steady stream of water tickled out of tiny holes in the corners of its green glass eyes. Its huge hands, cupped together to receive burnt offerings, stretched out between the towering shins. There was a long roll of parchment balanced across them over a bed of old ashes.

"Ah ha," said Jame. "There it is...or is it?" She stepped forward quickly, a frown growing on her face. Something about the length, the color of the paper...

"Marc, see if you can find another door. I think something is very wrong here."

While the big guardsman began a slow circuit of the room, Jame took the scroll out of the stone hands and carefully unrolled it. She examined it, then gave a low whistle.

"Marc, come and see this."

There was a scraping sound and a muffled grunt from behind the statue.

"What *are* you doing?"

"There's some sort of a lever back here. Maybe it controls a secret exit. I think I can..."

There was a crack, a deep gurgle, and a second later Jame sprang back, barely in time to escape a dousing as the glass eyes of the idol flew out of their sockets, closely followed by two thick jets of water.

Marc emerged from the shadows, looking sheepish. He held out a metal bar in the broad palm of his hand. "It broke off," he said apologetically.

"Never mind that," said Jame. "Better to be drowned than sacrificed anyway. Just look at this." She held the scroll out to him. He stared at the swirl of brightly inked words on it, making an obvious effort to focus.

"That isn't the Law Scroll," he said.

"I'll say it isn't. Do you see that?" She pointed to a line of runes drawn in magenta and gold. "A name: Anthrobar. This thing is the lost treatise on the bridging of the three worlds. Trinity knows how Loogan got his fat hands on it, or Ishtier ever found out that it was in Tai-tastigon."

"Is it important?" Marc asked, staring owlishly at the roll of paper.

"If the legends about it are true," said Jame grimly, "yes, very, and also very dangerous. Nine centuries ago the Kencyr scrollsmen on the border watches claimed that this bit of parchment held the secret to the destruction of the barriers between the worlds. If they were right and the barriers can be and are brought down, nothing, neither priest nor Law, will be left to stand between this cockleshell world and the three faces of god. It would be the ultimate disaster. Of course, the stories may be apocryphal, and perhaps Ishtier won't be able to read this—Trinity knows I'm not going to translate the parts I can make out for him—but it's too big a risk. I can't give it to him."

"It isn't the Law Scroll," said the guardsman, beginning to sway gently. "You don't have to give it to him."

"I swore to bring him the scroll in the arms of the idol," Jame said unhappily. "My word binds me."

Marc shook himself fiercely. "Aaaugh! But listen: if you take it now, lass, it will be stealing, not retrieving, and my word as a guardsman will bind *me* to turn you over to the merchants..."

"...who will be delighted to see me in the central square minus my skin, and probably without even the benefit of the flowers. Oh, what a mousetrap this is! I thought Ishtier was plotting something, but his confounded whispering had me too confused to guess what it was. I never dreamed it would be anything so magnificent. Look you: if I take him the scroll,

I may be opening the way to an incredible disaster; if I'm killed, he at least will have the satisfaction of my death; if I refuse, I'll be breaking my word and he will declare me a renegade, which would be a good deal worse than being dead. With you here, I get flayed alive if I do the former, and he has a Kencyr witness if I go the latter way. No wonder he decided to let you come with me. I could love that man for his subtlety…if only we weren't the ones caught by the tail."

At that moment, three things happened more or less simultaneously: the whole face of the image gave way, releasing a torrent of water into the already half-flooded room; the bar across the door began to splinter under repeated heavy blows from the outside; and Marc suddenly fell asleep standing up.

Jame looked around the room with raised eyebrows, and then back at the scroll in her hands. One complication would have been manageable, two a calamity, three ridiculous, but four? It would be an excellent time, she thought, to burn the manuscript and drown herself, but then there was Marc, who didn't deserve to die alone, much less asleep on his feet. Almost with a feeling of regret, she reached over and tapped the swaying giant on his chest.

"You'd better see to the door," she said. "I think we're about to have company."

"Zaugh…oh!" said Marc, blinking at her. He turned and waded through the water which now reached almost to his waist over to the opposite wall. While Jame took refuge on top of one of the statue's kneecaps, the guardsman began to wedge benches in front of the rapidly weakening door, handling their weighty bulk easily. As he was lifting the last one into position, he suddenly swore out loud and dropped it, creating a miniature tidal wave.

"Lass!" he bellowed over the roar of the water, splashing back across the room toward her. "I've got it! You can't steal the scroll, but I can!"

Jame saw his hand sweeping up at her out of the corner of her eye. She had been studying the manuscript intently and had only half heard him. Instinctively, she twisted away from what, from anyone but Marc, would have been a threatening gesture. The stone beneath her was slick with spray. The suddenness of her movement threw her sideways off her perch with a sharp cry into the surging water.

Marc fished her out and set her sputtering back on her feet. She swept a streaming lock of hair out of her eyes, gave herself a shake, and then stopped short with a gasp. Her eyes turned to him, enormous in her thin face.

"D...did you just say what I think you just said?"

The big guardsman shifted his weight uncomfortably, giving the impression that he would have liked to shuffle his feet if only there hadn't been so much water on them. "I wouldn't be stealing from a Kencyr, you know," he said in a half-pleading voice. "It wouldn't be breaking the Law, just...uh...bending it a little."

Jame's stunned gaze dropped to the soggy piece of parchment in her hand. She caught her breath, and then threw back her head with a sudden shout of laughter.

Marc stared at her.

She held the scroll out to him. Bright streaks of color spiraled across it into a muddy lower margin. Not a letter remained legible. "By Trinity, M'lord Ishtier may be subtle, but he's not omniscient. This is one solution he could never have foreseen. Here, take the thing! Only this once, I'll let you steal for me. Now in all the gods' names, let's get out of here."

"Uh, lass...how? There's only one door and no windows at all."

"Oh, use your head," said Jame, regaining her slippery perch on the stone kneecap with a spring like a young cat's. "Where there's fire," she pointed to the wet ashes in the cupped hands, "there's usually smoke. Where there's smoke, there had better be some sort of ventilation." Her finger traced a line from the offering bowl to the ceiling far above. "There. Do you see it? A hole, not very big, but large enough, I think." She began to pull small pieces of metal out of her belt and to fit them into a spidery form. "I thought we'd find at least that much of an exit before we walked into this place, but damned if I thought we'd have to use it." The grapnel complete, she unwrapped a line from around her slim waist and snapped it on. "Of course, we could wait for the room to flood completely, but you look ready to capsize as it is." On the third try, the hook shot straight up through the dark hole and caught firmly on something outside on the roof.

Jame threw the end of the line to Marc. "You go first, and try to stay awake at least until you get to the top. Remember, if you slip, I can only pick up the pieces."

Either contact with her had corrupted him, she thought as she struggled to anchor the line, up to her shoulders in water and half choked with the spray, or perhaps Kencyrs weren't quite what she had thought, and she wasn't so hopelessly tainted after all. At that moment something hard and cold began to dissolve inside her. She found herself singing out loud above the voice of the water as she followed her friend up the rope. By far the smallest part of her exuberance was due to the fact that she had not been obliged to commit suicide after all.

Marc, by some miracle, did not fall asleep half way up the line, nor as Jame guided him across the uneven roof tops of the city, nor even on the threshold of the temple of the Three-Faced God, though when the high priest snatched the limp scroll out of his hand, he very nearly pitched head-first after it. Jame led him out reeling.

As they passed out under the dark entry arch, they heard from the heart of the temple a high wail scarcely human in its disappointment and rage.

"That," said Jame, "is the best thing I've heard all evening."

They staggered home arm in arm through the festival crowds of night, both singing at the top of their lungs and both very much off key.

At the stoke of midnight, as Marc lay on his pallet snoring happily and the temples of Tai-tastigon heralded the new day with bells, chants, and laughter, the Talisman Jamethiel walked down the stairway with the traditional silver and black streamers of a senetha dancer flowing behind her, and the waiting crowd greeted her with a roar of welcome.

At his station across the room beside a huge keg of ale, Tubain beamed at her. Trust a Kencyr to always keep her word.

An introduction to "Bones"

This story grew out of a line in *God Stalk* about Penari's Maze being so complex that even its own architect got lost in it. From there, it just grew.

P.C.

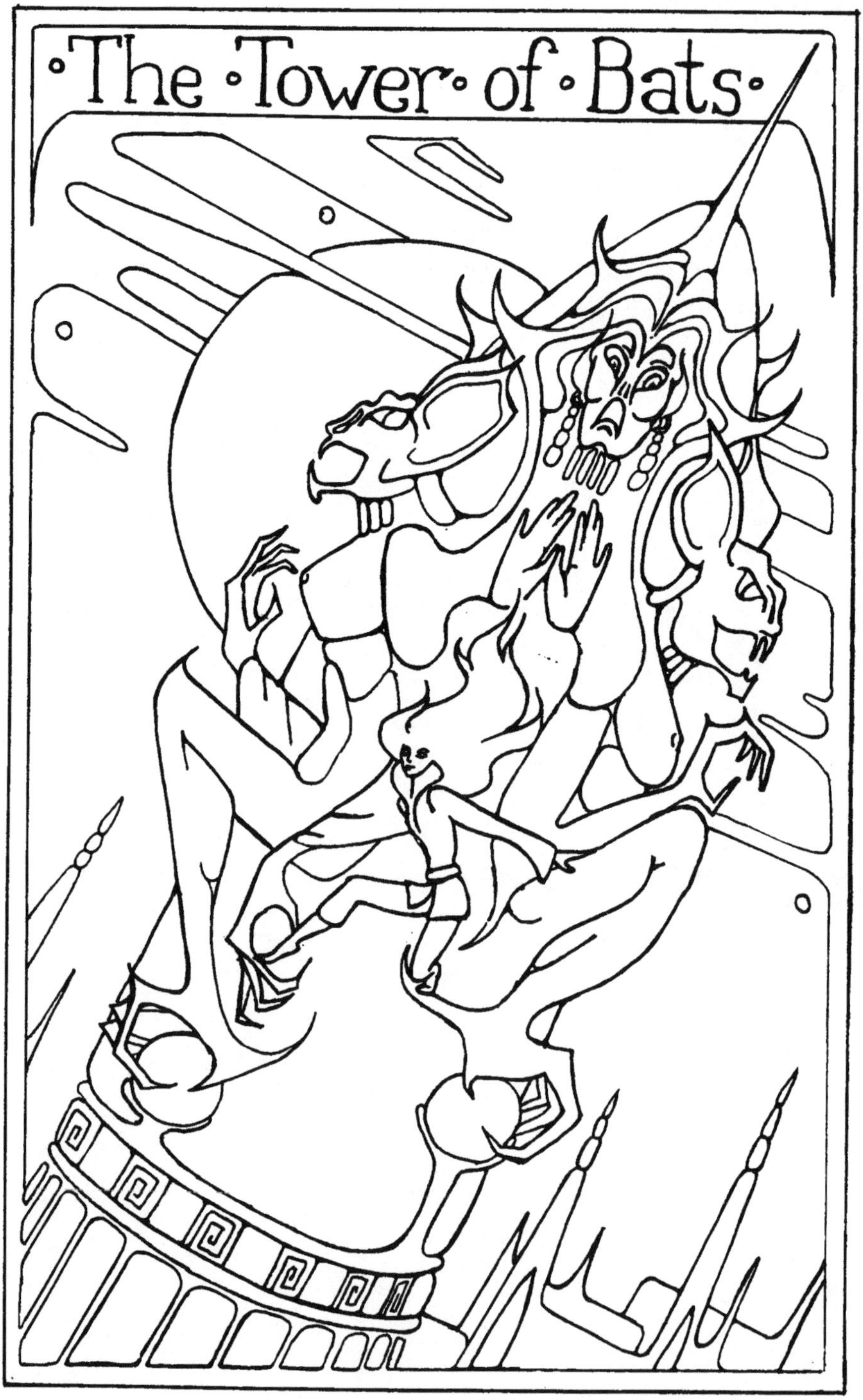
The Tower of Bats

BONES

It was nearly dawn in the city of Tai-tastigon. Birds had been chirping sleepily for some time as light seeped into the eastern sky, but the streets still lay drowned in shadows except where faint spheres of light shimmered against the walls. Down one such avenue in the Gold Ringing District came a hooded figure. It paused beneath each streetlight in turn, murmured "Blessed—Ardwyn—day—has—come" in a bored voice, and passed on, leaving darkness in its wake.

When the man was out of sight, Patches emerged from the shadows and resumed her vigil outside the gate of the mansion owned by Polyfertes, the Sirdan of the Lapidaries' Guild. While the plaster figures clustered around the house's lower windows were still indistinct, the young thief noted anxiously that up near the roofline the sinuous shapes of men, women, and beasts—all doing complicated, highly ingenious things to each other—stood out with far more clarity than they had only moments before. Even the black granite ravens on the gateposts seemed about to shake their wings and join the growing dawn chorus.

Gods, but it was getting late. Any minute now, a yawning servant would open the front door, and the guard, who was leaning against it, would tumble into the hall. As soon as they realized that his sleep had been deepened with poppy dust...

Jame—better known in the Thieves' Guild as the Talisman—was still inside that house. What the hell could she be thinking of, not to have made her escape before now?

At that moment, Jame's main thought was that she did not want to lose her fingers. Around her in the dim light of Polyfertes' treasure room glowed hundreds of gems, their erotic engravings intriguingly distorted by the horn glass of the cases that protected them. Securing each case was a box lock. Poised over each lock, out of sight within the intricacies of the box, was a weighted razor. An hour ago, Jame had edged her hand in under one such blade. She was still delicately probing into the lock mechanism beyond it, grimly suppressing tremors of fatigue. In the case before her, besides two gems, were twenty-five severed fingers, some half-decayed, all lovingly arranged on the cream velvet. Polyfertes collected more than gems.

There was a loud click. Jame caught her breath, bracing for pain. None came. The "thief-proof" lock had at last been sprung.

With a sigh of relief, she opened the case and removed the two jewels from their grisly nest. One was a magnificent sapphire, engraved with three women and a dog engaged in a rather peculiar activity. With this stone, Polyfertes had proved himself worthy of master's rank in the Lapidaries' Guild. The second jewel was a mere zircon. On it was the rough sketch for the masterwork. Jame turned the sapphire modestly upside down and pocketed the zircon, smiling faintly. Polyfertes wouldn't have to guess who had raided his treasure trove: the Talisman's eccentricities were by this time nearly as celebrated as her skill. Still smiling, she left the room.

Down below, Patches was chewing through the fingertips of her gloves, having forgotten that she had them on. Suddenly she stiffened. A line tumbled to the ground. Then a slim, dark form swung itself over the third-story window ledge and started down the rope, stepping lightly from plaster head to head.

"Talisman!" said Patches and, in the fullness of her relief stepped through the gate.

"*Thief!*" cried two raucous voices above her. Startled, she looked up and saw the gatepost ravens, stone wings spread, beaks agape. *"Thief! Thief! Thief!"* the warning cry came again from their motionless throats.

Jame was still twenty feet off the ground when she heard the guard wake with a snort. A pound of poppy dust blown straight up his hairy nostrils wouldn't have deafened him to an uproar like this. She pushed herself clear of the sculpted figures and let go of the line. The fall jarred her badly. Before she could recover, the guard was between her and the gate.

He lunged at her with his spear.

Jame sprang backward, twisting, and felt the cold breath of steel as the barbed head ripped at her jacket.

Patches yelped in protest.

"Stay where you are!" Jame shouted at her, and snapped at the guard, "'Ware truce, man: I'm unarmed!"

He lunged again.

God's claws, she thought, sidestepping. Didn't the idiot realize that if he spitted a thief without so much as a rock in her hand, the fragile nonviolence pact between thieves and guards would be shattered? Someone inside the mansion had begun to shout. Wonderful. The entire household would descend on her from behind if she let this moron delay her a moment longer.

Here he came again.

Right, thought Jame. *Unarmed isn't unable.*

She caught the spear shaft as it slid past and jerked the guard into a chin-strike that snapped his head back. Now, one more to teach him manners. She was poised to deliver the kick that would leave the man squeaking for a month when the ground suddenly lurched under her feet. All three, thieves and guard, found themselves on the pavement, bewildered. What the hell...

"Earthquake!" screeched the ravens. *"Thief! Earthquake! Thief!"* A second tremor wracked the courtyard. Looking up, Patches saw two intertwined plaster figures separate from the roofline. They were directly above the guard. Jame sprang at him as he sat gaping stupidly upward. Both disappeared in a cloud of dust and flying splinters as the figures crashed to earth.

Patches, choking on plaster dust, heard more shouts from the house, then her friend's voice at her elbow: "You were thinking, perhaps, of moving in? Come on!"

They ran. Behind them, the ravens were clamoring, *"Thiefquake! Earthworm!"* while Polyfertes' cook ran in circles beating a gong and bellowing "Fire!"

"I think we woke 'em up," said Patches when they had slowed down again several blocks later. "But why in Thal's name did you save that guard? The bastard tried to gut you."

"I hadn't his taste for truce-breaking. Besides, this isn't worth any man's life."

She dropped the zircon into Patches' hand.

"So you really did it," said the younger thief, awed, regarding the stone. Then she gave Jame a wary, sideways look. "Still mad at me, aren't you?"

"Mad? Why? All you did was let the other 'prentice thieves goad you into swearing that I could crack Polyfertes' treasure room. Well, I have. Your honor is safe, and so is my reputation—for once without bloodshed."

"Oh well," said Patches vaguely. "No omelets without broken eggs."

Jame turned on her. "Remind me, if you please, what happened to Scramp, your brother, only three months ago."

"He challenged you to rob the Tower of Demons," said Patches, squirming. "The demon nearly made fish bait of your soul, but you got away with the Peacock Gloves."

"And then?"

"Scramp's master disowned him."

"And then?"

"Scramp hanged himself. And then," said the pug-faced thief, rallying, "you gave me the Gloves so that I could buy my way into the Thieves' Guild."

"And that, I suppose, puts the egg back together again. You don't understand, do you? I might as well have put that rope around your brother's neck myself. As for tonight, couldn't you see that the other 'prentices were setting you up—and me, too—exactly the same way they did Scramp? If you ever put me in a situation like that again, we're through; I'll be damned if I'm going to cause another death in your family."

With that, Jame turned on her heel and walked away.

She had gone quite some distance into the bustling labyrinth that was Tai-tastigon before the haze of rage lifted, leaving her ashamed. Why had she torn into her young friend like that? Patches had meant no harm, either by accepting the challenge in the Talisman's name or by speaking lightly of spilt blood. She was simply a child of the streets, with neither time nor tears to waste on the dead. Jame had thought that she too had gotten over Scramp's suicide, but apparently not. Well, forget it. It was unprofessional to brood, and dangerous as well. Now she must report the evening's success to Penari, her master, whose instructions had made it possible.

The Maze, Penari's home, was one of Tai-tastigon's marvels. The old master thief had had the huge, circular edifice built some fifty years ago, just before the final, impossible theft that had made his reputation forever. Then he had retreated into it with his prize, the jewel called the Eye of Abarraden, thumbing his nose at the entire city. Since then many thieves had tried to track the old master to his lair to obtain his secrets, but the Maze had defeated them all. Besides Penari, only Jame knew the key to its twisting ways, and even she entered them this morning with trepidation, remembering how the building's own architect had once lost his way here and never been seen again.

Fortunately, the earthquake had done little damage...or so she thought until she finally emerged in the old thief's living quarters. These occupied the core of the building, a wide, seven-story-high shaft lit day and night by innumerable guttering candles and filled with the spoils of a lifetime. At the moment, virtually everything appeared to be on the floor. Icons, rare manuscripts, all the trinkets on the mantelpiece except for a solitary stone gargoyle, clothes, a shattered box with ivory inlay (formerly the resident of a high shelf), fragments of a roast goose...Jame sighed. What a mess. But where was Penari?

Molten wax splashed on the center table, followed by a shower of candles. Looking up, Jame saw that the huge chandelier had almost disappeared, lapped about in the folds of something white that undulated gently in the dim light.

"Monster?" she said incredulously, staring. "You idiot, that chain is ancient! Come down before the roof caves in."

The tablecloth moved. Jame threw it back and, crouching, found herself nose to nose with her master.

"About time you showed up!" hissed the old man. "Are we alone?"

"Why, yes—except for a forty-foot python suspended over your head."

"Never mind that." Penari scrambled out from under the table. Erect, the top of his head came to her chin and his cloudy, nearly blind eyes stared first through her collarbone, then wildly about the room. "Not here yet, is he?" he demanded, a touch of his usual self—confidence returning. "Good! I've time to thwart him yet. Now, have you seen his gargoyle?"

"I've seen *a* gargoyle," said Jame, bewildered. "Over there, on the...Why, that's odd. It's gone."

"Gone," he repeated querulously. "Of course. It would be. Quick now, have you ever come across any bones in the outer passageways?"

"Many time," said Jame, staring. "Rats, Monster's dinners, vhors..."

"No, no—*h u m a n* bones. A skeleton, say, with a finger missing."

"Bodies, yes, occasionally—when some fool wanders in and breaks his neck before we can escort him out—but bones...Wait a minute. I didn't exactly count phalanges, but did this particular skeleton have a medallion around its neck, a semicircle on a stem?"

"Yes, yes!"

"Well then, that would be Hervy."

"Who?"

"That's just what I call him," said Jame, with mounting embarrassment. "I came across him when you first sent me out to memorize part of the Maze and...well, he was such a clean-picked old gentleman that I used his bones to mark various passages. He's scattered all over the first level now."

"Excellent!" cried the old thief, to her amazement. "But do you remember where you left his head? Yes? Then go fetch the nasty thing, boy, and we'll smash it into toothpicks. Hurry!"

Jame went. Penari often left her speechless, but never more so than now. What did bones decades old have to do with a little stone statue that apparently moved about at will? Why was Monster, that venerable reptile, clinging to the chandelier, or his master, for that matter, cowering under a table...and would she ever get the old man to stop calling her "boy?"

The light of her torch danced on the bare walls. Dark, dusty, narrow—it was always rather like being buried alive here in the outer passages of the Maze. She went quickly, pausing now and then to listen for the sound of claws on stone. Not long ago, the labyrinthine building had suffered from an infestation of vhors—large, vicious rodents with a tendency toward demonic possession—and she was not sure that she and the priest lent to her by the Brotherhood of Sumph (Pest Control Chapter) had dealt with all of them.

Jame's destination was the intersection in the northwest quadrant of the Maze where she had originally found the entire skeleton. The bones were so old that she had never really thought of them as human remains and so had felt free to scatter them as she pleased, leaving only the skull undisturbed. She should have found it there now, but it was gone. Puzzled, Jame crouched beside the poor scraps of clothing that had survived time, rats, and her own meddling. Something glinted in the torchlight. She reached gingerly into the decaying rags and drew out Hervy's medallion. A semicircle on a stem...surely she had seen this emblem somewhere else, out in the city.

Suddenly Jame stiffened. Someone—no, *something*—was watching her. Firelight leapt on the walls. Dust drifted down from an overhead beam. The silence pressed in on her, broken only by the distant sound of dripping water and...what? The whisper of claws on stone? Vhors hunted in packs. When the madness seized them, they swarmed up from the sewers, engulfing anything alive that got in their way, passing their insanity on to it even as they died. Medallion in hand, Jame rose hastily and returned to the central chamber, making several quick but wary side trips.

"The skull is gone," she reported to Penari, "and so are many of the other bones. I didn't have time to check them all. Now, will you please tell me what's going on?"

But the old man didn't answer. He heard her news in silence, then began to pace back and forth, occasionally stumbling over out-of-place objects. Jame watched him, perplexed. This wasn't the first time he had kept a secret from her, but usually he did so with a kind of glee, daring her to solve the mystery for herself. That had been part of her training. But now he had apparently forgotten her presence altogether, and, for the first time since she had known him, he seemed to be badly scared. She was his apprentice, bound to him by law and respect. It was her duty to protect him, but from what?

The medallion grew warm in her hand. She didn't want to leave the old man, and yet...

"Sir," she said, "if you haven't any need for me here, I've an errand in the city."

Penari didn't seem to hear her. She was well out into the Maze when his voice, shrill with defiance, reached her. "You can't have them, do you hear me?" he was shouting, not at her, not, apparently, at anyone. "They're mine, I tell you, mine, mine, mine!"

Tai-tastigon, that great city, was wide awake now, shaken out of its predawn drowsiness by the tremors that had wracked it. The citizens of the night—thief, courtesan, and reveler—rubbed shoulders in the streets with merchants and craftsmen thrown prematurely from their beds. Pilgrims gawked at the damage. A fair number of these country-bred folk who know no better than to wander from their lodgings would not be seen again for weeks, if ever. Tai-tastigon the Labyrinth had swallowed even its own citizens before now, and possessed a floating, bewildered population of the lost whose patriarchs, some claimed, had been wandering the streets since the founding of the city.

Penari's Maze was more sparsely occupied, but in others ways it resembled the Labyrinth all too closely: one, in fact, was the miniature of the other. This was the greatest of Penari's secrets that Jame had yet learned, and it still awed her that a single mind could have stored up enough information about the city, street by street, level by level, to have drawn up from memory its map to use as the floor plan. She herself had only mastered a fraction of the Maze so far, but she did know how to match points in the building with their external counterparts. This bustling street, for example, equaled that dusty corridor; here she should turn just as she would in the Maze; there, go straight...and so on and on until some thirty minutes later Jame arrived at the spot in the northwest quarter of Tai-tastigon that corresponded to Hervy's original position in the Maze.

She was now in the heart of the temple district. All around her, chants and clouds of incense drifted out of open doors, fogging the air with sound and scent, while little troops of worshippers trotted past, some of them going backward in penance. Over the door of the temple facing her was the same emblem as on the medallion still in her hand. She saw, on this larger version, that the mushroom-shaped symbol was an instrument of some sort, marked with calibrations. She opened the door a crack and peered into the utter darkness of the sanctuary.

"Hello! May I enter?"

No one answered.

For a moment she stood there, undecided. It could be very dangerous to enter the temple of a god not one's own without safe conduct. Then, on impulse, she swung open the door and stepped over the threshold. Immediately, all outside light vanished. When Jame groped behind her for the door, nothing was there.

So much for thoughts of retreat.

Cautiously, she began to edge forward, hoping that this wasn't a sect that favored snake-pits. Then suddenly, as though an intervening corner had been passed, she saw what appeared to be a small, extremely detailed model of Tai-tastigon's Council Hall. Intrigued, she approached it. With each step she took, it grew remarkably, until, when she came up to its walls, they seemed every bit as high and solid as those of the original out in the city proper. Logically, the temple in which she stood could not have contained anything a tenth the size of this hall, and yet here it was. What was more, beyond it she saw another miniature structure—this time the Tower of Bats—and again approached to find it full-sized. This happened over and over until within a few minutes she had visited a dozen of Tai-tastigon's most notable buildings.

There was even a full-scale replica of Polyfertes' mansion. Jame circled it curiously, noting that here too parts of the ornate facade had fallen. The worst damage, however, was at the rear of the house where the servants' hall had partially collapsed. Then Jame saw something move in the ruins. It was a hand.

"Are you all right in there?" The hand had whisked itself back into a hole under a downed beam. Jame, peering in after it, saw nothing. "Hello?"

"Hello!" said a muffled, petulant voice. "Kindly get off my calculations."

Jame stepped back hastily. She had been standing on a set of mathematical figures drawn in the dust. The hand reappeared at a different hole, took several measurements with the now-familiar mushroom-shaped instrument, then added these numbers to those already on the ground.

"If," said the voice, "you were to take that board there, balance it on this stone here with the edge under this beam, and push down, you might do some good."

Jame complied, and a moment later a plump little man crawled out from under the rubble. "Well done. Thank ye," he said, brushing himself off.

"That's odd," said Jame, surveying the ruins. "Earlier this morning I...uh...had some business at this house—the real one, that is—and the earthquake had damaged it, too."

"Nothing odd about it," said the little man briskly. "Correspondences m'dear, correspondences. Naturally, the fall of one affects the other, and the same with cracks, crumblings, and other misfortunes. We even have a minor problem with pigeons. But see here: I'll show you what I mean."

He set off at a trot, obliging a perplexed Jame to follow. They passed many more buildings than she had as yet seen, a fair number of them recently damaged. Then, rounding another of those invisible corners, Jame found a tall, familiar pair of windows looming up before her, gorgeously tinted and ablaze with light. The architect priest threw them open. With a deepening sense of unreality, she followed him out onto the windy balcony of Edor Thulig, the Tower of Demons.

Tai-tastigon lay spread out far below them. Its streets hummed with life as the city's irrepressible citizens embarked on a new day of profit and pleasure. What was a mere earthquake to them? More untoward things happened in Tai-tastigon all the time...like stepping from the interior of one building onto the balcony of another blocks away. There to the northwest lay the Temple District. Jame was trying to pick out the architects' sanctuary—in which, a moment ago, she had been standing—when she noticed a dark scar cutting halfway across the entire district, a shadowy rift of downed buildings with shock lines reaching far out into the city.

"It was that damned Arthan," said the priest, holding down wind-torn hair with both hands. "A wild hill-god if ever I've seen one. His fool priests never told him they'd moved his house into town, so when he happened to come untempled this morning, of course he panicked. The biggest city he'd ever seen before probably had one communal privy. Why, the imbecile almost got as far as this temple! If you think the damage he did out in the city was bad, imagine what it would have been like if he'd gotten his big feet in among these models."

"You mean..."

"Yes, of course. D'you think the correspondences only work one way? Oh, we had a merry time getting that holy half-wit indoors again, and what should happen the moment I get home? Polyfertes' blasted house falls on me! I keep telling the architect who built it that he puts too much sand in his mortar."

Jame was leaning over the rail, staring down at the rose garden far below.

"A long way to the ground, isn't it?" said the priest behind her. "One hundred and fifty feet at least, and the Talisman jumped from here with the Peacock Gloves during the last Feast of Fools. Now there was a theft!"

"It wasn't from here," said Jame, still staring, surprised at how dry her mouth had gone. "It was from the south face down into the River Tone, which was quite bad enough, even at night, even without thinking. But there was no choice: the demon of the tower was a step behind me."

"You? Penari's Talisman?" She turned to find the little priest beaming up at her. "Well, this is an honor. We old men like to keep up on the doings of you young Guild bloods. I do believe the Talisman has stolen more supposedly inaccessible trinkets than anyone since the days of her master. Why trinkets, by the way? I've always wondered about that."

"For one thing," said Jame, "whatever I steal becomes my master's property, and Penari has all the riches he wants. For another, the only time I did lift something valuable—the Peacock Gloves, in fact—the affair ended badly. A boy died. No, you wouldn't have heard about that," she said with a sudden, bitter laugh. "He was only a shabby little nobody named Scramp, whose envy nearly cost me my soul."

"Good gracious!" said the priest, startled. "However did he do that?"

"By daring me to raid the Tower of Demons. The other thieves put him up to it, of course. They've never forgiven me for walking out of nowhere straight into the city's best 'prenticeship."

"And this boy?"

"He was an outsider too, trying to buy their acceptance at my expense. I could see what he was doing, and why, but I couldn't make him stop. Then, when I had carried off the Gloves, he lost his head altogether and accused me of cheating. We fought."

"You won, of course."

"There was no 'of course' about it," said Jame sharply. "He did very well. I hoped the others would honor him for it, but instead his master disowned him and...he hanged himself. Damn. I hadn't meant to think about that whole, rotten business again, much less to burden a stranger with it."

"Oh, I don't know," said the priest vaguely. "If you try to sit on something like that, it invariably bites you. I think I understand now why the Talisman has been taking such...well, suicidal risks these past three months. But I don't see why you feel so guilty about that boy's death. It wasn't your fault. If it had been, I expect your friend Scramp would have had something to say about it before now. In this city, the dead aren't always particularly docile, especially if they have a strong grievance against the living. I wouldn't worry about it so much if I were you. After all, anyone who can survive the Maze isn't going to fall easy prey to anything else. That building is a killer. I firmly believe that it was the death of Rugen, my old master, and he was the one who built it."

This apparently turned the little priest's thoughts in a new direction, for he abruptly swung around and trotted back into the darkness of the temple. Jame followed. She saw that they were approaching one last model, that of the Maze itself.

"Fifty years and more it's been since Master Rugen disappeared into that monstrosity," said the priest sadly, looking up at its blank wall. "A fierce old man he was—dangerous to cross but fair too, once the bloom was off his anger. I've never known him to hold a grudge against the innocent, or to forgive the guilty. This was the finest thing he ever built. He even cut off his little finger to lay under the center stone, saying 'Blood and bone bind.' I know he meant to be buried there."

"In the Maze?" said Jame, startled.

"Of course. We all make arrangements in the finest building we design—our end-work, we call it—but who crawls into a grave before his time? I still say he meant to come out when last he went in to see Penari."

"What if he simply got lost? Even if your master built the Maze, he could hardly remember every turn in it."

"He didn't have to. The floor plans were in his pocket. But then again, his gargoyle never came home. You know, one of those little stone beasties. Every master architect has one, and very useful they are, but impish too. Look the other way and you'll either find them gone or sitting on your head. They also guard their master's crypt. That's why some thought, when Quezal didn't come back, that Master Rugen had decided to lay his bones to rest with his lost finger in the Maze."

"Bones," said Jame uncomfortably, remembering what use she had made of them. "Well, he's there all right, but neither underground nor particularly quiet." And she told the priest about the events of the morning.

"Oh, ye galloping gods," he said when she had finished. "There'll be hell to pay over this. Master Rugen was never the sort to swallow insults, and fifty years of being dead won't have sweetened that foul temper of his. See here, you've got to do something about this!"

He grabbed Jame by the hand and began to half drag her around the curve of the model Maze to its western entrance.

"Wait a minute!" she protested, resisting. "I need some answers first. If Rugen really is Hervy, why has he waited so long to come back?"

"Who knows?" said the priest impatiently, trotting all the faster. "The point is, you've got to make peace between those two old men before they destroy each other and the Maze with them. Especially the Maze. If that goes, so may the city. Ah, here we are. Good luck, Talisman!" And he shoved her over the threshold.

"Dammit, wait!" Jame cried, but she was talking to herself. Behind her was not the darkness of the temple but the houses facing the real Maze. The priest had vanished.

"Marvelous," she said to the walls of the entryway. "Now what am I supposed to do?"

"Correspondences, m'dear, correspondences," replied the echo. *"Find Rugen's skull."*

Jame stood quite still for a moment. Then she plunged into the Maze. Equipped with one of the torches that were kept hidden near the entrance, she raced through the dark passages, checking off in her mind the places she had visited earlier in search of the bones. Someone, probably Quezal the Gargoyle, was gathering them together...but where? The obvious place would be Rugen's death-site, the original location of the entire skeleton, but not even the skull was there now. If Quezal was in a hurry, though, he might well be collecting the bones at some point roughly equidistant from the farthest reaches to which they had been scattered. That gave her several possible locations.

At the first three, Jame drew a blank. The fourth she approached more warily, not only because of her present search but because she remembered all too clearly the last time she had been in this part of the Maze. It was here that the vhors had trapped her, Monster, and the priest sent to exterminate them. In desperation, the priest had taken their madness into himself. Deprived of what had become their essence, they had promptly dropped dead while the poor man had plunged down the nearest sewer hole, headfirst. Jame hoped that his colleagues below had successfully exorcised him. Meanwhile, she had been left with several hundred vhor carcasses and forty feet of hysterical python. Nothing would calm Monster but the removal of the offending bodies, so Jame (not very wisely, perhaps) had thrown them into a nearby pit-trap and set them on fire. The resulting smoke and stench had made this section of the Maze unapproachable for weeks. It still stank.

Jame examined the corner where, months earlier, she had left a femur to mark her way. The bone was gone, but not without a trace: covering the floor where it had lain was a network of scratches just visible in the flickering light. In fact, the whole passageway was similarly scored. Surely it hadn't been like this the last time she had been here, Jame thought uneasily. With growing apprehension, she followed the marks back to the pit and peered down into it, noting the deep, fresh gouges that scarred its sides and lip. Not a bone remained in it.

Then, in the distance, Jame heard the sound that all this time she had half expected and wholly feared: the rasp of many, many claws on stone.

She tracked the noise by the marks on the floor. The sound grew, then abruptly faded away as she turned into the hallway where the last of Rugen's bones had been left. It wasn't there now. Standing in the eerie silence, Jame wondered how her reasoning had gone wrong, and what to do next. Then she heard a sound behind her, the faintest of scratches and turned to find the hallway full of vhors.

Not one of them had been alive for some time. Most were little more than charred bones held together by scraps of singed flesh. Torchlight gleamed off empty eye sockets, off naked claws and fangs. In all that decaying, fire-scorched mass, not one whisker moved.

Jame went back a step, then another. She couldn't take her eyes off that corridor full of death, couldn't even think. Then her foot hit something. She fell backward, the torch flying out of her hand and over the edge of one of the Maze's many water traps. In the total darkness that followed, the hall filled with the clatter of bones.

It took Jame a moment to realize that she hadn't simply tripped. Something was holding on to her ankle. The grip tightened. With a jerk she was dragged backward one inch, then another and another. The image formed confusedly in her mind of a shadowy side corridor which she had passed a moment before her fall. Something had been waiting for her there, was waiting still.

With an incoherent cry, she lashed out with her free foot. It didn't connect, but the grip on her ankle relaxed. Then it came hand over hand up her leg. The thing was on top of her now with its bony hands around her throat. Gasping, she struck out blindly again, and made contact. The bones fell apart. Each one still twitched with a fitful life of its own. Jame threw herself sideways away from them, colliding a moment later with the far wall. Something—a skull, from the feel of it—rolled under her hand. Snatching it up, she crouched there, ready to pitch her prize down the well if anything touched her, frightened enough to throw herself after it.

The darkness came alive with the sound of many objects dragging themselves over the stones, rasping, scratching, fumbling in the dark. Were they approaching, or drawing away? Ah, away. They were bound for the heart of the Maze, Jame realized. They were after Penari.

She would have to reach the old man first, without a light to show the way, over a course as complex as that from the Temple District to the Maze. *An exercise, Talisman.* She could almost see Penari grinning wickedly at her. *A simple little test, like so many in the past.* Well not quite, but close enough. She thought hard for a moment, selecting a route parallel to that of the disturbance, then rose and cautiously set out with the skull tucked under her arm.

An eternity later, Jame collided with a wall. This was hardly the first time in her blind journey, but now she groped along the upper edge and, to her relief, found the hoped-for depression. Something clicked, and a panel swung open. She stepped over the threshold into the heart of the Maze.

Jame had turned to secure the secret door when someone let off a shrill war cry almost in her ear. "Oh, no," she said out loud, and ducked as Penari's iron-shod staff whizzed over her head.

The old man shrieked again, advancing on her with flailing weapon. Obviously, in her absence, he had gone from terror to outrage—always a short step for him—and she now had something akin to a senile berserker on her hands. Jame retreated hastily to the middle of the room, and placed the skull on the table. Raising her eyes, she found herself face-to-face with Monster, who was hanging down from the chandelier. Apologetically, the snake flicked the tip of her nose with his tongue.

"You're no help at all," she told him, and then ducked again as Penari's staff hissed over her head, nearly braining the terrified python. Jame slipped under the old thief's return blow and, coming up behind him, put her hands over his on the staff.

"Sir, I'm back," she said in his ear.

For a second, Penari stood quite still, breathing hard. Then he twisted about and glared up at her. She wondered what he saw: a blur, probably, if even that.

"It's about time," the old man snapped. "Where in the seven hells have you been?"

Jame told him. From the faces he made, she gathered that he didn't like the direction her inquiries had taken, but the time for secrets was past. "And now, sir," she said, concluding, "will you kindly tell me just what the hell happened the last time Hervy—Master Rugen, that is—came to see you here in the Maze?"

"If you must know," he said petulantly, "we quarreled. That conceited jackass had the nerve to call this building his masterpiece. I ask you, where would he have been without my memory? I designed the Maze, dammit: he just put it together. And then he had the gall to claim that the final plans were his property. Of course, I didn't let him have them. He fumed about that for a bit and then he stormed out. And that's all there was to it."

"It couldn't have been," said Jame, staring at the door by which she had entered. "If so, why has he just come back?"

She had not had time to lock the panel. It gaped open now, and an indistinct figure stood on the threshold. Penari drew his breath in sharply. Nearly blind as he was, he couldn't see the form in the doorway or the horde of motionless shapes crouching at its feet, but he was no fool.

"Come back, have you?" he said through his few remaining teeth. "Much good that will do you now that I have your skull. Talisman, quick: Pick up the blasted thing and get behind me." With that, he scuttled to the far side of the table, clutching his staff.

Jame didn't move. Although she hadn't taken her eyes off that strange intruder or seen it so much as stir, it was now unmistakably several feet farther into the room. Its skeletal arm was half-raised. Where the ulna should have been were many tiny vhor bones laid joint to joint, and the fingertips ended in rodential claws. Instead of its missing skull, Quezal the Gargoyle crouched on its clavicle. The rest of the figure was wrapped in a winding sheet of some translucent material which Jame recognized as one of Monster's more recently shed skins. A burst of near hysterical laughter welled up in her, but she choked on it, one hand flying up to her bruised throat. Twenty minutes before, those taloned fingers had nearly throttled her. Not only that, but here were the vhors again, massed at the dead architect's feet, looking no more congenial than before. And they were much closer than they had been a moment ago. But she still hadn't seen them move.

Another fit of coughing seized Jame. When her eyes cleared again, the vhors and their master were within five feet of her. So that was it: Like Quezal, they could only move when unobserved. If she so much as blinked now, she was finished.

"Didn't you hear me, boy?" cried Penari behind her, clearly thinking that she was behind him. "I said smash it. Smash the skull!"

Without turning, her eyes still fixed on the architect Jame groped behind her on the table for the skull. Her hand touched it. A sudden wave of dizziness swept over her. In its wake, she saw standing before her not the grotesque, skeletal figure, but Master Rugen as he had been in life, richly clad, with Quezal perching on his shoulder. The architect was looking straight through her. His face was thunderous. Penari spoke behind her, his voice so oddly distorted that she couldn't understand a word.

"Sir?" she said, then caught her breath as the thief stepped into her line of vision. At least fifty years had fallen away from him.

He and the architect argued violently. Rugen brandished a packet in the thief's face, then thrust it back inside his robe, turned on his heel and stalked to the door. Penari stopped him on the threshold. The two exchanged more heated words, then Rugen, with a short laugh, disappeared into the Maze proper.

Jame followed him. He paced confidently through the labyrinthine halls, not pausing once despite the complexity of his path. And so it was that, without a break in his stride, he took his first wrong turn. Many more followed. At last the man stopped, looking aggravated, and reached into his pocket. His expression changed. The packet wasn't there. He tried to retrace his steps, stubbornly silent at first and then shouting angrily for Penari until his voice failed. When his torch also finally gave out he muttered a hoarse curse and sent Quezal for help. None ever came.

"Now I understand," said Jame to him. "You put the plans into your pocket, and Penari lifted them out again, there, on the threshold. Then, when you sent your gargoyle back to him, he imprisoned it. Because of that, you died of hunger and thirst in the dark. How...vile."

Abruptly, she found herself back in the heart of the Maze with her hand still on the skull and Quezal's grotesque face only inches from her own. Then something stuck her shoulder so hard that she was lifted off her feet and thrown sideways to the floor.

Damn, she thought hazily. *I must have blinked.*

Her eyes focused again and she was suddenly very still. The vhors were directly in front of her, close enough for her to see the grain of their yellow fangs and bits of rotting debris caught between them. Rugen might have spared her life, but his creatures assuredly would not. Not that the architect had been all that gentle. His claws had apparently slashed through her jacket, because her shoulder had begun to sting and blood was running down her arm inside the sleeve. She couldn't even take her eyes off the vhors to check the extent of the damage. And her back was turned toward the architect. What was he doing now? All she could hear was Penari, alternately shouting insults at Rugen, encouragement to her, and counting to himself as he went through the steps of a quarterstaff drill in gleeful preparation for mayhem. For some reason, Rugen hadn't attacked the old thief yet. She had to get him under observation again before he did. Carefully, Jame rose and backed away from the vhors, her eyes still fixed blinkingly on them.

The table brought her up short. Rugen bent over it, his hands almost on the skull. Facing him and inadvertently immobilizing him was Monster, who had again lowered his head and about ten feet of body from the chandelier. *How fortunate,* thought Jame, *that snakes don't blink.* Any second, however, the python would probably spot the vhors and panic again. *Right,* she thought, taking a deep breath. *Now I earn my wages.*

She launched herself onto the tabletop, rolling over her right arm, hissing with pain as her weight came briefly to bear on her injured shoulder. Rugen seemed to pinwheel past. She snatched the skull from between his skeletal hands and half-fell off the far side of the table, landing on Penari. For a moment, no one's eyes were on the architect. As she disentangled herself from her master, Jame heard the table crash over. Then she was sitting on the old man with the skull in her hands and Rugen bending over her.

"If you really want me to destroy this thing," she said unsteadily, glaring up at the architect, "move."

"Smash it, smash it!" cried Penari's muffled voice through the rucked-up folds of his robe. "What are you waiting for?"

Jame raised the skull, then hesitated. If she did manage to shatter it on the stone floor, that presumably would be the end of Master Rugen...unjustly slain a second time. Then too, what had that little priest meant when he had spoken of these two old men destroying each other, the Maze, and perhaps even the city? That would only make sense if...

"Uh, sir...I think we have a problem. Remember those models I told you about in the temple that fell down because their counterparts in the city did? Well, the priest told me that the reverse could also happen."

Penari paused a moment in his furious thrashing. "Umph?" he said irritably, from the depths of his own clothing.

"Since the Maze is a three-dimensional map of Tai-tastigon," said Jame slowly, "it might well be considered a model of the city. In that case, to damage the building would be to endanger the entire town. The priest thought that your quarrel with Rugen might put the Maze in jeopardy, and he sent me to find Rugen's skull, just as you did. But I don't think he wanted me to destroy it. I mean, here's the man who built the Maze, who bound himself to it with blood and bone. Couldn't you say that his mind was the Maze? Then this skull would be its physical emblem, its model, if you will. So if I destroy it, what happens to the building...and to the city?"

"What?" snapped Penari, his head finally popping into sight. "Oh! Those damned correspondences again. If we're playing that game, I should think that my head would be worth any number of his. But then, that was the original argument, wasn't it? Who is the Mastermind of the Maze? You claimed you were, didn't you, you old fraud?" he suddenly shouted up at the architect. "You were so cocksure that you didn't need any help to get out of here.

"Why do you want the plans, then? I say to you.

"'Oh, I have a special use for them, but it isn't to find my way. Never think that. This building is my end-work. I know every turn in it.'

"And, the gods help us both," said Penari, his voice suddenly sinking, "I took you at your word."

Jame had been staring up unblinkingly at Quezal's devilish face, haloed by the chandelier that hung above them both. The mass of wax and metal moved slightly, groaning. Monster must be shifting. Then the import of what Penari had just said sank in.

"Do you mean that you didn't intend...But what about Quezal? Didn't you realize that something was wrong when he came back?"

"I thought that Rugen had left the Maze, discovered that the plans were missing, and sent his pet demon back in to steal them. The robber robbed. That would have appealed to the old bastard. So, just to teach him a lesson, I grabbed his gargoyle and popped it into my ivory inlay chest. Then, well, I was a busy man in those days."

"In other words, you forgot about it."

The old man nodded miserably. "Months later, I came across Rugen in the Maze. Nastiest shock I've ever had in my life. So I'm sorry, but that doesn't change anything," he said, abruptly rallying. "The plans are still mine—I say!—and you can't have them. Put that in your back teeth and chew on it!"

You see how it is, said Jame silently to the skull. *He didn't mean to kill you, but you still died—just as Scramp did because I failed him. Penari's pride in the Maze and mine in my reputation made us both...careless. But how long do we have to go on paying for that? Only you can tell us, and you'll have to do it now because I can't keep you at bay any longer. Your old apprentice said you were a fair man, so to hell with mercy. Give us justice.*

Then she closed her stinging eyes and waited.

A long, nerve-wracking silence followed, broken by a deep groan from above.

Something slammed into Jame. She was sent flying backward head over heels with the skull still in her arms and, a second later, Penari's sharp elbows in her ribs.

A tremendous crash shook the floor. Dust filled the air, half choking both master and apprentice as they tried to sort themselves out by the far wall. Jame felt a sudden weight on her good shoulder. Startled, she looked up to find Quezal the Gargoyle perched there. *What the hell?*

"Here," she said, shoving the skull into Penari's arms.

With the gargoyle still clinging to her and vhor bones crunching underfoot, she waded into the cloud of dust, batting at it ineffectively. She almost hit Monster. The albino python loomed up in front of her, his head a good two feet above her own. But this time his other four-fifths were on the floor. Quezal's claws tightened painfully as the giant snake made a tentative effort to wrap itself around Jame's neck.

"If you're that upset," she said crossly, pushing him away, "go cuddle your master. What have you done to the chandelier?"

It lay before her, a great mass of twisted metal and smashed candles with its broken chain draped over it. Underneath was a rectangular hole in the floor. Penari, blundering up from behind, nearly fell into it before Jame could stop him.

"Where's Rugen?" the old man demanded. "And what's become of my center stone?"

"Center stone!" Jame repeated, startled. She peered down into the hole, and at its bottom saw the splintered remains of Rugen's skeleton.

"When the chandelier fell," she said, thinking out loud, "it must have triggered some counterweight hidden in the floor. The stone tilted, and the bones slid into the grave prepared for them."

"The grave? *Whose* grave?"

"Why, Rugen's, of course. Remember, this was his endwork."

"He wanted to be buried here, in *my* Maze?" The old man, began to bristle again. "Why, the nerve of the man! But that's just like him: he always did treat everything as if it belonged to him. No one else was to take any credit at all—oh, no! Arrogant old bastard. Serves him right that even his own gargoyle deserted him in the end."

Jame had been regarding her master oddly as he stomped back and forth. "Sir, you don't understand. Quezal may have pushed me out of the way, but it was Rugen who saved you."

"*What?* Oh, hell." Penari stopped short and seemed visibly to deflate. "Oh, bloody hell. He would turn noble on me at the last minute. Well, two can play at that. He can stay here if he likes and...and what's more, he can have the damn plans." He fished about impatiently in one of his voluminous pockets, at last jerking out a familiar packet tied with a dirty string. "It's not as if he were going anywhere with them, is it?" he demanded, glaring up defiantly at Jame. "Just the same, you do the honors: he'll never be able to say that I handed them over."

Jame unwrapped the packet. It contained not the sheaf of papers she had expected but a fine linen cloth with the plans drawn on it. So that was why Rugen had been so determined to keep possession of this thing: it was his shroud. She jumped down into the grave with it. In one corner of the hole lay a small object wrapped in silk: Rugen's missing finger, almost certainly. Jame placed it with the other bones on the burial cloth, finally adding the skull, handed down by Penari, to the top of the heap.

"I'm sorry that I mistreated your bones before, and called you Hervy," Jame said to the skull. "Sleep quietly at last, master architect." And she folded the cloth with its intricate drawings over the fleshless face.

"Well, that's that," said Penari with relief when they had put the center stone back in place. "A sticky business, on the whole, but I think I handled it rather well. Let that be an example of what courage can accomplish. Stay with me, boy: I'll make a man of you yet."

And with that, the old thief gave Jame a hearty slap on her injured shoulder.

She stepped hastily out of his reach. Rugen's claws had caused more mess than damage, luckily, but the scratches still stung. In another sense, though, Jame would hardly have cared at that moment if they had cut to the bone. For the first time in three months, the weight of Scramp's death was gone, and she felt almost light-headed with relief.

But there was still one loose end.

Penari broke off his panegyric of self-praise as she headed for the door. "Here now!" he called after her in sudden anxiety. "Aren't you going to help me clean up this mess?"

"Later, sir. Just now, I owe a friend an apology. Maybe Quezal will lend a hand until I get back."

Between one blink and the next, the gargoyle shifted from her shoulder to Penari's head. He flailed at it, squawking, then went off in a sort of war dance about the room, making loud, semi-articulate declarations that he would not be sat on it his own hall, thank you, and would Quezal please sit somewhere else.

Jame regarded her whirling dervish of a master, the vhor bones piled high on the floor, and Monster nosing cautiously among them, obviously ready for a precipitous retreat if any of them should move.

Ah, home, she thought. *How nice to have everything back to normal.*

Then she went out into the Maze and beyond that into the sun-washed streets of Tai-tastigon in search of Patches.

An introduction to "Stranger Blood"

This was my second story about Jame. As in "Child of Darkness," I still couldn't get into her mind, so the point of view, again, is that of a boy reacting to her. It's also a story set years later than *Seeker's Mask*, although you can see where some of the fraternal tensions in that novel are going. Fair warning: Things between Jame and Tori are going to get a lot worse before they get better.

P. C.

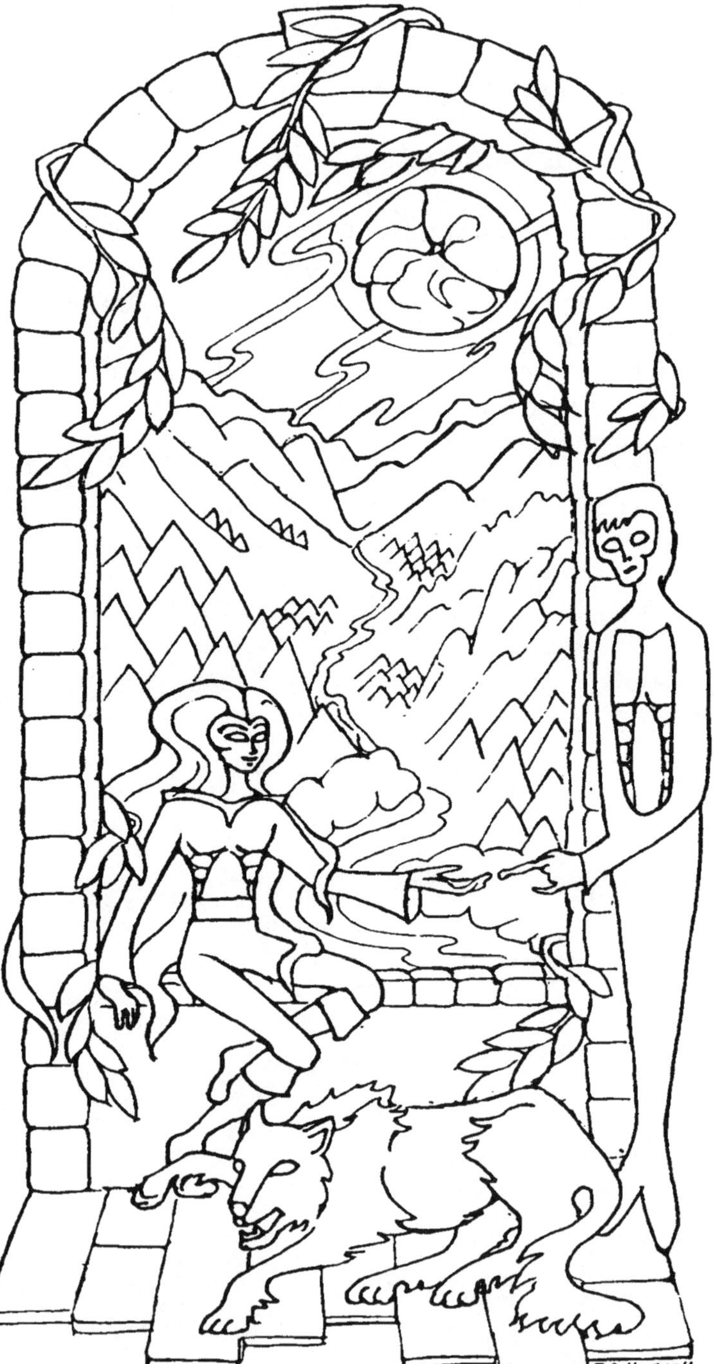
P.C. Hodgell

STRANGER BLOOD

The Master of Knorth, High Lord of the Kencyrath, a proud man was he. Power he had, and knowledge deeper than the Sea of Stars. But he feared death. A bargain he made with Perimal Darkling, ancient enemy. His people he betrayed to win life unending. A house he built under eaves of darkness, and shadows crawled therein...

Damn. The ink had begun to clot again. Arie poked at it with his quill pen and upset the bottle. Oh, what was the use? It was too cold up here in the northwest turret of the High Keep to write anyway, especially about so dark a subject.

Arie glanced northward between mountain peaks to where the Barrier loomed up as far as the eye could see like a wall of mist. On the other side lay Perimal Darkling. Nearly thirty millennia ago, the darkness had first breached the greatest barrier of all between the outer void and the series of linked dimensions known as the Chain of Creation. At that time, the enigmatic Three-Faced God had bonded together the three people of the Kencyrath—Highborn, Kendar, and catlike Arrinken—to stop the shadows' spread. Then, apparently, the god had left his chosen people on their own. Their contest with Perimal Darkling had become a long, bitter retreat from threshold world to world down the Chain. Arie knew the old songs about every fleeting victory, every final defeat. They made a grim record, but the ones that hurt the most told of the Master's treachery. For the first time, a Kencyr had turned on his own kind and, moreover, caused nearly two-thirds of the Kencyr Host to fall with him. The remnant—Arie's ancestors among them—had fled here to Rathillien, the next threshold world, and raised the Barriers not only against the shadows but against their own fallen kinsmen as well. More than three thousand years had passed since then, but the shame and anger remained, especially at a border outpost like the High Keep. Other Kencyrs snug in the Riverland to the south could perhaps afford to forget, but not those left to guard the Barriers. Here the past still lived. Rangers even claimed that a man could walk right through the mist into the fallen world, into Perimal Darkling. Certainly, poor, warped creatures sometimes made their way out of the shadows to this side. The head of one was nailed to the northern battlement now, surrounded by gorging crows. At least this time it was clearly an animal. Just after Mid-Winter, the last patrol before storm season had brought back something that looked almost human.

Those same rangers were in the lower ward now, at maneuvers on a field of melting snow. They were mostly hoary veterans and boys Arie's age—the old and the young, all with the grim, pinched faces of those sworn to maintain the millennia-old watch of the High Keep Kencyrath down through the white years, though blood should freeze and hearts crack.

Arie knew he should have been one of them, riding, turning, fearing...fearing...the sweat of the colt, the wild force between his knees, rising, rising...Kethra was shouting at him...up, over, down...crushing pain, darkness...

The quill pen snapped in his shaking hand.

Fit for nothing, said Kethra's voice in his mind. For nothing, for nothing, Arie whispered back.

In the distance, a guard's horn sounded. The boy started. Was it an attack? Twisted figures crawling down from the north, from Perimal Darkling...The horn sound again, closer, from the south.

Arie heaved himself up and hopped on one foot to the window. Below, Waning Valley plunged down from New Moon Pass, bending southeastward toward the Riverland, home on Rathillien of all the major Kencyr houses. It was nearly two hundred leagues from the High Keep to Gothregor, the High Lord's citadel. Scarcely anyone had come north to this desolate outpost since the downfall of Ganth High Lord nearly forty years ago. Lord Min-drear of the High Keep had stood by Ganth in that last terrible battle among the White Hills and afterward had ridden slowly home, a broken man carrying the ashes of his five sons in a silver box.

Now horsemen rode into the outer ward from the south behind a gray-cloaked figure on a mare the color of fresh cream. The rangers' shaggy mountain ponies snorted and bowed their heads as the mare passed. She was a Whinno-hir, a Highborn's mount. Arie let his breath out slowly. So. The moment everyone had dreaded since Mid-Winter was at last at hand. From the south came riding the end of everything the High Keep Kendar had fought millennia to preserve.

Arie leaned his head against cold stone. Below lay the inner courtyard with Kendar, alerted by the horn, hurrying across it to their various posts. A week, a month, a year from now, what would he see if he again looked down from this perch? These familiar faces, or only those of usurping strangers? He willed himself to see, willed it until the blood hummed in his ears and his sight blurred, but nothing came. Of course not, he thought bitterly: His visions chose their own time, and then they never showed him anything real.

Below, the sun-shadows had moved and a thin, keen wind sprung up. No keep Kendar were in sight now. Instead, just within the gate stood two strangers. One, clearly a Highborn, seemed to smolder against the dark stones in his rich coat of crimson. He was pulling off gold-studded riding gloves. Beside him stood a second visitor, painfully thin, clad in dusty black, whose rank was harder to guess. Both were staring across the courtyard. Following their eyes, Arie saw the stranger in the gray cloak, already half way to the great hall's door.

Near the door was a ramp leading down into the keep's subterranean chambers. From the depths came a sudden hollow clang and an answering howl. The figure in gray stopped abruptly. Arie caught his breath. It was the mid-hour of the afternoon, he remembered. Every day at this time the war hounds were loosed to hunt their food in a yammering pack through the dark mountain forests. No one in his right mind would stand in their way, but no one had apparently warned the visitors, and the huntsmaster in his subterranean kennel didn't know they were there—or, worse, perhaps he did.

The gray bitch leader burst into pale sunlight from the mouth of the ramp, the rest of the pack baying behind her. They were all of the Molocar breed, four feet high at the shoulder and strong enough to bring down a charging warhorse. The stranger stood directly in their path. In a moment, he was surrounded. The hounds surged about him, baffled by his stillness, goaded by their hunger. In their midst, he and the gray bitch faced each other as though carved from stone. Now the stranger was moving. Very, very slowly, he peeled off his right glove, and held out his hand. The bitch leaned forward as though to sniff. Then, with a sudden sideways lunge, she snapped her jaws shut on it. Arie thought he heard bones crunch. He saw the shoulders of the figure jerk.

Too late, Kethra's voice roared across the courtyard. A hound yelped. A moment later the pack was in full flight from the only person who could make them shiver at a word. The Warder of High Keep stood in the hall doorway, her expression nearly as black as the randon scarf knotted around her strong throat. What she saw made her scowl deepen even more.

The pack had fled, but not the gray bitch. She stood as if frozen, the stranger's hand still gripped in her jaws. Drops of bright blood splashed on the flagstones between them. A cold breath of wind swept through the court, stirring gray cloth, ruffling gray fur. Then the hound released her grip and, with a sigh, sat down at the stranger's feet.

Kethra stepped back into the hall without a word, leaving the door open behind her. The stranger followed with the hound trotting at his side. At the gate, the crimson-coated Highborn at last angrily shrugged off the hand with which the other had held him back when the pack first erupted into the courtyard. As he and the thin man crossed to the door, Arie saw that the latter cast no shadow. All disappeared into the hall.

Arie grabbed his crutch and hopped as rapidly as he could down the stairs, across the courtyard, through the door. Inside, he slipped to the right, into shadows. The hall was thick with them. It was a high vaulted room, built for feasts and laughter. Some forty years ago, it had heard its last war song, raised in honor of its lord and his five bright-faced sons. Now the sons watched the hall blank-eyed from their memorial tapestries, woven of threads taken from the clothing in which each one had died. Similar death banners lined the upper reaches of the hall, pair after pair of the distinctive Min-drear hands held open-palmed in frozen, possibly futile benediction. Lady Shian, Lord Min-drear's consort, was there. Only Min-drear himself and his aging sister Nessa were absent.

Kethra stood before the fire, her body hard-edged and unyielding against the fitful flames. Old Tarin, steward of the hall, had put the customary flask on the table before her before slipping back into the wall niche that was his post. The bottle was uncorked but still full. The Warder had offered the visitors no welcome cup.

"I tell you again," she said to the gray-cloaked stranger who faced her across the table, "Lord Min-drear sees no one. Tell me your business and I will inform him of it if I can."

"What, without seeing him?"

The stranger's voice surprised Arie. It had such a curious huskiness that he couldn't tell if a man or woman spoke—not that any Highborn lady would come among them like this. The visitor still wore cape and hood. His hands were clasped behind him, hidden in the folds of the gray cloak.

"Kendar, remember your place!" snapped the crimson-coated man.

"Hush, Kracarn. This *is* her place and we are guests. Warder, tell your lord that I have come to summon him to council at Gothregor a month hence."

Kethra gave a harsh laugh. "A summons from Gothregor! After all these years! The last time we answered, Highborn, how many of us ever returned? The White Hills are thick with the ashes of our dead and our hall is empty except for those." She gestured toward the tapestries. "Who would you have us send this time? Who is left? Old men and women, children, cripples...?"

Involuntarily, her glance flickered past the visitors to Arie standing in the shadows by the door. He flinched, and so did she. Rage at her slip made the Warder turn all the more fiercely on the strangers.

"Five Highborn and a hundred Kendar gone from this hall," she said savagely, taking such an abrupt stride toward the intervening table that the gray bitch sprang up with a snarl. "We have paid our debt in blood to Ganth of Knorth's house. Leave us in peace!"

"Gently," murmured the visitor, dropping a hand, the left, to soothe the hound. "Others have loved Ganth as little as you. He erred badly in the White Hills. He had just come from Gothregor where he found his family slaughtered and rotting in the sun. He was not sane when he led your people against his massed foes. He was not sane later when, in exile, he drove the daughter of his second wife across the Barrier into Perimal Darkling. He was neither sane nor forgiven. He died with blood in his throat.

"But now Torisen, Ganth's son by that second wife, occupies the High Lord's seat. This council summons comes from him, although he never thought it would travel so far. I will speak plainly with you, Warder. My lord Torisen would do as his father did: gather the Kencyr Host and march against our foes here on Rathillien. He forgets, as his father did, that the true enemy is Perimal Darkling and that only border posts such as this keep the Barriers strong. Perhaps your lord can remind him of that. Otherwise, soon, the war summons may come again, and you will have to answer or be foresworn."

Kethra shook her head as if to clear it. That husky, purring voice had slid like velvet between her thoughts, half deadening them. "Torisen, Torisen...he was born in the Haunted Lands during his father's exile, returned to claim Ganth's power, wielded it as High Lord in a great battle at the Cataracts...So a wandering singer told us."

This time, she shook all over like a bear rousing itself. A look almost of fear came into her eyes.

"He had a sister. Some say that her father cursed her as a hell-spawn and cast her out. She fell into the Master's hands, but not even he could manage her and she escaped from his house back into Rathillien. They say that she can blood-bind, and that she has spoken the Master Runes so often and so recklessly that some of their power has bled into her voice. They call her the Darkling. Now in Trinity's name, *who are you?*"

Then, abruptly, there was someone else in the hall. Highborn and Kendar both pivoted to face the thin, white-gowned figure bearing rapidly down on them.

"Lady Nessa." Kethra gave Min-drear's sister a shaky salute.

"Have you found my brother yet?" The white figure fluttered anxiously about them like some ghostly moth. Only her anxious, red-rimmed eyes showed through the slits of her veil-mask. "Oh, I've looked everywhere, everywhere!"

"Even on the foundation level, lady?" the Warder asked with a note of desperation.

"Clever Kethra! No, but I'll search there immediately. Oh!" She stopped short, noticing the strangers for the first time. "Who are you?"

All three visitors bowed. "That is Kracarn of Tagmeth, that, Bender," said the Highborn, shaking back the gray hood. Underneath was a thin face marked by silver-gray eyes and high cheekbones, one of them with the faint white line of an old scar cutting across it. She gave Kethra a lopsided, almost rueful smile. "And I am Jamethiel Priests'-bane, the Lordan of Ivory...the Darkling."

"I am honored to meet you," said Nessa in a preoccupied way. "Now excuse me. I must find my brother." With that, she darted away, followed at a tactful distance by a Kendar attendant.

"Have you misplaced Lord Min-drear?" Jamethiel asked Kethra politely.

The Warder made an inarticulate sound. She suddenly stepped around the table, grabbed the other's arm, and wrenched her right hand into the light. Arie felt his stomach turn.

"You said only scratches," Kethra said fiercely. "By God, Ganth's daughter or not, you will carry no infection forth from this house!"

With that, she swept the flask off the table and emptied its fiery contents over the mangled hand. The Highborn shuddered violently but made no sound. Nor did she try to withdraw from Kethra's grasp any more than she had from the hound's jaws earlier. For a long minute, Highborn and Kendar locked eyes as liquor dripped unnoticed into a black pool on the floor between them. Then Kethra dropped the hand with an oath, hurled the bottle into the fireplace, and stormed out of the hall without a backward glance.

"Border hospitality," said Jamethiel. "I have on occasion been made to feel more welcome."

Kracarn came forward quickly, wrenching a white scarf from his neck. "Damn these people anyway, Highborn and low," he said angrily, wrapping the scarf around her hand. "I think they must all be mad! Why did you let them treat you that way—you, the High Lord's sister!"

She flexed her hand carefully, painfully. "There. More mess than damage, I think. That Warder is so upset she hardly knows what she's doing. But why? Something is very wrong here, Kracarn. When I know what it is, I'll know how to react, won't I?"

Tarin emerged from his recess, expressionless, and gestured to the woman to follow him. As she left the hall with the gray dog still at her side and the thin, silent man at her heels, Arie saw that she was absentmindedly licking the last traces of liquor and blood from the tips of her long, white fingers.

In her wake, the hall seemed very empty and silent. Silent? No. There was a throbbing, a deep pulse. Arie felt as if his head was swelling with it. He desperately willed it to stop, willed himself not to see, but already the hall before him was fading. In its place was a much larger, grander hall, its high roof supported by black marble columns, its floor paved with green-veined stone. Thousands of death banners lined its walls. Tapestry faces grimaced. Threadbare hands clutched at rotting fabric. All was dead fiber, and yet the walls beneath were stained with blood.

Arie backed away. "No," he said out loud. "No, it isn't there. It isn't *real.*"

He tripped on steps, then turned and scrambled blindly up and up, past the second level gallery, into the close turnings of the highest tower. The wind came whistling down to meet him.

At its summit, the tower opened out on all four sides. Arie sank down beside the sheer drop, trembling. Then he began to cry. It wasn't fair. He hadn't asked to be so weak, or crippled, or—or cursed with these visions. No one here understood what that was like. Kethra certainly didn't. He hadn't even dared to tell her when he had begun to see things. She would think he was feeble-witted on top of everything else or, perhaps, going mad.

Arie rested his cheek against the cold stones and closed his eyes. The wind rushed about him, slowly stripping away his fears. He began to sing to himself, very softly, first songs that the wandering singer had brought to the keep more than a year ago and then songs of his own. The wind deafened him to his own words but seemed to make them ring all the more clearly in his mind. He worked them this way and that, changing, polishing them, and for a while was content.

It was nearly sunset when he opened his eyes again. Light streamed between the two opposite peaks to the west and shadows slowly rose in the Pass below. To the north, a premature darkness clouded the Barrier. Its surface moved restlessly in patterns that must have been miles across, and lightning flickered inside. There almost seemed to be something solid within the mists. Each flash half defined shifting outlines as of roofs and chimneys and gables as if at any minute the haze would roll back and there would stand the Master's House, looming over the mountains, the High Keep, over all Rathillien. It was a mirage which often appeared before one of those terrible spring storms from the north, from Perimal Darkling, that shook the keep down to its very roots. Arie picked up his crutch, shivering. It was more than time that he went below.

As he stepped out of the stairwell onto the second level, he heard his name called. Here the western wall opened into a long, rib-vaulted gallery lined with windows through which light poured. Someone sat under the center arch in the heart of the blaze.

"You sing well," said the High Lord's sister.

"Y-you heard me, lady?"

"I have a good ear for a wind-borne voice. Sing again."

Arie surprised himself by obeying, and even more by using the words he had been trying to write down earlier that day. Since then, the song had grown. As he sang it, he strained to make out the figure against the white flame of the sun. The gray cloak was thrown back now, revealing cream-colored riding leathers, a short byrnie of rathorn ivory, and high buff boots, all travel stained. Arie had never seen any Highborn lady but Nessa, and very little of her. This woman seemed impossibly slim compared to the powerfully built Kendar among whom he had grown up, and infinitely more graceful, with a hint of underlying tension. Even in repose, she seemed poised for sudden movement.

"Very good," she said when he had finished. "You have the true singer's voice—and sight. How did you know that the Master's hall is paved with green-veined stones?"

Arie gaped at her. "I—I didn't know. I just saw..."

Then stammering, he told her about his visions—the corridor extending into infinity, the window opening on such a landscape as Rathillien had never known, the black marble staircase ascending to a doorway barred with red ribbons as if it led to a lord's bridal chamber.

"I remember those stairs," said Jamethiel in a low voice, as if to herself. "Someone was waiting beyond those ribbons, and perhaps still is. When did you see these things?"

Arie told her.

"So," she said thoughtfully. "It all began when the patrol brought back that wretched 'almost human' creature from near the Barrier soon after Mid-Winter. Yes. That makes sense...but what a half-witted thing to have done!"

"Lady?"

"Nothing—I hope. Arie, how long has it been since the High Keep had a direct clash with the Master's folk?"

"Centuries, I think. Lady, it's been so long since the Master's fall. Is he really still there beyond the Barrier, still waiting?"

"Oh, yes. Listen to your own song. The man bargained for immortality and got it, he and his people both, after a fashion. Then, too, time passes more slowly in Perimal Darkling than here. The Master can and will wait until we forget him, as my brother has, until we lower our guard. But your leg hurts, doesn't it? What did you do to it?"

"Kethra put me on a half-broken colt when I was a child. I—it reared and fell on me."

"I see. Come to the window."

Arie hesitated, then limped shyly forward, only to stop again abruptly. The darkness at the Highborn's feet had risen. It was the gray bitch.

"Give her your hand," said Jamethiel.

Arie would rather have bolted. Instead, he found himself holding out a shaking hand, bracing himself for the pain which he felt sure would come. The dog sniffed it. Then, incredibly, his fingertips were wet from her tongue.

"Good," said the Highborn. "Now, after me, you are her master. Sit down...please."

Arie sat on the window ledge. He could see the visitor's face clearly now in the failing light. It looked very young and tired.

"Does your hand hurt much?" he blurted out.

The thin lips lifted in a wry smile. "Considering the things that have happened to me and that I've done to myself—yes, including that idiotic recklessness with the Master Runes that left me croaking like this—these wounds hardly count." She raised her bandaged hand and looked at it. Her smile slipped away. "In fact, compared to the binding of a creature's body and soul, these scratches are beneath contempt, and I have forced this hound to sell its freedom for a few drops of blood!"

Her long fingers curled stiffly into a fist.

"Lady!" Arie cried, and caught her injured hand in both of his as if to prevent it from striking out at the nearest stone. Its warmth and the feel of fine bones just under the skin startled him. Somehow, he hadn't quite believed before that this strange woman was mere flesh and blood, however much of the latter he had already seen.

"Sorry," she said with a crooked smile, withdrawing her hand. "But this keep. It's so old, so…fragile. Like an eggshell. I can feel darkness tapping on the outside, tapping at my self-control, too. How easy it would be to fall in a place like this. Arie, listen: to protect yourself, you have to know what's going on. Somehow, the will of this keep's defenders has been badly undermined, so much so that Perimal Darkling lies just beneath the surface here. Patrolling the Barrier is hardly enough when that sort of rot sets in. And each time the rangers bring back a darkling, things get worse because every creature out of the shadows brings some of them with it. That 'almost human' thing certainly did. So far, no one but you has seen these visions, but soon everyone will if this goes on. This entire keep is in danger of becoming no more than a shadow of that greater fortress in Perimal Darkling, the Master's House."

Arie wrestled with this. "Then, when I saw the room with the green-veined floor…"

"It was because Bender and I had just been in your hall, the counterpart of the Master's," said Jamethiel bitterly. She glanced at the gallery wall. Arie, also looking, started violently. The rapidly fading daylight cast both their shadows on the stones, but the Highborn's was darker and had a human face. There stood Bender, as he must have all this time.

"That is an unfallen darkling," said Jamethiel. "I am another one. We both were inmates in the Master's House. Neither of us consented to his evil, but we were both changed nonetheless. Bender is...as you see him. And I?" She shivered suddenly, and drew her cloak around her as if for warmth. "I have darkness in my veins now. Enough to blood-bind this poor brute to me body and soul. Enough to cast the very shadows I fight."

Thunder rumbled nearer, louder, and a cold northern wind breathed down the gallery. It was nearly dark now. To the north, verdigris lightning played across the Barrier as through the heart of a black opal.

Then from below came a booming sound. It echoed up the stairwell like some great shout of warning from no human throat and the gallery rang with it.

Jamethiel sprang up. "What in God's name is that?"

"The alarm, lady." Arie lurched to his feet. "Someone has sounded the Keepguard Horn in the lower hall. We must be under attack."

Below, the large room was rapidly filling as the keep Kendar poured into it in answer to the alarm, hurriedly buckling on armor as they came. Kethra stood by the extinct fire, silent and grim. Before her on the table lay something long and pale. It was Nessa's body.

The crowd parted for Jamethiel. She bent over the still form.

"Dead," said Kethra thickly.

"Yes, and already beginning to stiffen." She reached for the mask, which, out of respect, no one else had touched.

"But where is her gown?" asked Arie in a thin voice from the foot of the table.

Kethra looked at him, then at the corpse. What she had taken for the familiar garment in the stress of the moment was in fact only the first of many under-tunics.

"I'm afraid that isn't the only thing missing," said Jamethiel, and turned back the veil. Shock rippled through the hall. Under the silk was a grinning, bestial face whose eyes long since had gone to feed the crows. "I suggest you look on the northern battlement for the head of this poor lady," the Highborn said soberly. "Now. Before dawn brings back the birds."

Kethra turned on her, shock and rage at war in her face, but before she could speak, a Kendar burst through the crowd and threw himself gasping at her feet.

"Warder! In the lowest corridor by the western foundation...Tucor, Erlik, and I on guard duty...we found Lady Nessa's servant all broken and then...w-we saw her in the shadows, beckoning. Erlik and Tucor went to her. I-I saw her put her arms around them and then...she began...to squeeze. Warder! She crushed them, she crushed them both. I-I ran. Forgive me, but I couldn't fight *her*."

"Who?" roared Kethra.

"I-I think it was the High Lord's sister, but she wore Lady Nessa's gown..."

The rustle of cloth as Jamethiel swung her gray cloak over the body caused the guard to look up. His jaw dropped when he saw them both.

"One thing at least is certain," said Jamethiel grimly. "The dress was hers."

Kethra turned on her again, seething. "Battlements, cellars, exchanged heads—how much of this do you understand, Highborn?"

"Sweet Trinity, less than you should," said the other in exasperation. "Warder, do you know what a changer is?"

Kethra gave her a startled look and then almost by reflex began to recite the ancient lesson: "'In the Master's House there were those who embraced his evil. To them also life unending was given, but they purchased it with the corruption of body and soul until they could take on the mockery of any form but hold none that was true. So were the changers born.'" She gave a harsh laugh. "Are you saying that's what our guest in the cellar is, Darkling? After all these centuries, and on a night when you just happen to be our guest, too?"

Kracarn put a hand on his lady's arm almost pleadingly. "Jamethiel, it's beneath your dignity even to talk to this madwoman. Kendar!" He raised his voice. "One of you go summon your lord. God's claws, his sister has just been murdered!"

No one moved.

"Kracarn, please. Warder, if I'm right, this keep last saw a changer not centuries but only months ago when your patrol brought back the head of that 'almost human' thing to grace your battlements. Yes, that's what I think it was."

Kethra snorted. "D'you think we wouldn't know a changer if we saw one?"

"I don't think you would recognize one if it threw you down the stairs. Remember, these creatures can counterfeit any appearance. But they were also once like us and still are in some respects. What would *y o u* do if someone fed your kinsman or friend or lover to the crows like a common piece of carrion without benefit of death rites or pyre?"

"Do?" The Warder stiffened at the very thought of such an abomination. "*Do?* Why, I would tear down the bastard's house stone by stone and stake him out among the rubble. I would give him his own blood to drink..." She stopped short. "Sweet Trinity. Is that what we did?"

"I think so. And now with the same spring thaw that brought me comes that poor creature's avenger to breach *y o u r* walls and spill *y o u r* blood—although, being a changer, he goes about it rather more obliquely than you would."

Throughout the hall, Kendar shifted uneasily. More than one made the Darkwyr sign both against this avenger out of the shadows and against the evil which they themselves might unwittingly have committed. But Kethra looked at the still figure on the table and her expression hardened.

"Whatever we may or may not have done, this poor lady was innocent. Now her blood is a stain on our honor until we avenge her death." She turned to the uneasy crowd and raised her voice. "Hear me! We may have a different kind of quarry tonight, but it is still quarry and we are still hunters and warriors. This creature will die with blood in its throat, so I swear! Re-Kencyr..."

"Warder!" Jamethiel's voice cut across the ancient battle cry. "You have no idea how different a hunt this will be. I do. Leave it to me."

Kethra gave her a scornful look. "I'd as soon send this boy. Crippled as he is, he's at least as strong as a poor stick like you."

"Ancestors preserve us," said the Highborn, exasperated. "What has strength got to do with it? You'll never slay this creature by force anyway. God's claws and toenails, what do you think will happen if the lot of you go charging down into those cellars? Think of the confusion. Think of this creature's powers. It may even be one of the breed who can snatch the very thoughts from your mind. Down there in the dark, how long will you be sure that the person coming up behind you is really your brother, your sister, your friend? Then the killing will start. I tell you, the changer has set a trap for you all, and that," she pointed at Nessa's corpse, "is the bait."

"Bait?" Kethra started forward, big hands flexing. "*Bait*? The last of the Min-drears..."

An abrupt silence fell on the hall. No one even seemed to breathe.

"You had better tell me," said Jamethiel. "Whatever it is, you can't hide it forever."

The Warder had turned away, shoulders bowed. "Lord Min-drear is dead," she said in a choked voice. "His poor sister couldn't accept it, but it's true. We gave him to the pyre on Mid-Winter Day."

"And kept it a secret all this time?" Kracarn was outraged. "The news should have gone to Gothregor months ago! Lord Torisen will have to assign this keep to another Highborn family and they, of course, will bring in their own Kendar. You should all have made arrangements to leave by now!"

A low growl rose from the assembled Kendar. They closed ranks around the two Highborn. Arie began to shiver. He saw something in those familiar faces that he had never seen there before, and it terrified him.

"Kracarn..." said Jamethiel. "Shut up." She looked with amazement at the wall of hostile faces ringing her in. "My God, what are you people thinking of? D'you really believe that killing us will keep the news from Gothregor forever? And when my brother hears, what then? I give you fair warning: he annoys easily. But I still don't entirely understand. The last of the Min-drears? This boy..." she looked at Arie. "He has the build of a Highborn and the Min-drear hands. Isn't he the old lord's son?"

"Yes," said Kethra, as if the word hurt. "But not his consort's. Enough! For the moment, this is still our home and we will defend it as we see fit, without the help of one who once ate that Master's bread and might, for all we know, still earn it."

"Warder!"

Kethra spun around, aware that she had really overstepped herself this time and prepared to bluster. Instead, her eyes met those of the visitor, and she fell back a step.

"Threatening my life is one thing," said that husky, purring voice. "Questioning my honor is another. At the very least, to do so is...unwise. Shall I remind you of your manners, Warder? Yes, I believe I will. Three times within one day you have ignored the cup rites. Once for my arrival. You will forgive me if I fail to count the bottle which you so graciously emptied over my hand. Once for your slain lady. Her parting cup should have been drunk before she grew cold. Once for the hunt. Vengeance must be sworn and sanctified in proper form."

"Lady, now is not the time," protested Kethra, thrown on the defensive and more than a bit shaken.

"I say it is. Moreover, all must take part and each rite must last its full hour. Let everyone in the keep assemble here. Steward, bring all the ale you can find. Bender will help you. The rest of you, prepare the hall."

There was a moment's startled hesitation. Arie felt as if someone had kicked the feet out from under him and suspected that others felt the same. It was a long time since the full, innate power of a Kencyr Highborn had been exercised within these walls. Kethra opened her mouth, shut it, opened it again. If Jamethiel's demands had gone any further, she would have rebelled, but the customs invoked had weight with her, and so did the other's manner.

"I think one of us really has gone mad," she said. "All right. Do as she orders. The changer can work no mischief down there by itself. Our hunt and our vengeance are only delayed."

In short order, the hall was made ready. A hundred men and women sat on the benches, each with an ale mug in one hand and a naked sword in the other. All turned grim faces toward the head table where the Warder and Arie sat with the visitors. Nessa's body lay in state on a trestle between the high table and the benches. A thick candle marked with hour bands burned at her head, now retrieved from the battlements.

Kethra rose and growled the code of welcome. The response was muttered sullenly through the hall and the drinking began.

Bender put a small cask on the table in front of the Warder.

"A guest-gift," said Jamethiel. "My cask of wine for your flask of liquor. I occasionally remember my own manners, such as they are. You may have a taste," she added to Kracarn, "but then you must drink the common ale. There is little enough of this."

They poured and drank. Arie knew that he had never tasted better wine.

There was silence in the hall at first, broken only by the splash of ale. Outside, the storm rumbled closer. Fitful gusts of wind breathed through the hall's small upper windows, stirring the banners. Candles flickered and a pool of molten wax began to form beside Nessa's head. Arie drank more wine.

The first hour passed at last. Kethra stood and gave the call to mourning.

The voices in the hall were louder now, raised as though to compete with the approaching storm. The stones of the keep shivered as the thunder spoke again. In the lulls, Arie became aware of Jamethiel's quiet, slightly husky voice reciting the ancient stories of betrayal and flight and Rathillien, the new world, of striving and suffering, joy and triumph. Kethra relaxed and listened as the noises in the hall mounted unnoticed. Arie drank more wine.

The second hour passed more quickly. The summons to vengeance was greeted by a low, hoarse roar and the raising of many cups.

Kethra sank back in her chair. That husky voice had caught her now, all the more so because this time it told a story she had heard before only in fragments. Arie also listened, rapt. As the Highborn described it, he seemed to see that great mass of people known as the Horde slowly circling, circling in the Southern Wastes as they had for centuries past. But then, abruptly, the circle broke and the Horde began to more northward, three million strong, toward the Riverland. The Kencyr Host led by Torisen High Lord marched south to meet it. Host and Horde came together at the Cataracts. Battle followed on the narrow stair beside the falls, and confusion and carnage.

As Jamethiel spoke, Arie almost thought he heard other, nearer sounds: shouts, oaths, a bench crashing over. Out of the corner of his eye he caught movement, as though many figures were weaving about in confusion. Shadows leaped and, crying, fell.

But the voice went on, quiet, husky, arresting. It spoke of a girl escaped from darkness who came in search of her brother and found him in the chaos of battle at the Cataracts. It described their reunion, her doomed attempt to live as the Kencyrath said a Highborn woman should. Then followed flight, friendship among the scrollsmen, randon training, and much else besides in a life as breathless as a midnight race along the edge of a precipice.

"Except," said Jamethiel with a sudden smile, "when I occasionally fall on my head and so manage to get a little rest."

"A Highborn woman, uncloistered, unmasked." Even with the evidence before her, Kethra still found that hard to believe. "Has the Kencyrath changed so much since your brother became High Lord?"

"No," said the other, a bit sadly now. "Not really. But there are new possibilities. As for me, my brother hasn't exactly been pleased with my path, but he hasn't done all he could to stop me either."

"I should think," said Kethra wryly, "that it would take a great deal to do that."

Just then, Kracarn slid out of his chair and under the table, still clutching an ale mug. Arie started to laugh. Then, for the first time in hours, he looked past the Highborn to the hall beyond and his mouth dropped open. Half of the High Keep Kendar were sprawling on the floor and the rest slumped over the low tables.

"Oh, yes," said Jamethiel quietly, sipping her wine. "Very little stops me. That, however, might." She lowered her cup and regarded the sword point which Kethra had leveled at her throat.

"No more stories," grated the Warder. "No more honeyed voice. What have you done to my people?"

"Gently, gently. They only sleep, like my companion here, thanks to the phial which Bender poured into their ale. My congratulations on their hardheadedness, by the way. I demanded the full rites, but never really thought it would take all three hours for the potion to work. You have a choice now, Warder: strike, or finish your wine and come with me." She gave a sudden wry grin. "You might at least give me the benefit of the doubt. For once, I know what I'm doing—I hope."

For a moment, Kethra stood glaring. Then she drained her cup with a gulp. The two rose and crossed the body-strewn floor to the stairs leading downward. Bender and the gray bitch followed them.

Arie was left at the table, staring blankly at Lady Nessa's body. The third hour passed in a slow stream of hot wax running down the thick candle at her head. Then the rising storm slammed into the keep with a shout of thunder. The hall doors burst open. Wind came questing into the hall, licked back Nessa's veil. For a moment her pale face, oddly tranquil, caught the light. Then the candle blew out.

Arie grabbed his crutch, with something almost like a sob, and stumbled after the others toward the stair. The murk of the subterranean levels received him soundlessly.

The first basement was occupied by the winter stables and the kennels. As he went, half falling, down the stairway, Arie heard the uneasy movements of horses and a dog whimpering somewhere in the dim maze of wooden partitions.

He caught up with the others halfway down into the second basement where the fire timbers towered fifty feet from brick floor to ceiling. Impossible to ignite by accident, these huge logs had only been made to burn after a year of dropping hot coals into their hollowed-out trunks. It had taken the largest of them many generations to burn through to the bark. Their dusky orange glow lit the hall, but Arie could feel little of their warmth. Someone had left open the trap door in the southwest corner which led down to the foundation level. Chill air rose from the black hole, heavy with the smell of earth. The stairway went straight down into it.

A moment later, they were all standing on the dirt floor of the keep's lowest level with the torchlit passage stretching out before them along the western foundation wall.

Kethra and Jamethiel went first. The Warder still carried her sword naked in her hand and used it to cut tangled webs from their path. The Highborn, unarmed, kept her left hand locked in the gray dog's fur. Arie limped after them, still wine-befuddled, wondering if any of this was actually happening. The torches bracketed at intervals in the outer stonewall had begun to burn with a bluish tinge. High above in the hall, the death banners must be flying over the drugged Kendar, but only a dull vibration in the stones and a groaning from the inner wall of ironwood—like that from the timbers of a ship at sea—marked the presence of the storm. Not even the voice of the thunder could reach them in this grave of narrow passageways.

They found Nessa's attendant at the mouth of the third corridor leading off under the main body of the keep. As the guard had said, she was horribly broken, as if someone had taken great pains to snap every bone. Beyond lay Erlik and Tucor. They had been crushed together face-to-face, tooth uprooting tooth, shattered rib bursting through flesh and armor to lock with rib in a horrible parody of a lover's embrace. The ground all about them gleamed darkly in the torchlight.

Kethra swore out loud.

The gray bitch suddenly strained forward under Jamethiel's hand, growling. The next moment she broke free and disappeared down the side corridor.

"After her!" cried Jamethiel.

They ran, the Highborn and the Warder racing on ahead. Arie stumbled. Bender's thin hand closed on his elbow and drew him on. Surely they were going downhill now, but he had never heard that these passages sloped. The ceiling and walls also seemed wrong, as though the former were rising and the latter opening out between the islands of torch-cast light into shadowy depths. He caught glimpses of high vaulted chambers, arcades, and halls where there could be nothing but ironwood and ashlar walls.

These are shadows of the Master's House, he thought dizzily. But in the presence of three darklings, they were rapidly becoming more than that.

Then from ahead came a scream of canine agony.

Kethra sprang forward with a hoarse shout, brandishing her sword. Jamethiel tripped her. When the Warder tried to rise, a slim arm snaked around her throat, deft fingers barely touching the pressure points. Kethra gasped.

"You fool, not with the sword!" hissed Jamethiel's voice in her ear. "Remember, this creature's blood is utterly corrupt. It *burns*."

Kethra shook off the Highborn and rose, seething. "One more trick like that, Darkling..."

"And you'll feed me to the chickens. Just as you wish, but later. Here it comes."

The two swung about to face down the passageway. Arie peered around them. He could no longer trace the phantom outlines of the openings, but the sense of open space remained. They stood under a torch between solid walls. Beyond, however, the brands were nothing but blurs in midair, bobbing in the cold wind that slid past where no wind had a right to be.

From ahead in the gloom came a faint rustling sound, moving closer, closer. Something pale entered the farthest circle of light. Arie gulped. That was Nessa's gown, but what in all the names of God was wearing it? The advancing form looked like that of a woman, but even as he watched it thickened, the curve of breast and hip becoming less distinct. Seams ripped. The dim blur of a face swam closer in the murky light. The Warder drew in her breath sharply.

"Kethraaaa..." came a low, hissing and yet horrible familiar voice from the shadows. "Keeeethraaa..."

"Min-drear?" the Warder whispered. "No, *No!*"

She lunged forward, steel flashing. Her sword bit deeply into the shoulder of the advancing changer. A few drops of blood spattered on the ground, on her hand, and ate hungrily into both. The awful wound closed around steel, burnt it away. Kethra found herself clutching only a sword hilt. The creature grinned down at her with a face rapidly becoming more and more like that of her dead lord.

"Keeethraa...have you missed me? Cooome, and embrace for old love's sake..."

It had caught hold of her arms and now began to squeeze. Her coat split down the back. Bones creaked. Arie started toward her with a cry, but Bender held him fast.

"Warder!" The Highborn's voice cracked off the stonewalls. "It takes its form from your memories. Think of something else!"

The creature faltered, its face beginning to lose definition. With a snarl, it thrust Kethra aside.

"Soooo...the Master's toy. What do *you* remember, changeling?"

Arie saw its features begin to alter again as it shambled forward, cheekbones becoming more pronounced, silver-gray eyes widening. Jamethiel went back a step.

"I deny you," she said hoarsely. "I damn you."

Her hands jerked up, bandaged fingers separating stiffly. With horror, Arie saw her start to make the Darkwyr sign in reverse.

Bender caught her arm and sent her spinning backward. She collided with Arie, knocking him into the wall. The stones against his back felt strange—sheet ice over deep water, about to crack. He pushed both Jamethiel and himself away from them.

Bender completed the mirror sign. The wind stopped. Cold grew. In the uncertain light, it looked as if what little flesh the man still had was melting away as from someone years dead, but his hands held the sign without a tremor.

The changer had halted uncertainly in front of him. Now it reached out as if to grab the man, and its own fingertips shriveled at the touch. It turned, snarling, thwarted. Behind it lay Kethra. She had fallen against the wall at the edge of the light. Arie could see her left arm and the lower part of her body clearly, but the rest was indistinct. Instead of stones behind her, there seemed to be pavement, stretching back out of sight, marked with strange patterns. Kethra was straining to pull herself out of the darkness. She would not succeed before the changer reached her.

Without thinking, the boy released Jamethiel's arm and slipped past Bender. The face and form of the changer were in motion again even as he threw himself between it and the Warder.

"Cripple," it said, almost in Kethra's voice. "Worthless little cripple." Then it burst into long peals of jeering laughter.

"Shut up, mother!" he screamed at it. "Shut up, shut up!" He swung his crutch.

The pain of splinters ripping into his palms as the shaft was wrenched out of them brought him to his senses with a gasp. It was towering over him, chuckling now with a sound like bubbles rising through quicksand. He stared up at it, too appalled to move.

Behind him, Kethra staggered to her feet.

"Now!" cried Jamethiel. "Hellbender, bring it down!"

The man dropped his hands. Kethra swept Arie aside. The changer had half turned at the sound of the Highborn's voice. Now it swayed and toppled as both Bender and the Warder hit it simultaneously. Each pinned down an arm. Arie, to his amazement, found himself trying to control one of its legs. The limb slowly writhed in his grasp. He felt a terrible strength gathering in it.

Jamethiel dropped to her knees beside the misshapen head. She tore the white scarf off her hand, hooked her fingernails in the half closed wounds, and ripped them open. Blood spiraled down her wrist. Bender forced the changer's mouth open and she held her hand over it. Blood streamed off the heel of her palm down into the working throat.

The changer gagged, and then it convulsed. A knee smashed into Arie, knocking him two paces down the corridor. Caught by a whiplash arm across the face, Jamethiel staggered back into the wall under the torch. Her head struck the stones sharply. Bender drew her clear.

Convulsion followed convulsion. Nessa's gown was ripped apart in seconds. Beneath it, the pale flesh twisted and writhed, as if each sinew was a separate thing. There was a dull crack as a bone snapped in the midst of a muscular contraction, then another and another. Still, it wasn't until the shattered end of a femur tore its way out through the side of one leg that the thing began to scream. There were words mixed in that rush of agony and dark blood. The changer was begging for death, begging despite its torment in the correct ritual terms. Only a Highborn would use that formula. Only a Highborn had the authority to grant what was asked.

Jamethiel stood over it, her bruised face very still. "Bring me fire," she said in a low voice. "Hurry."

Bender took the torch out of its socket and put it in her hand. She extended it to the distorted thing on the floor. Its hand shot up and gripped the burning wood. Flames leaped down the ruined sleeve of the gown. In an instant, fire clothed the entire form. Flames spread, covering walls, floor, ceiling, and yet none of them burned. It was as if the shadows themselves were being consumed. The heat and stench of the pyre drove Arie and the others back to the western foundation. It was there, when at last the flames and the unnatural wind died together, that they realized Jamethiel was not with them.

They found her sitting on the stairs, hands clenched together with no regard for the torn flesh. Orange light from the fire-timber hall spilled down the steps around her, casting her shadow black on the floor. Bender stood in it. *Of course,* thought Arie with a kind of light-headed omniscience, *that's because he has no shadow of his own.* Kethra regarded the Highborn belligerently, fists jammed on hips.

"Well?" she demanded.

"That all depends," said Jamethiel bitterly. "As you may have noticed, I nearly got you killed. That damned sign. I always was too quick with my hands. This time, at the very least it would have cost me my soul or Bender his—if he still had one. Instead, I've killed a Highborn, one of my own blood, with my blood. Set one to catch one, eh? Perhaps, after all, there isn't that much to choose between two shades of darkness."

Kethra regarded her soberly for a minute more. Then she unknotted the black scarf of office around her neck.

"I make my choice," she said and, taking Jamethiel's injured hand, carefully wrapped the cloth around it.

Arie woke the next morning in a corner of the lower hall, groggy with wine and dreams. He remembered finding Jamethiel on the steps and the long climb upward. He remembered his mother and the Highborn sitting at the head table drinking the last of the wine, talking through the last long hours of the night while the storm slowly spent itself outside. He *thought* he remembered scraps of their conversation:

"*A keep is more than its Highborn. My brother and I still agree on that, if on little else.*"

"*The boy is weak. Brave, yes, but weak.*"

"*So am I—physically. Strength isn't everything. Then, too, he sees things, true things. A singer with the sight can be very powerful, very...dangerous.*"

"*To you?*"

"*Perhaps. Someday he may see more in me than I care to know about myself, but no one can stop a true song or, I hope, a new idea.*"

"*Still, a half-Kendar lord...*"

That last must be a dream. Arie had fallen asleep to the sound of their voices. His last clear memory was of a fur robe dropping over his shoulders.

At last he opened his eyes, and found that not all the warmth of his makeshift bed came from the robe. The gray bitch lay curled up beside him. Her right paw was bandaged and there was a lump on her head. Something in the protective curve of her great body told him that the hound had been assigned a new master. Timidly, he reached out and stroked her gray flank.

It was still very early morning, barely past daybreak. Most of the Kendar still sprawled snoring on the floor and Nessa kept her solitary state, but a voice spoke in the courtyard. It was Kethra, pledging the rider's cup. Arie threw off the robe. He and the hound limped to the door together.

Jamethiel sat her Whinno-hir in the courtyard, one hand still wrapped in the Warder's black scarf resting on the mare's neck. Bender and Kracarn waited nearby, one as inscrutable as ever, the other clearly feeling very ill-used. Kethra was offering them the cup.

Jamethiel saw Arie and smiled. "Mind you," she said to the Warder, "no promises. All I can offer is a new possibility, and hope."

"Hope." Kethra put her hand rather awkwardly on Arie's shoulder. "Yes, we can live on that—as long as necessary. In the meantime, a month from now I and my son will come south to your brother's council. Then, if Arie wishes it, he will stay with you for a while. There are things you can teach him that I can't."

"Do you wish it?" Jamethiel asked.

Arie could only nod.

"Very good. Your songs will help us all push back the darkness. In a month, then!" She raised her bandaged hand in farewell, turned the mare, and in another minute had disappeared through the main gate.

"A month," said Kethra. "Not much time. Still, we will make it count. You will sing for us often, I hope. The shadows have been too long in these halls."

They went back into the keep together, the Warder, the lame boy, and the gray hound.

An introduction to
"A Ballad of the White Plague"

This story is an oddity: one of my rare, non-Jame pieces. I was challenged to write about Sherlock Holmes, so I did, although the result is less detective than gothic. Its genesis was a conversation at Wiscon, the feminist science fiction convention, when friends linked tuberculosis (the so-called "White Plague"), vampirism, and a particularly gruesome nineteenth century folk song. I took it from there.

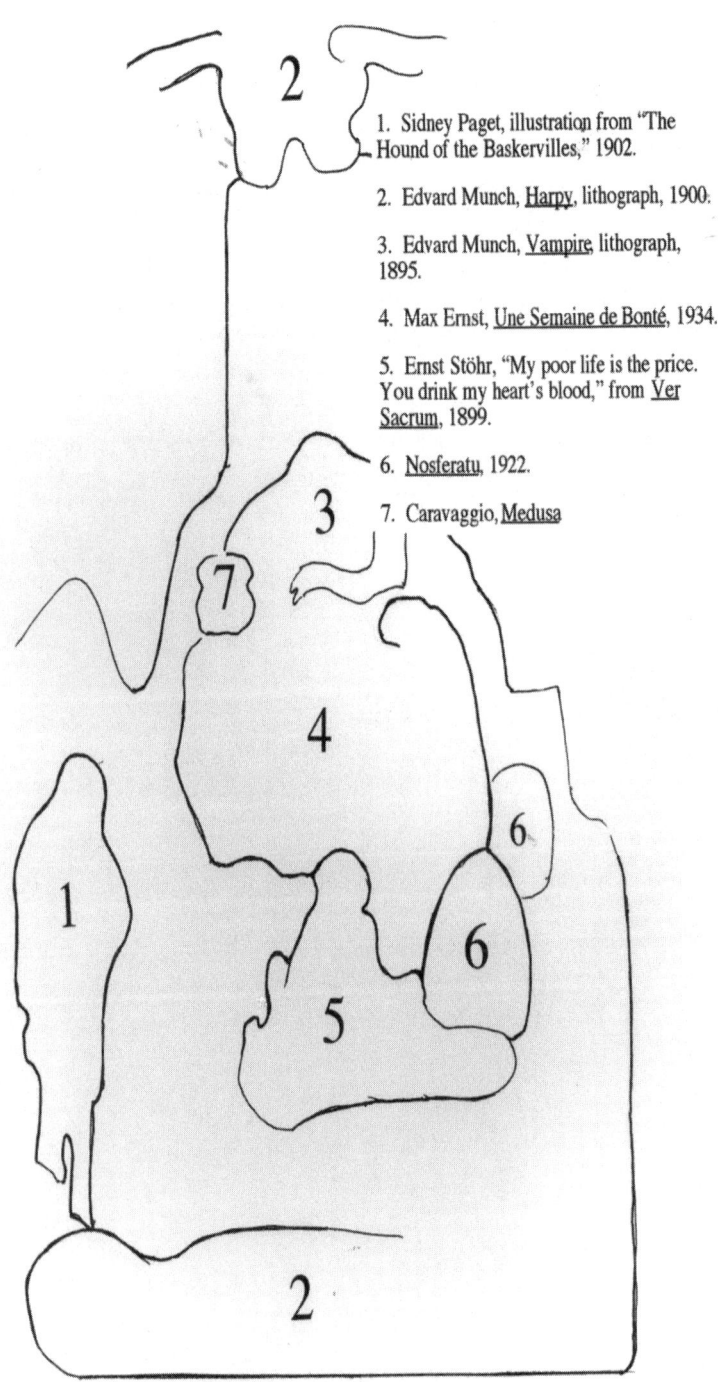

1. Sidney Paget, illustration from "The Hound of the Baskervilles," 1902.

2. Edvard Munch, <u>Harpy</u>, lithograph, 1900.

3. Edvard Munch, <u>Vampire</u>, lithograph, 1895.

4. Max Ernst, <u>Une Semaine de Bonté</u>, 1934.

5. Ernst Stöhr, "My poor life is the price. You drink my heart's blood," from <u>Ver Sacrum</u>, 1899.

6. <u>Nosferatu</u>, 1922.

7. Caravaggio, <u>Medusa</u>

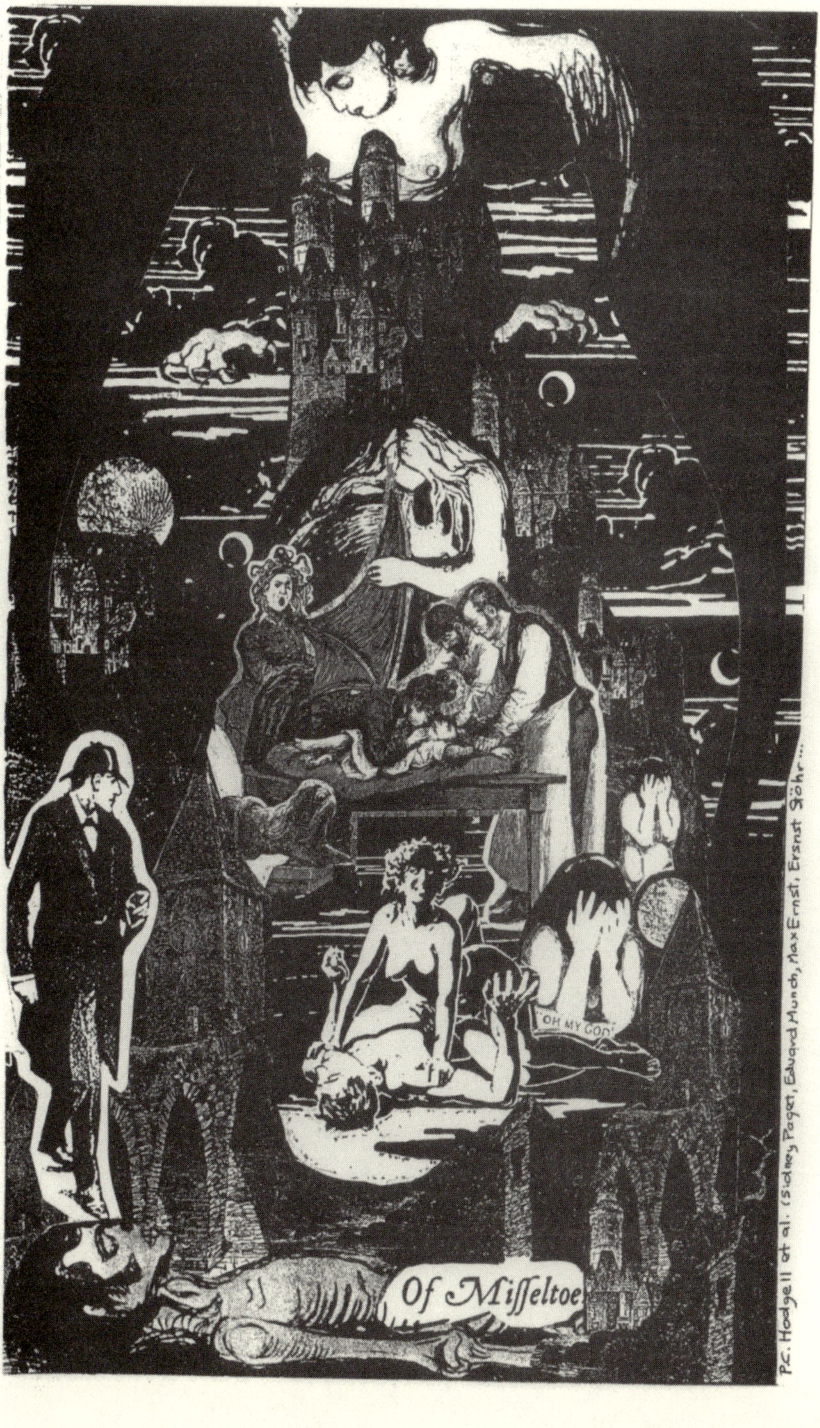
"OH MY GOD!"
Of Misseltoe
P.C. Hodgell et al. (Sidney Paget, Edvard Munch, Max Ernst, Ersnst Göhr...

A BALLAD OF THE WHITE PLAGUE

"*Denn die Todten reiten schnell*,'" Holmes quoted in a sudden, mocking voice. "'The dead travel fast.' My dear Watson, we are not dead yet, but that may soon be remedied if you overturn us in a ditch."

I was almost startled enough to do exactly that, so long had it been since last he had deigned to speak to me—as if our current plight were entirely my fault!

Lightning flared to the north, broken forks seen through a black canopy of oak leaves, and a moment later thunder rolled down on us like a run-away cart full of rocks. The pony's hooves clattered nervously on the rough stones of the old roman road. Our rented trap bounced and swayed. With nightfall, a cold wind had pushed aside the heat of the August day, and now we stood a good chance of being half drowned, if not pelted with hail or struck by lightning.

"My dear Holmes," I said, mimicking his tone to cover my own quite natural nervousness. "You must admit that our situation approaches the gothic, if not the ludicrous. Lost in the wilds of Surrey! What time is it?"

"The dead of night," he replied in a hollow voice. "The third watch. The witching hour."

"In other words," I said crossly, "about midnight. At this rate, we will never make Bagshot in time to catch the last express to London."

"It was your idea to drag me off for a drive in the country."

"And yours that we return through this wretched wilderness...oh really, this is too much!"

"'The children of the night!' Holmes quoted again, listening to the distant howl. "'What music they make!'"

The howl ended in a most unromantic yelp, some exasperated farmer probably having clouted the hound. We were, after all, only five or six miles from civilization, cutting across the woodland that surrounded Surrey Hill. Sandhurst lay to our southwest, Ascot to our north, and Bagshot to our east. If we followed the Roman road far enough, we would rejoin the world, but not in time to return our rented trap and catch the last train home or, it seemed, to escape a drenching. On top of that, Holmes was in a strange, wrangling mood that made me long to shake him.

"You may jeer at my romantic tastes and complain that I reduce your cases to mere sensationalism," I snapped, "but you yourself have just quoted from Bürger's 'Lenore' and *Dracula*. Now, admit: sensational or not, Bram Stoker knows how to tell a tale."

Holmes snorted. "A tale of arrant nonsense. The living dead...ha! Some people will devour any story if it is sufficiently fantastic, as your readers have repeatedly proved. Sometimes I wonder how gullible you yourself are. Next, you will claim that, once upon a time, we really did confront a vampire in Sussex."

"I never thought so, anymore than you did. That was real life, not fiction."

"I am glad that you acknowledge the difference," said Holmes tartly.

"Nonetheless," I said, pursuing my own thought, "there are sometimes curious coincidences between the two. For example, take names: Carfax Abbey, where Stoker's undead monster lay hidden in his coffin by day, and Lady Francis Carfax, whom we plucked living from the tomb only a month ago."

When Holmes made no reply, I shot him a look askance. The brim of his hat was pulled down over his eyes, and his chin had sunk into the collar of his gray traveling-cloak, leaving only the predatory hook of his nose. He was ignoring me again.

I knew that the Carfax case still bothered my friend. At first, I thought that that was because he had so nearly failed to deduce Lady Francis's whereabouts in time to prevent the villainous Holy Peters and his female accomplice from burying her alive. As it was, we had barely removed her from the coffin in time to prevent her asphyxiation from the chloroform with which she had been drugged.

The Carfax case took place in July of this year [1902].

Soon after, I moved to my own rooms on Queen Anne Street and for a fortnight did not see my friend. When we met again, I was disturbed by his haggard appearance. He had not been sleeping well, he said, and muttered something about a recurrent dream. In it, his fear apparently was not that the lady would fail to escape her premature grave but, oddly, that she would succeed.

For the intensely rational Holmes to admit to any dream was rare. Far worse was his tacit admission that one was actually robbing him of his sleep. True, I had known him to stay awake for days on end when working on a case, but this case was over, successfully solved, if at the last minute.

It had crossed my mind that Lady Francis might have stirred a latent taphephobia in Holmes. By 1900, the fear of premature internment had grown to epidemic proportions. Recently, an elderly female patient had presented me with a first edition of Tebb and Vollum's *Premature Burial and How It May be Prevented*. If she died while in my care, so great was her fear of waking in the grave that she strictly charged me to cut her throat before allowing her to be buried. Glancing through the book's bibliography, I had counted no less than 120 works in five languages on the subject, in addition to 135 articles, 41 university theses, and 17 pamphlets published by the "London Association for the Prevention of Premature Burial." By God, that gave *me* nightmares, before I ever heard of Lady Francis Carfax.

But Holmes had never shown any such weakness, nor did it seem likely with his cool, almost clinical approach to any case. In short, I was at a loss to know why the Carfax affair still haunted my friend, and I was worried. Hence my ill-fated attempt to divert him with a country drive.

"Turn here," said Holmes suddenly.

I could see no crossroads, but to the right there was a dark break in the trees. At a tug of the reins, the pony swung down off the causeway, the trap lurching after him. We would end in the ditch after all, I thought, but then the wheels crunched on unseen gravel. We were following a hidden drive through a tree-lined tunnel of darkness. High grass swished around the pony's legs. Branches scraped the trap's sides. The first fat drops of rain began to tap imperiously against the over-arching leaves.

"Holmes, I don't think that this is the road to Bagshot."

"No. It is, however, the road to shelter, if you don't mind a ghost or two."

I was about to demand what he meant when we emerged from the trees. Ahead, indistinct against the dark flank of Surrey Hill, sprawled an enormous building. Then a lightning flash revealed my mistake: the house itself was fairly small, a country manor in the Georgian fashion. Surrounding it, however, like a series of broken eggshells set one inside another, were the ruins of at least three far older structures. Then the darkness fell again like a thunderclap, and again the house seemed huge and misshapen, devoid of light or life, yet watching, waiting.

The wind swooped and rain came spattering down, mixed with a handful of stinging hail. As I secured the pony in the lee of the house, Holmes disappeared inside. Following, I hesitated in an entry way as black as the bowels of the earth, stinking of wet wood and rot.

"Holmes? Holmes! Where are you?"

His voice came hollowly from within: "Welcome to Morthill Manor."

As I groped toward him, the storm breathing loudly down the hall at my back, his words reached me in snatches:

"The name or some variation of it...said to date back to Neolithic times, designating the huge barrow mound which itself is the hill. Druids...circle of standing stones within the oak grove on its summit…60 A.D., human sacrifice there to ensure Boadicea victory in her revolt against the Romans…Following her defeat, Roman soldiers slaughtered the priests, overthrew the stones, and cut down the sacred oaks to build a country villa…said to have sealed Celtic infants alive under the floor as foundation sacrifices…Watson, you spoke?"

"No," I snapped. I had run my thigh hard against a table and sworn, as much at Holmes and his ill-timed games as at the pain to my old war injury, already aching with the change of weather.

My left hand lost contact with the wall. I stood in the doorway of a long dining room, its dimensions briefly defined by a flash of lightning outside tall, broken windows. Holmes was moving about at the room's far end, apparently in search of something, still lecturing like some infernal cicerone:

"Many structures have risen on this site since then, each built with the bones…I mean, the stones of its predecessor, each with its foundation sunk deep into the same thirsty darkness. In the Middle Ages, a convent rose on the villa ruins, but was abandoned because of 'straunge noises under-ground.' Later, it was learned that the abbess had ordered thirteen young novices to be walled up alive for 'consorting with the dead of the mound.' During Elizabeth's reign, the house was rebuilt, but again abandoned after tainted water from a new well shaft killed nine children. In 1645, Roundheads burned it to the ground under the impression that the wife and children of a Royalist supporter were hiding inside. Unfortunately, they were. Ah."

A candle flared. The light flickered across Holmes's sharp-boned face, and then across that of the young woman behind him. I could not suppress a cry, even as I realized what I was seeing. Holmes turned and looked at the portrait over the fireplace. I believe that its sudden, spectral appearance startled him too, though the only sign was a quiver, instantly controlled, in the hand which held the candle.

"The current structure dates from 1725," he said. "Its last owner, to my mind, was its worst. There, if you please, is the portrait of a true vampire."

The light called her forth from the shadows, ghostly in her pallor, yet strangely, avidly alive. The pose and style were reminiscent of da Vinci's "Mona Lisa." Her hair, the shade of anemic strawberry, was pulled back from a broad, white brow to tumble luxuriously down below her waist. Her eyes were a pale, almost luminous green. White teeth—the incisors, not the canines—showed between unexpectedly full, red lips. She was smiling. I thought, despite myself, that she looked hungry, and Walter Pater's description of that famous painting came unbidden to my mind:

She is older than the rocks among which she sits; like the vampire, she has been dead many times, and learned the secrets of the grave.

No. This would *not* do.

"Really, Holmes. Next you'll claim to have known this lady."

"Of course I did," he snapped, turning. "Her name was Blanche Vernet. She was my cousin."

Then a strange expression flickered across his face. He was staring at something above my head. Hastily, I crossed the threshold and turned to look up. Over the doorway, chained to the lintel, hung a giant, skeletal branch of mistletoe. It moved slightly in the unaccustomed draft rushing in from the hall, its leafless fingers scraping on stone.

"'The mistletoe hung in the castle hall.'" Holmes quoted the old ballad in an odd tone, as if surprised to remember it. "'The holly branch shone on the old oak wall...'"

His voice faltered. For a moment, he looked..."haunted" is the only word—but that moment quickly passed.

"You have heard me mention my maternal great-grandfather, the French painter Carle Vernet," he resumed briskly. "Besides his son Horace, also an artist, he had another son, Charles, who became a doctor."

"Your great-uncle," I said, working this out.

"Yes. For a doctor, he seems to have been singularly unfortunate: his first wife, a French woman, did not survive Blanche's birth. His second wife, the daughter of a minor Wallachian diplomat, died some twelve years later under similar circumstances, leaving behind the twin infant girls Alice and Alyse. That was in 1853, I believe, after the family had moved to London... Watson, am I boring you?"

"What?" I jerked my attention back to him, away from a second face that stared grimly from the end wall opposite Blanche out of the heavy gold of a mock Byzantine icon. "Holmes, who is *that?*"

"Irisa," he said curtly, noting the direction of my gaze. "The second wife's sister and the twins' aunt. She descended suddenly from some aerie in the Carpathians and stayed to tend house after her brother-in-law removed his family here in the summer of '62."

Severe, black clothing, an ornate Greek cross on her breast, black brows drawn together over inimical black eyes... she was like the shadow cast by Blanche's hectic light, watching her niece down the length of the dining room with the unfathomable stare of a death's-head.

Sodden branches lashed the windows. Atop Surrey Hill, the druids' desecrated grove seemed to pull lightning down from the sky.

Flash. CRACK.

I blinked in the after-glare, seeing not the room but its image burned into my mind, stark black and white. Instead of portraits, the family themselves stood silent and watchful against the walls: black-browed Irisa, pale Blanche, and two little girls in white, side by side in a corner, regarding us solemnly... but then my sight cleared and again they were only paint on canvas with dust-blurred eyes. Of the two girls, however, there was no sign.

I cleared my throat. "Dr. Vernet painted these?"

"He did," said Holmes. "Art in the blood will out, one way or another. His last portrait was that which you see over the mantel, but his true masterpiece was its original: his eldest daughter, Blanche."

"'The baron beheld with a father's pride,/ His beautiful child, young Lovell's bride,'" I quoted the ballad's next verses sarcastically, still half-convinced that Holmes was pulling my leg, not wanting to prove myself as gullible as he thought or as I had just been given reason to fear.

"Oh, yes," he said, ignoring my tone. "He doted on Blanche, for whom nothing was good enough. My father, on business in London, wrote home that Blanche's coming-out ball was the hit of the season and she the nonpareil, upstaging even that other 'Pocket Venus,' the notorious Florence Paget. Oh, my lovely cousin had many admirers, but, as women will, she fixed her wild heart on the least suitable and seduced him."

This was blunt, even for Holmes, surprising bluntness from me in return. "Who?"

He ignored my question.

"In the midst of her triumph, she contracted a cough which proved to be consumption. At that time, Dr. Vernet sold his London practice, bought Morthill, and moved his family here in a desperate attempt to find a cure."

In this, Dr. Vernet had my sympathy. The only "cure" for tuberculosis is fresh air and sunlight, but most victims die anyway, usually from inanition, sometimes from drowning as bodily fluids flood into their destroyed lungs—a far cry from the romantic image of the disease in Dumas's *Lady of the Camillias* or *La Bohème*. In the mid-nineteenth-century, the disease which we now call the White Plague killed millions, if not tens of millions, with no end in sight even today.

"I fear," I said, "that Dr. Vernet's effort was gallant, but doomed."

"Call it rather his obsession, matched only by his daughter's ferocious will to live. Tiny as Blanche was—hardly taller than a child—she proved remarkably tenacious of life. Summer passed, and then fall. In the last, bleak days of the year, a black-edged envelope finally arrived—sent by Blanche to announce her father's death."

"Of consumption?"

"Yes. Remember, this was before Villemin proved tuberculosis to be contagious, although it had already been noted that while the disease dawdled with some victims like a fond lover, it galloped off pell-mell with others. This had been Dr. Vernet's fate. Moreover, Blanche informed us that she had inherited all her father's assets, including a large debt owed by my father to hers. She asked—no, demanded—that Father immediately attend her here at Morthill to discuss terms. And so, perforce, he came, bringing me with him."

Holmes looked up again at the leafless branch chained and creaking over the lintel.

"Forty years ago on Christmas Eve, when I was a boy of eight and that bough was fresh . . ."

* * *

Viscum album, the boy Sherlock thought, regarding the spiky greenery over the door. The traditional kissing bough. How seasonal.

He tried to keep his thoughts on this subject—*parasitical, sacred to the Druids* . . .—but unease gnawed at him, as it had all that long, dark day on the increasingly silent drive to his cousin's house.

Looking back, it seemed that none of their household had been easy since Father's return from London the previous spring. That was when the letters had started to arrive. At first, awkwardly joking about some "damned importunate suitor" in a civil case, he had carried them away to read in private.

Finally, in a stony voice, Mother had said, "Burn them."

From then on, self-consciously, he had—unopened, in full sight of the family—until they had slowed and stopped at summer's end. Intrigued, the boy had slipped back into the breakfast room to rescue the last one from the grate. All that remained was a piece of red paper, ripped on one side and charred on the other, overlaid with a filigree of light ash.

Then, that morning, another envelope addressed in that same impetuous hand, edged in black, lay beside Father's plate.

"Open it," Mother said, and he had.

As he read, his face had blanched. "My God. So much money. This will ruin us." He had looked at Mother, turning paler still. "I must go."

Mother had been silent for a moment and then had suddenly said, "Take Mycroft with you."

Mycroft had looked grim at this. At fifteen, seven years his brother's senior, he took their mother's side in whatever-it-was that had upset her since the previous spring. Father had glanced at him and then quickly away.

"No. I will take Sherlock. A child may soften her."

Now here they stood in their cousin's cold, disordered dining room, beside a long table laden with dirty dishes. Their pony and rig were tied at the outer door; no one had come to take charge of them, the servants having all fled.

"A plague house declares itself," that grim woman in black (Aunt Irisa?) had said as she let them in. Then she had seen Sherlock, and drawn her breath in sharply. "You fool, to bring a child here! Do you know what happens to children in this house?"

The boy wondered about his two little cousins, Alice and Alyse. As he entered the dining room, he thought he had seen the white hem of a child's dress flick out by the far door. *Girls are timid*, he reminded himself, clutching for the warmth of superiority. Cold as the room was, Mycroft would laugh at him if he shivered: *What are emotions to the superior mind? What is physical weakness?*

Father hid his emotions poorly. He was pacing now, shooting glances at the door.

Quick footsteps out in the hall, a flurry of white—Blanche stood there, breathless, under the bough, corsaged with holly and crowned with mistletoe. Once she had been as tiny and perfect as a porcelain doll. Now her unbound hair, thinned by illness, floated up about her in the draft from the hall and her eyes glistened. When she looked at Father, the tip of her pale tongue slid as if with a life of its own across the bruised ripeness of her lips. Then she saw the boy, and the smile froze on her face like ice mantling over a corpse.

"What a dear little chap, Siger!" she cried with feigned delight. "My cousin Sherlock, is it not?"

She embraced him as if she would gladly have broken him in two. There was strength there yet, though he felt the rack of her bones beneath the white shroud of her gown and smelled the sweet rot of her flesh, mingled obscenely with attar of roses. Then she began to cough and pushed him away. Flecks of her blood speckled his face.

"How shall we...entertain you?" she cried, collapsing into a chair, struggling to catch her breath. "I know...a treasure hunt! There is a paper...a promise in writing to repay my dear dead father...oh, such a great amount of money! Find it, and perhaps you may keep it." She clasped her hands against her wasted breast, gazing at his father. "Look for it...under a broken heart."

The boy left the room by the far door, forcing himself not to run. A stair led upward to the second floor. He climbed.

The window at the far end of the upper hallway was small and round, silvery with twilight. It seemed a great distance away, and yet Morthill was not large. After all, it only had two central corridors, one on each floor, with rooms opening off to either side. It should be easy to find his cousin's bedroom. Women liked to keep their secrets hidden close. He hesitated a moment, uncertain, and then turned to the first door on the left, which stood half open.

His boots crunched on broken glass as he stepped inside. The door closed behind him. He edged forward in utter darkness, his feet now rustling as if through fallen leaves. He ran into something, hard. A table edge. More glass fell and broke.

Now he could see the vague outline of a window. Advancing on it, he pulled down the black velvet which muffled its long, narrow frame.

Twilight glimmered into the ruins of Dr. Vernet's laboratory. Here was the squat hulk of an alchemist's athenor; there, rows of shattered retorts like jagged, crystal teeth; everywhere, the pages of books ripped out and strewn in drifts about the floor. Chemical formulae, astrological symbols, and Celtic runes tangled in black charcoal across the whitewashed walls.

Bon sang ne peut mentir, read one notation. *Le sang c'est la vie*, proclaimed another—and a third, simpler and more raggedly written: *Sangsue*. Leech. Bloodsucker.

Scrawled over it all, in letters almost too large to read, was a single, repeated word: NON, NON, NON . . .

There were secrets here, but they belonged to the doctor, not the daughter. He must look elsewhere.

The boy dragged the door open again, grating over shards of glass. Beyond, however, lay not the hall but another, smaller room. He must have lost his bearings in the dark, he thought. Thin light showed him two iron cots, bolted together side by side. One was draped with leather straps. The floor beneath it was dark, and greasy, and there was a smell.

The boy paused, thinking that he heard the distant voices of children, singing. Alice and Alyse must have come upstairs before him. This was a cold, lonely place. He would find his little cousins and ask for their help.

But each door only led to another room, never to the hall.

As night fell, the boy wandered on, deeper and deeper into the house. How cold it was and how silent, except for a chill winter's rain stealthily tapping on the windows. Where were his cousins? Where was he? Maybe he was no longer even in the same house which he had entered—oh, such a long time ago, it seemed. What if tonight all the Morthill manors down through the ages had come back, stone, and oak, and human bone?

(*"Do you know what happens to children in this house?"*)

What if, even now, black-robed monks were walling the little novices up alive? In the dark, gagged and bound, they beat their heads against the newly set stones: *Ta-thump, ta-thump*...and from within the mound came the slow, heavy answer: THUMP. THUMP. THUMP.

What if, even now, Roman soldiers were bending the limbs of a child to fit into an oak-lined cavity under the floor? "The earth is still hungry," the centurion in charge would say—in Latin, of course—and they would come tramping through the house, looking for another child to bury alive...

Then, to the boy's relief, he heard the singing again, closer now, almost clear enough to understand the words. They were playing hide and seek with him. He hurried on through door after door, room after room, following the thread of song, until at last he entered a chamber which reeked of roses.

At the foot of an unmade bed was an oblong chest, the size of a child's coffin. Was this what his little cousins had wanted him to find? He listened for them, but only heard the rain, tapping on the windowpanes. The box was oak, black with age, bound with iron. He traced the crude carving on its lid—a spray of mistletoe, split by a finger-wide crack. Then, gingerly, he opened it.

Within lay a welter of Blanche's under-garments.

At first the boy thought that the bosom of the negligee uppermost was soaked with blood, but then he saw that the red was the backing of a lace paper valentine, ripped down the middle. He had found Blanche's broken heart, whose other half his father had burned almost but not quite to ashes.

The boy looked on, detached, as his hands shredded the paper. *(What are emotions to the superior mind?)* Crimson fragments fell into the chest like a sprinkling of blood.

Then he knelt to burrow beneath the shattered "heart," through layers of not-very-clean linen. The smell made his head swim. Breathing through his mouth, he clambered inside the chest so as to be done searching as quickly as possible. Camisoles, chemises, drawers, petticoats, no, no, no...yes! Here was a legal document: his father's promissory note, tucked into the bodice of a peignoir.

Then the chest's heavy lid crashed down on his head. Darkness. Pain. Confusion. Fear.

The reek of sweat and perfume clotted his lungs. He...couldn't...breathe. Her arms were wrapped around his neck, tightening as he struggled . . .

Don't struggle. Listen. The children are singing:

> *The mistletoe hung in the castle hall,*
> *The holly branch shone on the old oak wall,*
> *The baron's retainers were blithe and gay,*
> *Keeping the Christmas holiday...*

Mistletoe. He was inside the mistletoe chest, tangled up in his cousin's clothing. There was a crack in the chest's lid. He was not going to suffocate.

Be calm, he told himself, still more than half dazed. *Breathe deeply. Never mind the woman smell. Mycroft says women will kill you if you are weak...if you feel...*

Then, when his heart finally stopped hammering and he had caught his breathe, he tried to lift the lid. At first it resisted and he thought (...*be calm* . . .) that someone was sitting on it, but it was only stuck. At last he was out of the chest, of the room, down the stair, into the hall . . .

Blanche sat on the dining room hearth, beneath her portrait. Father bent over her. She had looped her long, pale hair around his neck and he was staring down at her like a rabbit at a snake. The boy's eyes were dazzled—by the firelight, he groggily supposed—but it seemed to him that a darkness loomed over them both, as if the house itself stood there, watching, waiting. Then Blanche drew his father down. They kissed. And the darkness smiled with Irisa's thin, cruel lips.

The boy heard a strange sound, then realized that he himself had made it.

Father broke away from Blanche, as glad of the interruption as of a rescue. He fussed over his son, brushing fragments of red paper out of the boy's hair, staring when his fingers came away stained with blood. The chest lid had struck hard. The boy looked blankly down at his own hand, at the stiff legal paper which he still clutched.

He heard singing. No, he was singing:

> *The baron beheld with a father's pride,*
> *His beautiful child, young Lovell's bride,*
> *While she, with her bright eyes, seemed to be*
> *The star of that goodly company,*
> *Oh, the mistletoe bough!*

Blanche stood rigid, glaring like a Gorgon at father and son. "Siger, why did you bring this brat? Was it to remind me how false you are, what other bed you have shared?"

Darkness moved. For a moment, the boy stared directly into Irisa's black eyes, inches from his own, and then she had retreated, taking the promissory note with her.

"Go," she murmured in Blanche's ear in her heavily accented English. "Take this. Lure him to your narrow bed. The song guides you."

Blanche looked blankly at the paper which her aunt had thrust into her hands. Her full lips framed the song's next line. Then she caught her breath in a gasp of laughter and began raggedly to sing:

> *I'm weary of dancing now, she cried:*
> *Here tarry a moment, I'll hide, I'll hide,*
> *And Lovell, be sure thou'rt the first to trace*
> *The clue to my secret lurking place.*

"The clue, 'Lovell,' the clue!" she cried, waving the note in Father's face as he stood as if turned to stone. "Find me and—perhaps, perhaps—you may keep it!" Then she thrust the paper into her bosom and ran from the room, her aunt following like her shadow. And again the boy sang, as if possessed:

> *Away she ran and her friends began*
> *Each tower to search and each nook to scan,*
> *And young Lovell cried, oh where dost thou hide?*
> *I'm lonesome without thee, my own dear bride,*
> *Oh, the mistletoe bough!*

But the boy was singing to himself. Siger Holmes had left the room. Trailing after him, Sherlock found his father standing irresolute at the foot of the stair, listening to the voices above—the aunt's low and intense, her niece's shrill with rising anger.

"Leave me alone!" Blanche suddenly cried out-loud. "Why do you prattle of the dead? The dead are nothing! Only life matters. I am alive, and I will live, do you hear? *Arrêtez! N'y touchez pas...*"

A hollow thud cut off her words.

Father ran up the stairs. The boy stumbled after him. Irisa stood in the upper hall before the closed bedroom door, stern as Fate, implacable as Nemesis.

"Leave," she said. "She is my business now and none of yours, nor should she ever have been. Leave, and the debt which you owe this house is buried forever."

"What have you done with her?"

"Can you not guess? Sing, boy!"

And the boy sang:

> *They sought her that night, they sought her next day,*
> *They sought her in vain when a week passed away,*
> *In the highest, the lowest, the loneliest spot*
> *Young Lovell sought wildly, but found her not...*

"Stop!" cried Father. "I cannot...I will not understand! Why are you doing this?"

"In my homeland, we know how to deal with such heartless *stregoica* as she, who must feed their lust at whatever cost to others, who prey upon those whom they should first protect."

"You think her a *vampyre*, like Polidori's Lord Ruthven or Prest's Varney?" Father tried to laugh. The boy could see that he thought her mad, and that she frightened him. "Come, the pallor of her cheek and the blood upon her lips are the curses of her illness, nothing more. You are an educated woman. Surely you cannot believe such wild tales!"

She smiled, and her smile was a terrible thing.

"I believe in evil. I believe that no place on earth is immune, including your oh-so-civilized England. Do you think that only *nosferatu* prey upon the innocent? Shall I tell you why this woman still lives while her little sisters lie side by side in the grave? Because that hero of science, their father, stole the blood from his infant children's veins to transfuse into hers. There."

A black-gloved finger stabbed like a lance at the laboratory's closed door across the hall.

"He took and took and so did she until there was nothing left to give. Too late did I understand those devils' marks scrawled across the wall, those iron beds of pain. Too late, his remorse, too late. Oh, my dear little nieces, my sweet Alice and Alyse . . .

For a moment, grief cracked the dark mask of her face and something darker still glared through, beyond reason, beyond mercy. Then by ruthless will alone she pulled herself back together.

"Leave," she said again to Father, with such awful, cold scorn. "You weak, foolish man. Once you willingly embraced her corruption and now she has breathed death into your mouth. I know. I saw. Leave. Soon enough, you will join her in the grave's narrow bed. Listen: already she calls to you."

And they heard. Inside the bedroom. Muffled. Raging. Thuds. Long, scraping sounds. Fists beating again the coffin lid. Nails scratching…

Father made a choking sound. Then he snatched up his son and fled. Behind them, Irisa laughed and laughed.

No one ever saw Blanche again.

* * *

> *And years flew by, and their grief at last*
> *Was told as a sorrowful tale long past,*
> *And when Lovell appeared the children cried,*
> *See the old man weep for his fairy bride,*
> *Oh, the mistletoe bough!*

The echo of Holmes's voice died in the room, swallowed by its dank decay. The storm was muttering off into the distance, leaving the melancholy drip of water outside the manor and in.

"Curiously enough," he said, with a shaky return to his normal, dry manner, "that ballad is based upon a tragedy which befell a family in Rutland named Noel. We cannot seem to escape it or the Christmas theme—or can we? Gone she was, but my father did not weep. He died within four months, coughing blood. I nearly followed him. As I lay ill, I overheard that Irisa was also dead, of self-inflicted starvation. A refusal to consume, if you will. Nonetheless, some curses are…very persistent. Even now, in my dreams, I hear it: fists beating against the coffin lid, nails clawing…"

I stared at him, speechless, then blurted out the first question that came into my mind. "B-but what about the two little girls?"

Holmes drew a thin hand over his face. "How can I have forgotten? Of course, they were already dead. I saw their gravestones among the trees as we drove away."

This was too much for me. "And they, I suppose, are the 'ghost or two' which you promised me before we entered this foul place, not to mention a Wallachian madwoman, an evil scientist, and a vampire in the linen chest. Oh, well done, Holmes. Bravo! And you call *me* romantic!"

His attention sharpened and he threw up a hand for silence. I, well trained, instantly obeyed.

We listened. Water dripped, the wind soughed, the old house creaked...and then it came again, from above us somewhere on the second floor: a faint rasp, a muffled thump.

"Oh, really!" I exclaimed.

Snatching the candle from his hand, I limped hastily down the hall to the far door. There was the stair, with water cascading down the steps. The decayed remains of a carpet made them as slippery as moss in a riverbed as I climbed, clinging to the banister.

I did not want to believe my friend's story. It frightened me the way he had groped after details, not as if making them up but as if drawing their memory out of a half-forgotten childhood nightmare like splinters from a long neglected wound. And such details! Was I really to believe that...no, I would not.

But I had to be sure.

Here was the upper hall as Holmes had described it, eerily long, lined with doors. I hesitated on the upper landing, suddenly unsure. After all, here I was, with a guttering candle, in the upper storey of an abandoned house miles from anywhere, on a dark and stormy night, hunting ghosts. For all I knew, we might instead be sharing Morthill with an escaped ax-murderer—which, at that moment, I would almost have preferred.

The first door to the left stood half open. From the darkness within came a furtive rustle, as if of shifting paper.

A hand closed like a vise on my arm. "Don't go in there," snapped Holmes.

I was startled, so quickly and quietly had he come up the stair on my heels, and I was annoyed to find myself whispering. "Why not?"

"Because the way in may not be the way out. And besides," he added, somewhat lamely, "the floor may be unsound."

"A fine time to think of that. Very well, then; if not this door, which?"

He would not answer me, but his eyes betrayed him, sliding involuntarily to the first door on the right. When he made no move to open it, I pushed past him and gripped the knob. It came off in my hand.

I glanced back at Holmes, suddenly as reluctant as he. Candlelight flickered across his face, shadows pooling in the hollows beneath cheekbones and eyes. He stood as if rooted before the door from which his father had fled.

There was no way forward but one.

I set my shoulder to the warped panels and pushed. The lock broke in a shower of rust and the door squealed open on clutching hinges. Mindful of the house's tricks, I reached blindly inside, fished out a high-backed chair, and wedged the door open with it. Holmes stared into the darkness, then entered, as if drawn. I followed.

Candle light flickered on moldering clutter: a disordered bed whose canopy long since had fallen down across its foot, rags of once-elegant clothing strewn about the floor, a pair of long, dingy gloves draped like flayed skin over the back of a chair. More confusion littered the dressing table—age-dull bottles, lotions, notions, and trinkets tumbled together.

One of Carle Vernet's lithographs hung on the nearby wall, depicting an extravagantly dressed eighteenth-century belle seated at her dressing table, admiring herself in its large mirror.

"The picture is called *Vanity*," said Holmes, behind me, "not that Blanche probably understood why. She had a certain imitative cleverness—like a monkey—but no real imagination."

I looked again, and recoiled. The mirror's rounded shape was that of a naked skull, the twin images of the woman's head and her reflection its hollow eyes, the cosmetic bottles her teeth bared in a cryptic smile. This print, not the *Mona Lisa*, was the original of Blanche's portrait in the hall below.

"*Sangsue*," her dying father had scrawled in horror over his meticulous notations. Bloodsucker. *Non, non, non* . . .

A long, scraping sound made me start. It came from the window. Outside, the fingers of a dead oak again drew restlessly across the glass and tapped against the pane.

I turned to Holmes in triumph, just as he threw back the collapsed canopy. At the foot of the bed was a chest, no bigger than a child's coffin. A crude spray of mistletoe was carved into the age-blackened oak of its lid. At its farther end, caught in the crack, were several long strands of pale hair.

Holmes hesitated a moment. Then he gripped the lid and, with a sudden effort, attempted to lift it. It rose a quarter inch and stopped with a jar that dislodged his fingers. Belatedly, he looked at the key, still turned in the lock. For a long moment we stood there, he staring at the key, I at him. It had grown very quiet outside. Inside, all I heard was the distant, forlorn drip of water. Then Holmes sighed.

"No ghosts need apply," he murmured, turned, and walked past me out of the room.

I suppose I stood with my mouth open a good ten seconds, and then I swallowed. There was the chest; there, the key. Stealthy moonlight pooled about it on the floor, and a breath of air sighed through the broken window. The strands of pale hair stirred...

I ran down the treacherous stair after my friend, in danger of adding one more ghost to the house by slipping.

Below, the dining hall had filled with shifting moonlight and shadow. I paused in the hall doorway, searching the walls not for the painted smile of a "da Vinci" or an icon's baleful glare, but for those two white blurs in the corner, forever side by side. They were not there. Something outside the window caught my attention. There they stood, white frocks glimmering among the moon-silvered birch, watching, waiting...for what, or whom? Their pale, unblinking eyes gazed upward, as though toward the window of a second story bedroom.

Cold water dripped on my head. I started and looked up. Above me hung the mistletoe, that filthy parasite, each bare twig glistening with a drop of condensation like so many sparkling poison berries.

When I looked out the window again, and cursed my gullibility. Not children but two small, white gravestones leaned toward each other in the family plot, almost touching.

We reached Bagshot in time to catch the last train. Holmes slept all the way to London.

* * *

We have never spoken of that evening again.

Was the whole adventure a practical joke—Holmes's attempt to cure me by surfeit of my foolish romanticism? I want to think so, but I cannot shrug off the story. It haunts me. In my dreams, I wander through endless, dusty rooms, sometimes hearing distant song, sometimes distant laughter. Last night, all too close, there was a muffled voice crying and the sound of nails breaking against wood as hard as iron...

Let me out, let me out, let me out...

Thus, I have felt compelled on this Christmas Eve to make what sense I can of that strange night four months ago. Perhaps I have read more into my friend's words and especially into his silences than he ever intended. Perhaps he is waiting for me to publish this fantastic tale to have the last laugh. Perhaps, in the beginning, that was his only goal.

I believe, however, that he found himself telling a deeper story than he intended, digging up the buried horror that poisoned his sleep. What he cannot endure is the inexplicable, the irrational. Mere ghosts will never bother him, for he does not believe in them. For him, the mystery is solved. That is enough.

In that, he is more the detective than I have proved the storyteller. Before that sullen, silent chest, my courage faltered, and the story's end remains untold.

[1902]

ADDENDUM

Storytellers die, but do stories ever really end? If you are reading this, then I too am dead, and the guardianship of these hitherto unpublished accounts passes to you.

Whatever my other failings, I have found myself too much both the storyteller and the detective to destroy evidence. At the bottom of this old, tin dispatch-box is the last stanza of "The Mistletoe Bough," wrapped around a key—two keys, as it were, to a single mystery. The dispatch-box itself sits upon a oblong chest made of age-blackened oak, bound with iron, with a crude mistletoe carved into its cracked lid. Without telling Holmes, I had carters convey it unopened from Morthill Manor to the vaults of Cox and Company Bank.

Here, then, are the ballad and the key; there is the chest. As my dear, late friend once said of another case, "It can't hurt now." We all sleep as quietly as our several lives allow beyond, at least, any earthly harm. Do what you will.

> *At length an oak chest that had long laid hid*
> *Was found in the castle, they raised the lid*
> *When a skeleton form lay moldering there*
> *In the bridal wreath of that lady fair.*
> *Oh sad was her fate, when in sportive jest*
> *She hid from her lord in the old oak chest,*
> *It closed with a spring and a dreadful doom*
> *And the bride lay clasped in a living tomb,*
> *Oh, the mistletoe bough!*

[1929]

MAPS

(Included in this section are the othr maps that P. C. has drawn over the years to show the lands of Jame's world, that were not used as one of the short story locations.)

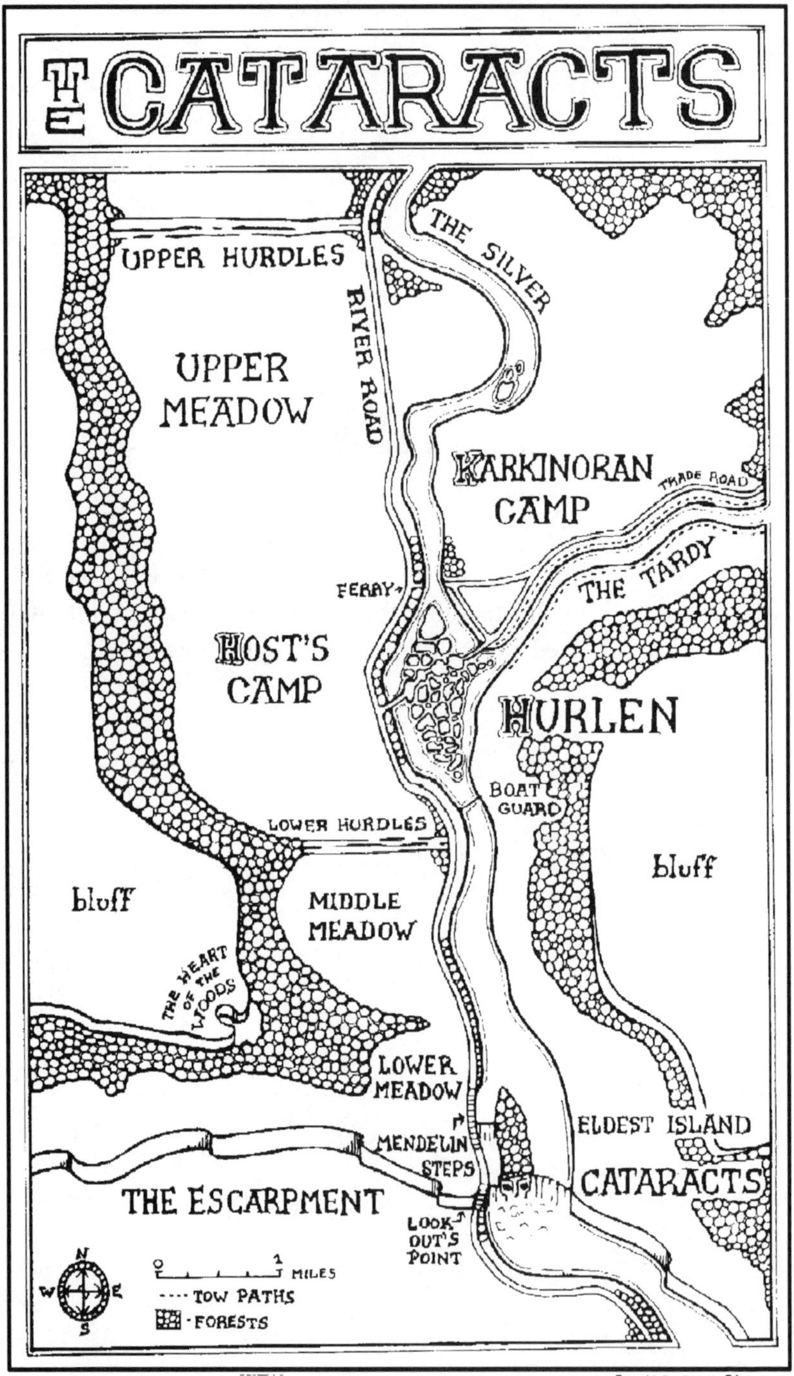
THE CATARACTS
UPPER HURDLES
RIVER ROAD
THE SILVER
UPPER MEADOW
KARKINORAN CAMP
TRADE ROAD
FERRY
THE TARDY
HOST'S CAMP
HURLEN
BOAT GUARD
LOWER HURDLES
bluff
bluff
MIDDLE MEADOW
THE HEART OF THE WOODS
LOWER MEADOW
ELDEST ISLAND
MENDELIN STEPS
CATARACTS
THE ESCARPMENT
LOOK-OUT'S POINT
N
W
E
S
0
1
MILES
TOW PATHS
FORESTS

P.C. HODGELL - 1984

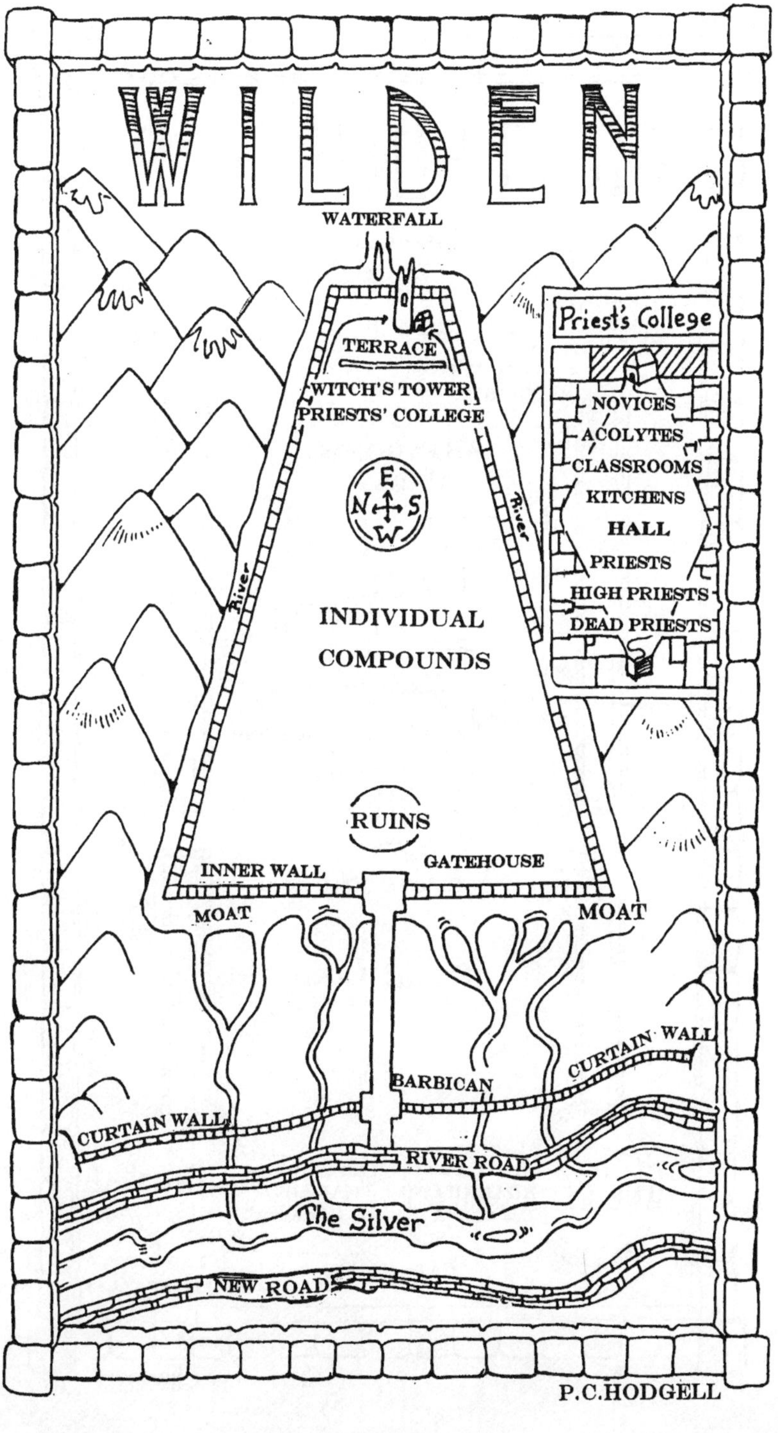
WILDEN
WATERFALL
TERRACE
WITCH'S TOWER
PRIESTS' COLLEGE
E
N
S
W
River
River
INDIVIDUAL
COMPOUNDS
RUINS
INNER WALL
GATEHOUSE
MOAT
MOAT
BARBICAN
CURTAIN WALL
CURTAIN WALL
RIVER ROAD
The Silver
NEW ROAD
Priest's College
NOVICES
ACOLYTES
CLASSROOMS
KITCHENS
HALL
PRIESTS
HIGH PRIESTS
DEAD PRIESTS

P.C.HODGELL

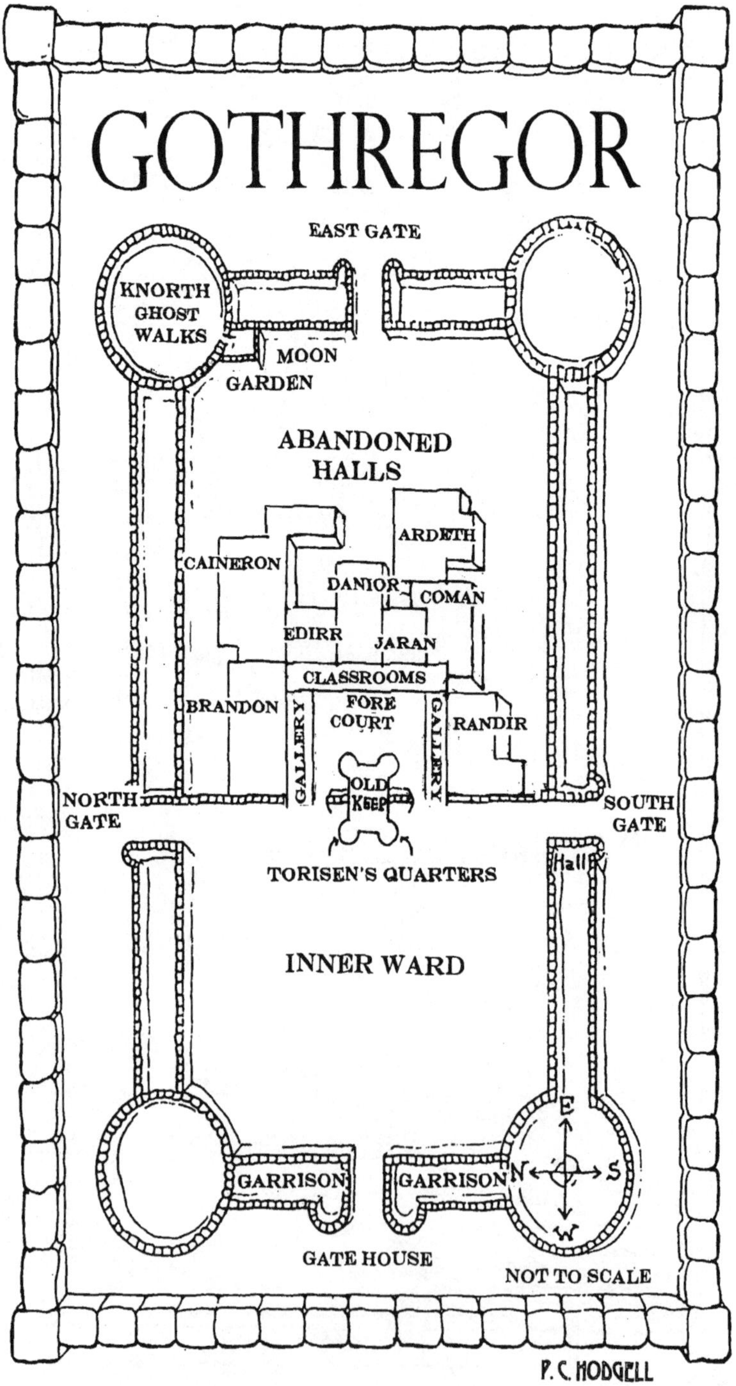

GOTHREGOR
EAST GATE
KNORTH GHOST WALKS
MOON GARDEN
ABANDONED HALLS
ARDETH
CAINERON
DANIOR
COMAN
EDIRR
JARAN
CLASSROOMS
BRANDON
GALLERY
FORE COURT
GALLERY
RANDIR
OLD KEEP
NORTH GATE
SOUTH GATE
Hall
TORISEN'S QUARTERS
INNER WARD
E
N
S
W
GARRISON
GARRISON
GATE HOUSE
NOT TO SCALE
P. C. HODGELL

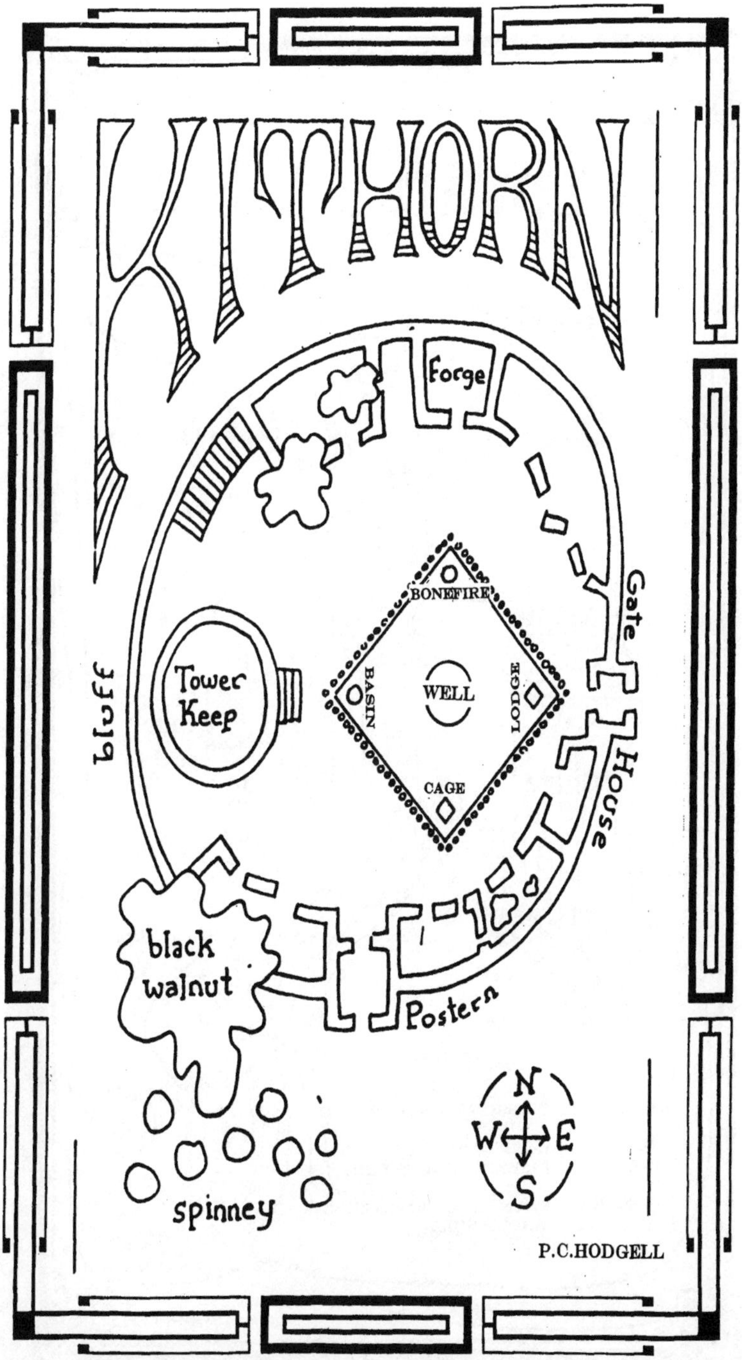
KITHORN
Forge
Gate
BONEFIRE
BASIN
WELL
LODGE
CAGE
Tower
Keep
bluff
House
black
walnut
Postern
N
W
E
S
spinney
P.C.HODGELL

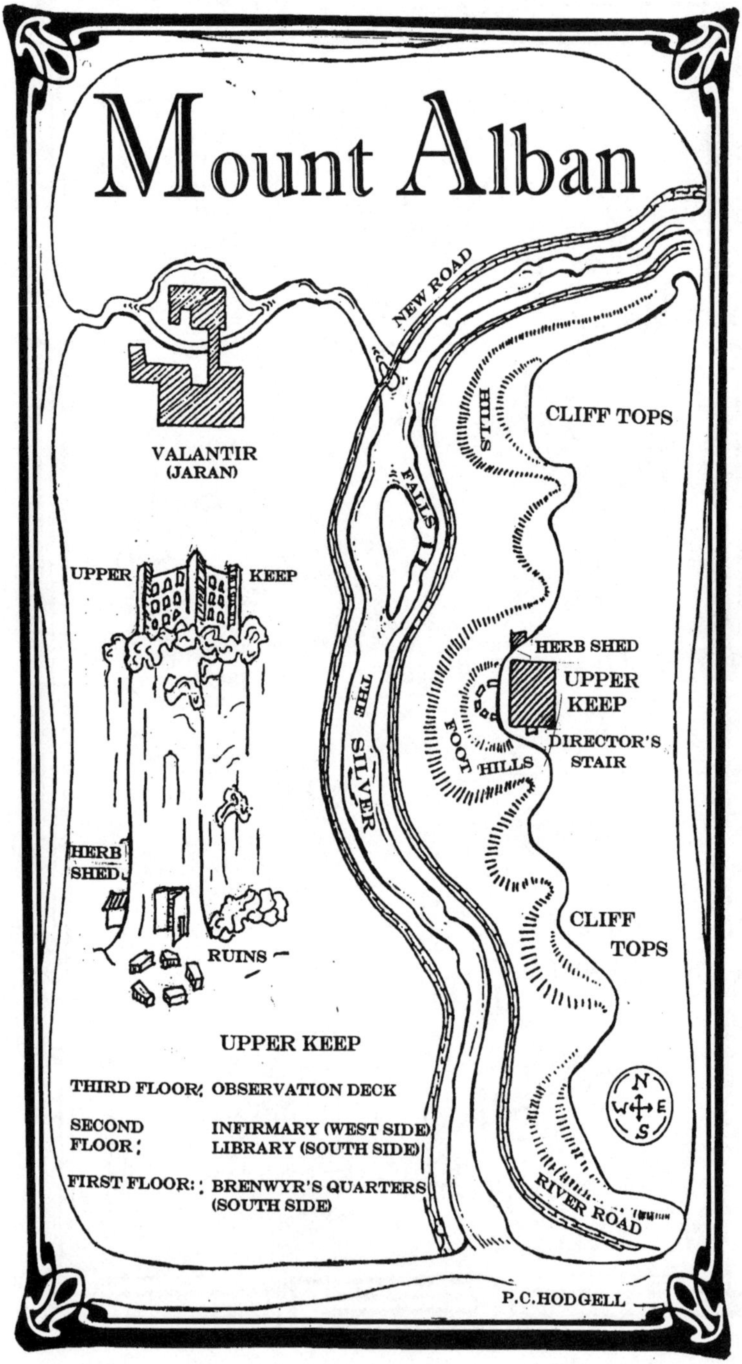

Mount Alban
NEW ROAD
VALANTIR (JARAN)
HILLS
CLIFF TOPS
FALLS
UPPER KEEP
THE SILVER
HERB SHED
UPPER KEEP
FOOT HILLS
DIRECTOR'S STAIR
HERB SHED
RUINS
CLIFF TOPS
N W E S
UPPER KEEP
THIRD FLOOR: OBSERVATION DECK
SECOND FLOOR: INFIRMARY (WEST SIDE) LIBRARY (SOUTH SIDE)
FIRST FLOOR: BRENWYR'S QUARTERS (SOUTH SIDE)
RIVER ROAD
P.C.HODGELL

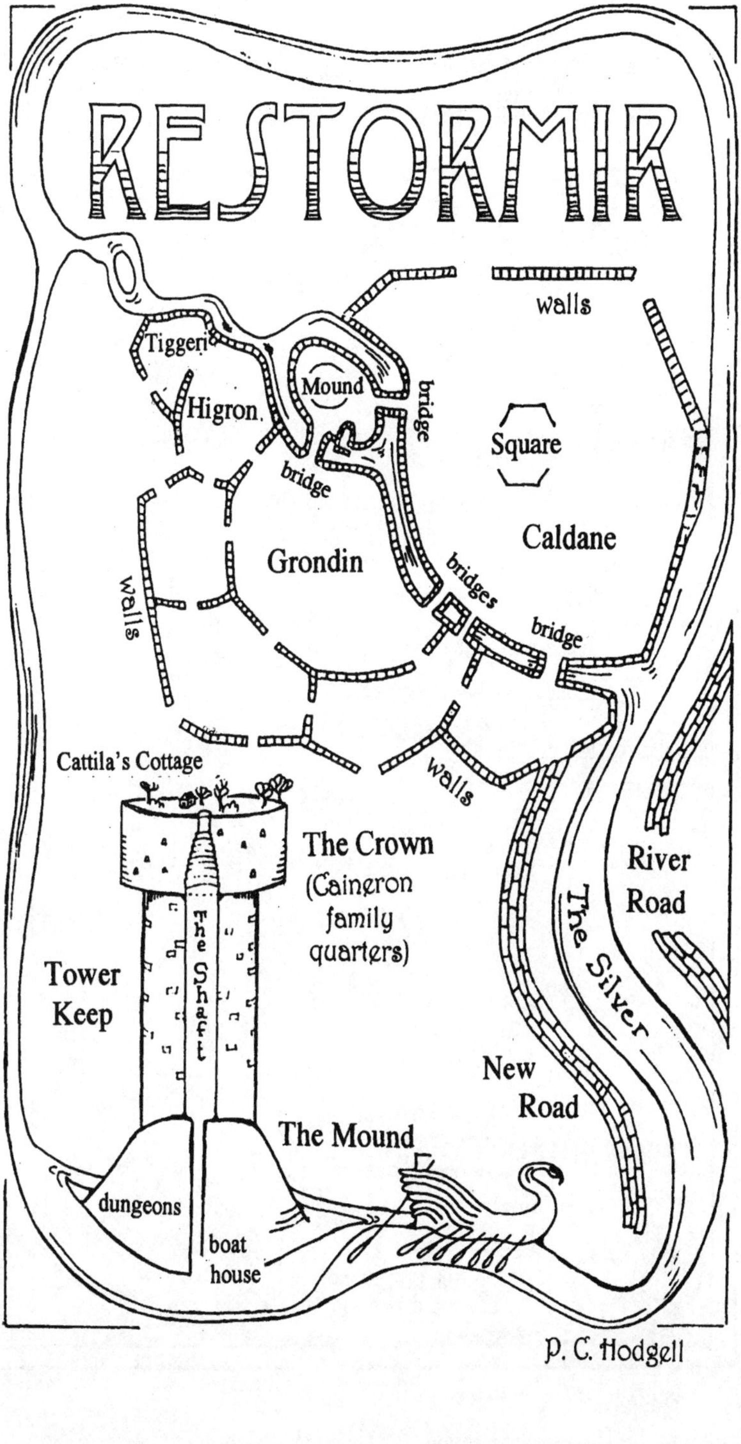
RESTORMIR
walls
Tiggeri
Mound
bridge
Higron
Square
bridge
Caldane
Grondin
bridges
walls
bridge
walls
Cattila's Cottage
The Crown
(Caineron
family
quarters)
River
Road
The Shaft
The Silver
Tower
Keep
New
Road
The Mound
dungeons
boat
house

P. C. Hodgell

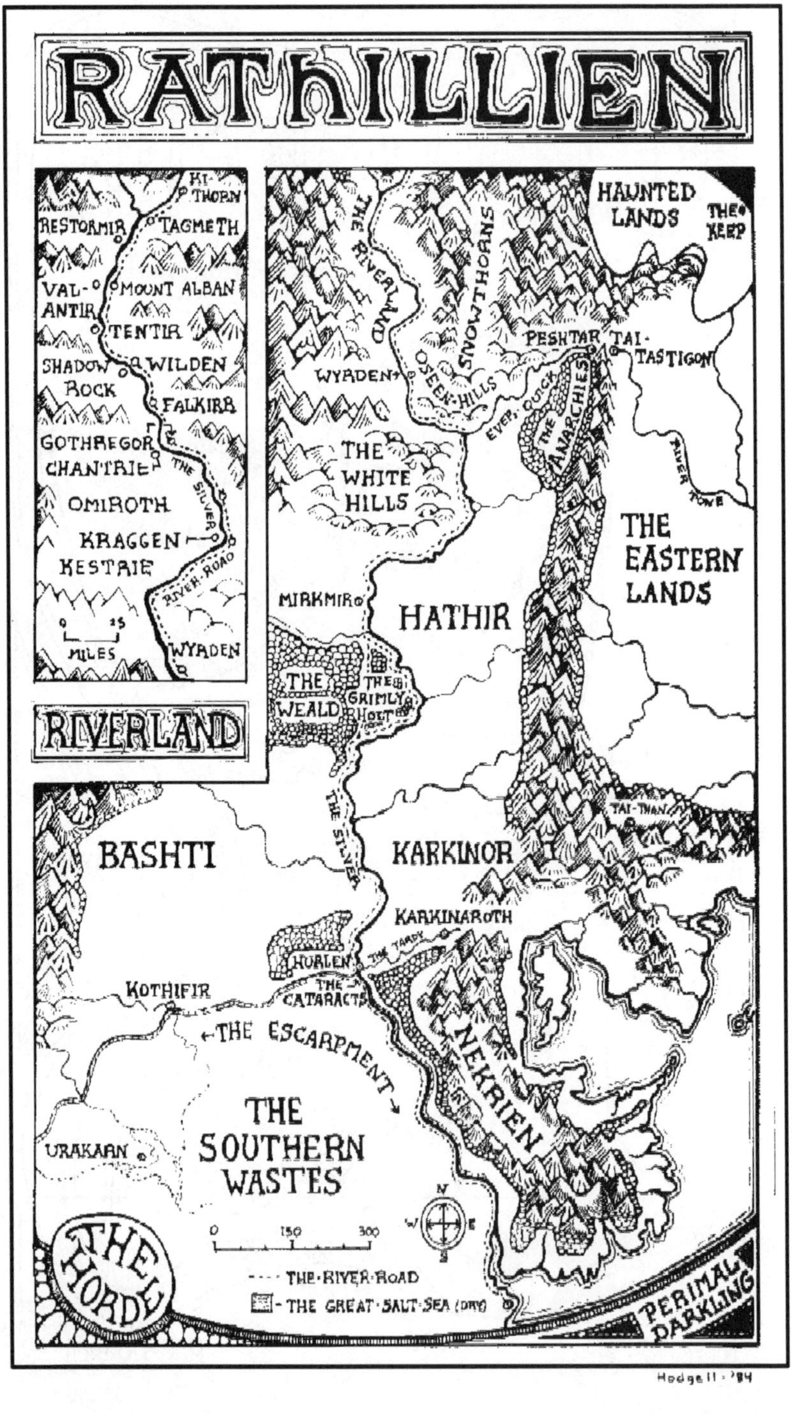
RATHILLIEN
RIVERLAND
KI-THORN
RESTORMIR
TAGMETH
VAL-ANTIR
MOUNT ALBAN
TENTIR
SHADOW ROCK
WILDEN
FALKIRR
GOTHREGOR
CHANTRIE
THE SILVER
OMIROTH
KRAGGEN
KESTRIE
RIVER-ROAD
0 25
MILES
WYRDEN
THE RIVERLAND
SNOWTHORNS
HAUNTED LANDS
THE KEEP
OSEEN-HILLS
PESHTAR
TAI-TASTIGON
EVER-QUICK
THE ANARCHIES
RIVER TONE
THE WHITE HILLS
THE EASTERN LANDS
MIRKMIR
HATHIR
THE WEALD
THE GRIMLY HOLT
THE SILVER
TAI-TIAN
BASHTI
KARKINOR
KARKINAROTH
THE TARDY
HURLEN
THE CATARACTS
KOTHIFIR
←THE ESCARPMENT→
THE SOUTHERN WASTES
URAKARN
NEKRIEN
N
W
E
S
0 150 300
THE HORDE
---- THE·RIVER·ROAD
- THE GREAT·SALT·SEA (DRY)
PERIMAL DARKLING

Hodgell · '84

ART

(Enclosed here are some of the various sketches and drawings that P. C. has done throughout the years of Jame and others.)

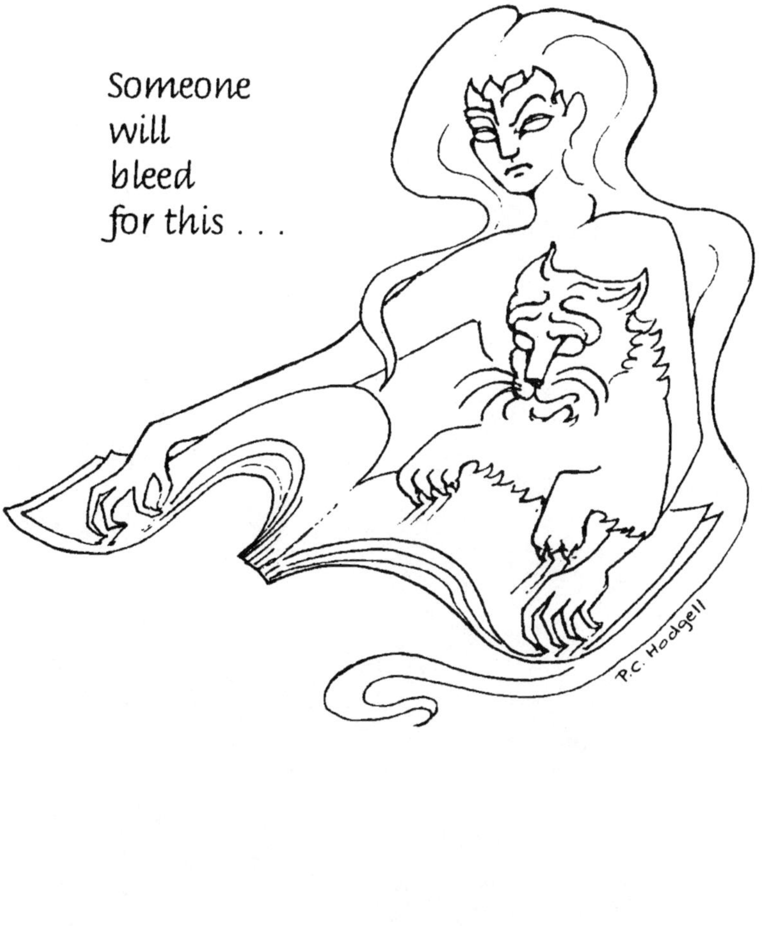
Someone
will
bleed
for this . . .
P.C. Hodgell

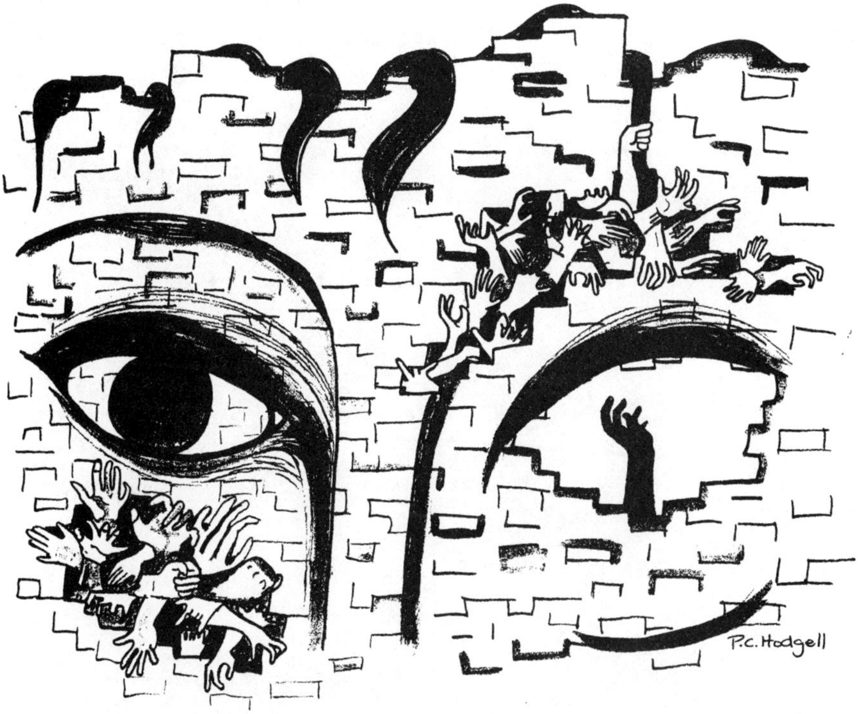
P.C. Hodgell

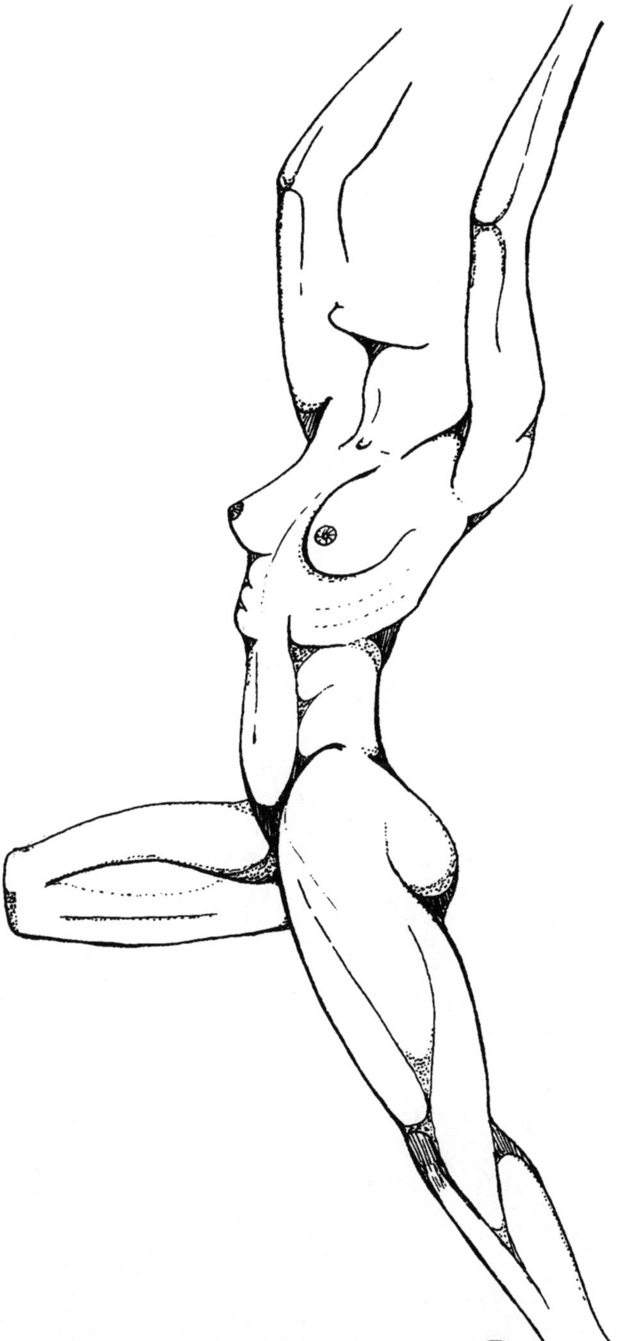

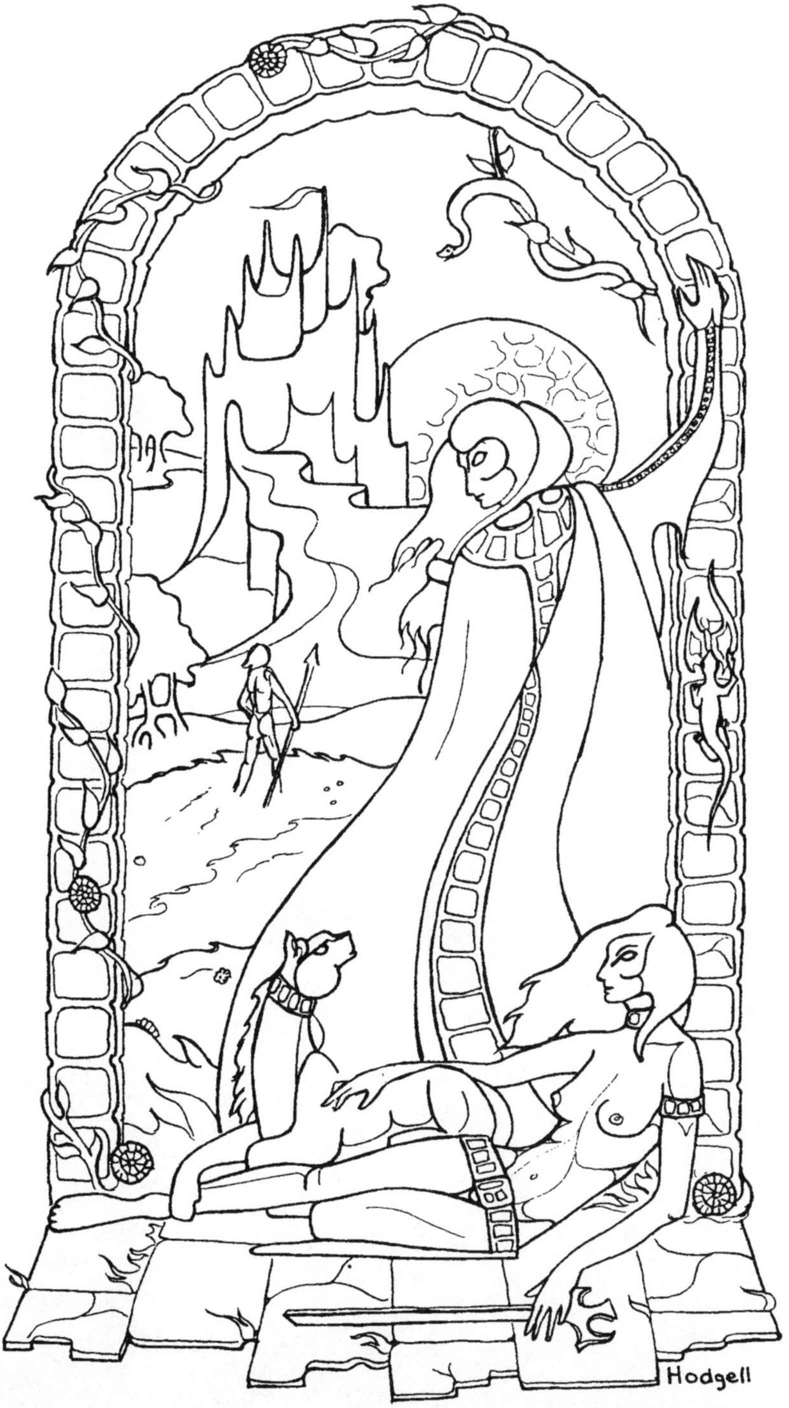
Hodgell

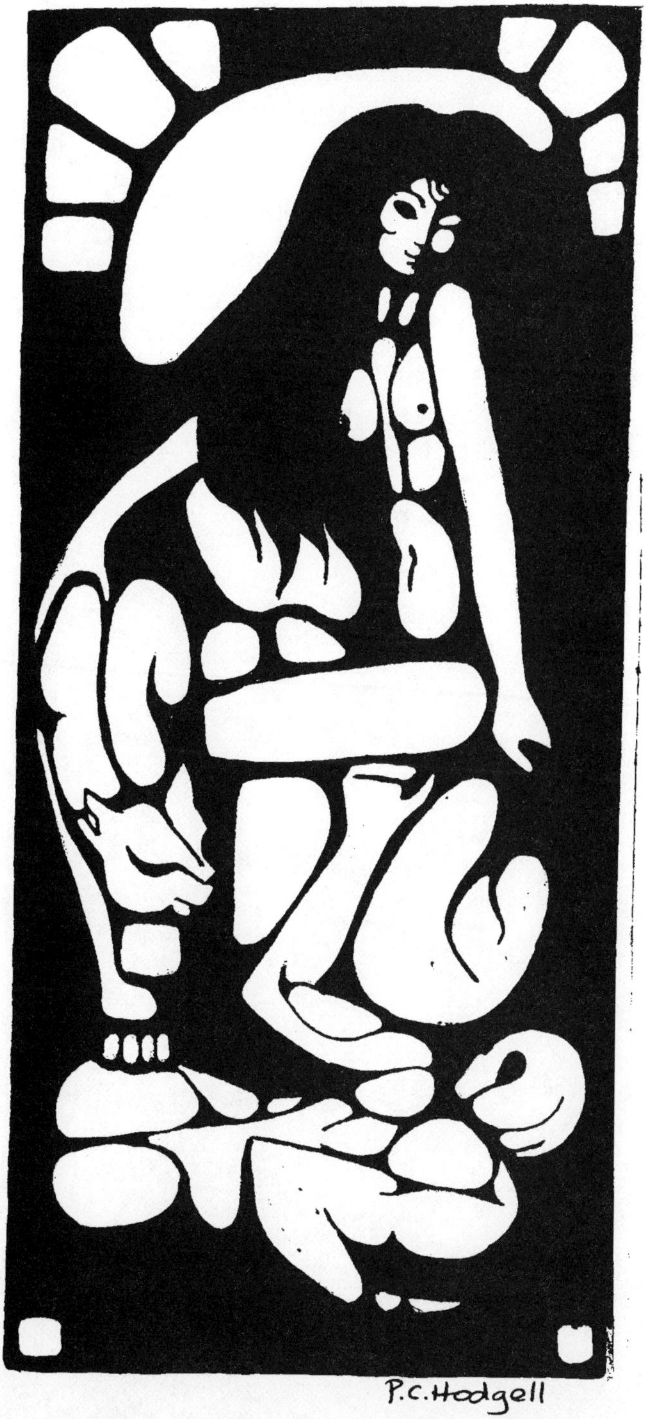
P.C. Hodgell

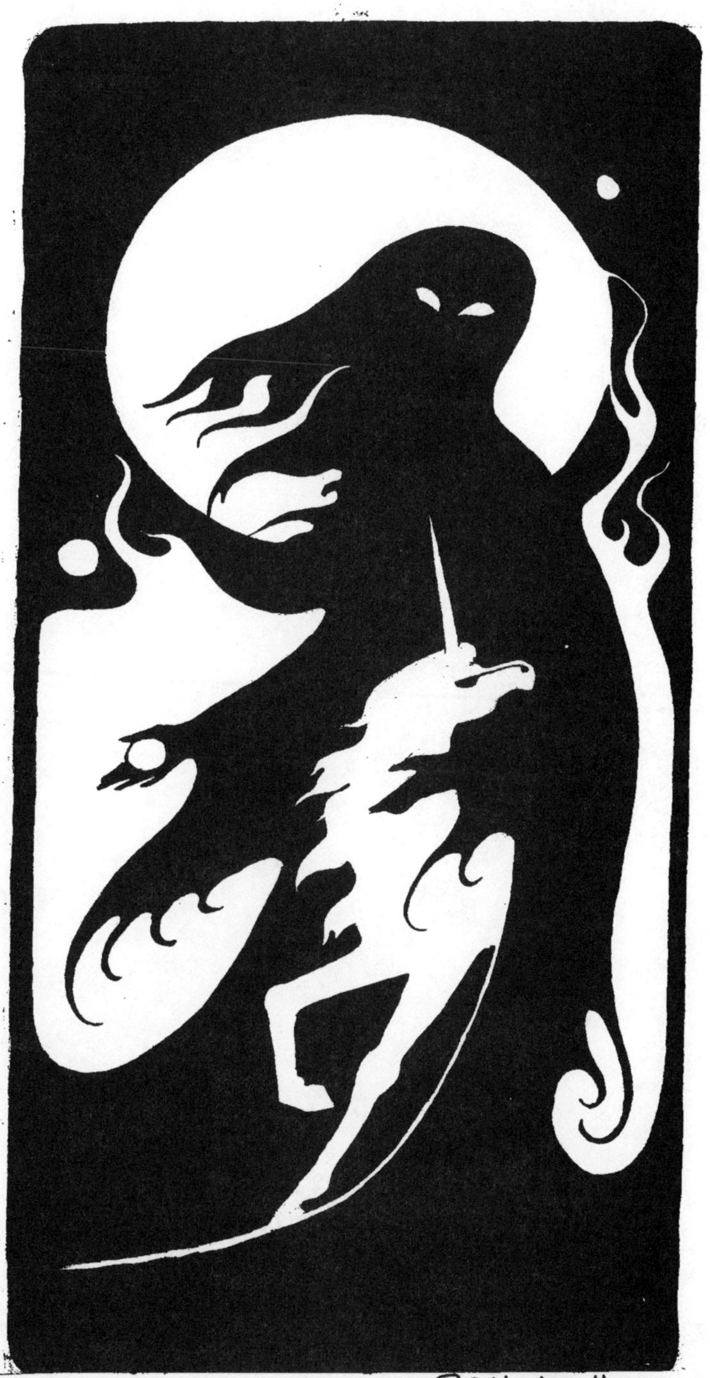
P.C. Hodgell

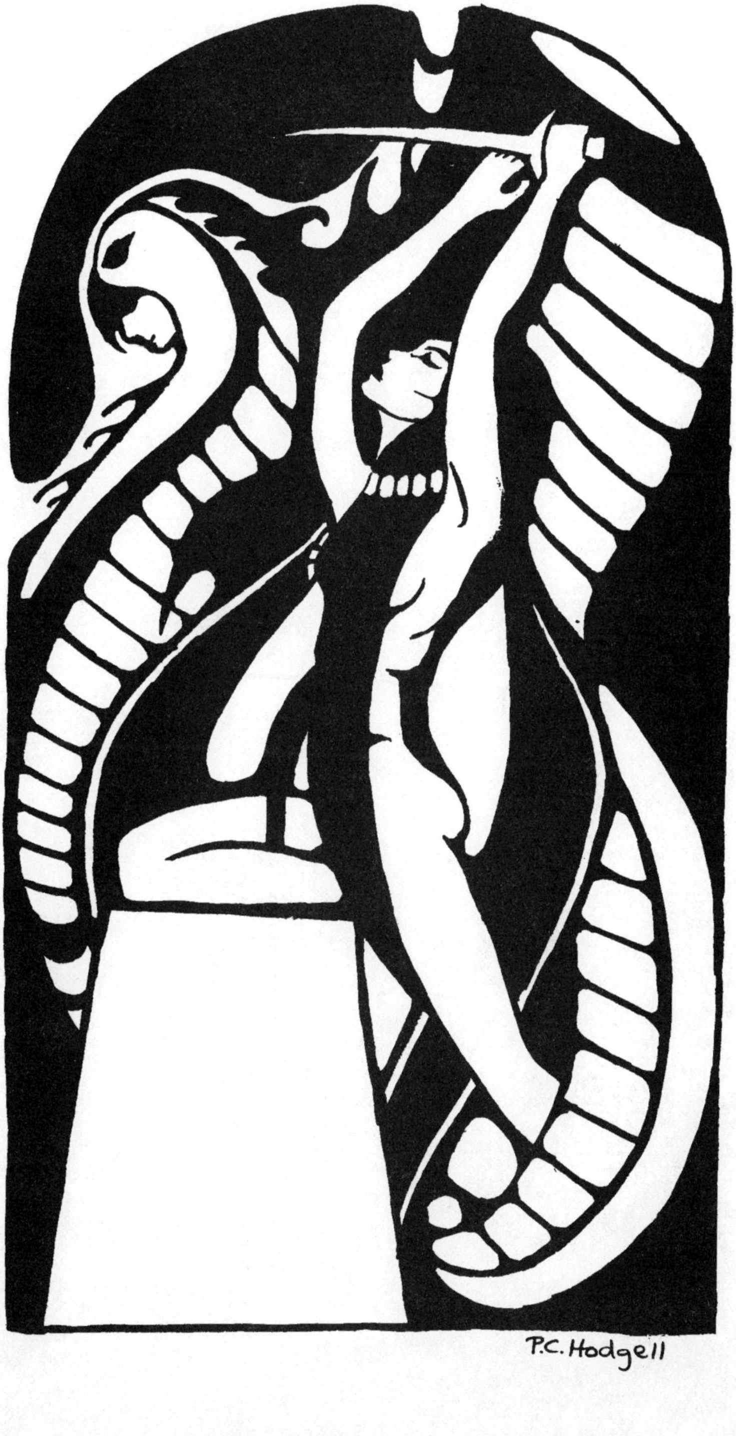
P.C. Hodgell

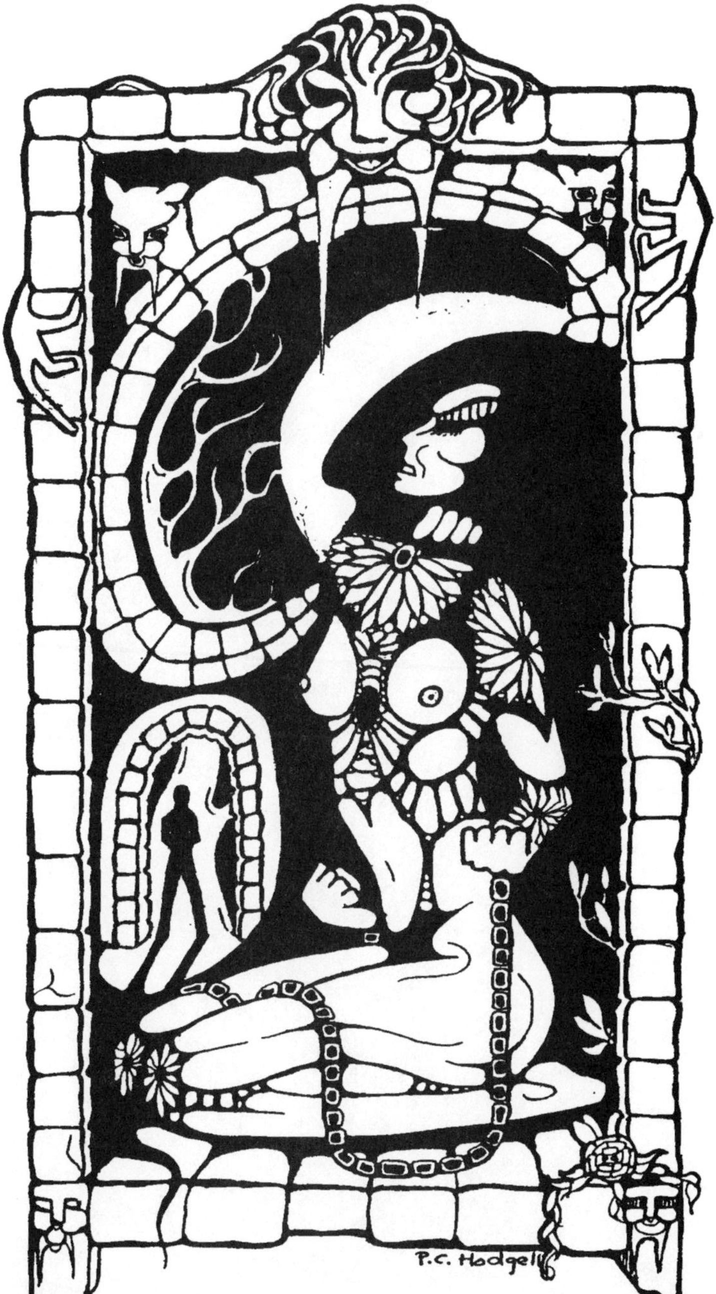
P.C. Hodgell

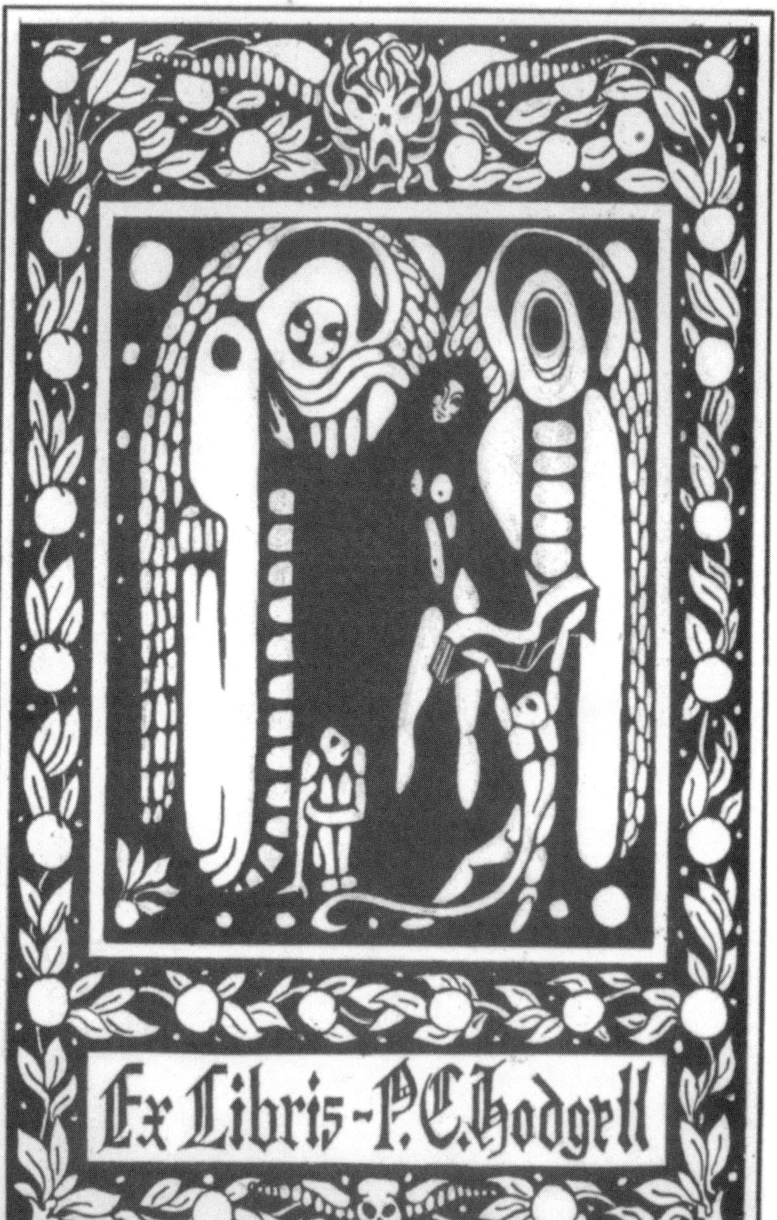
Ex Libris - P. C. Hodgell

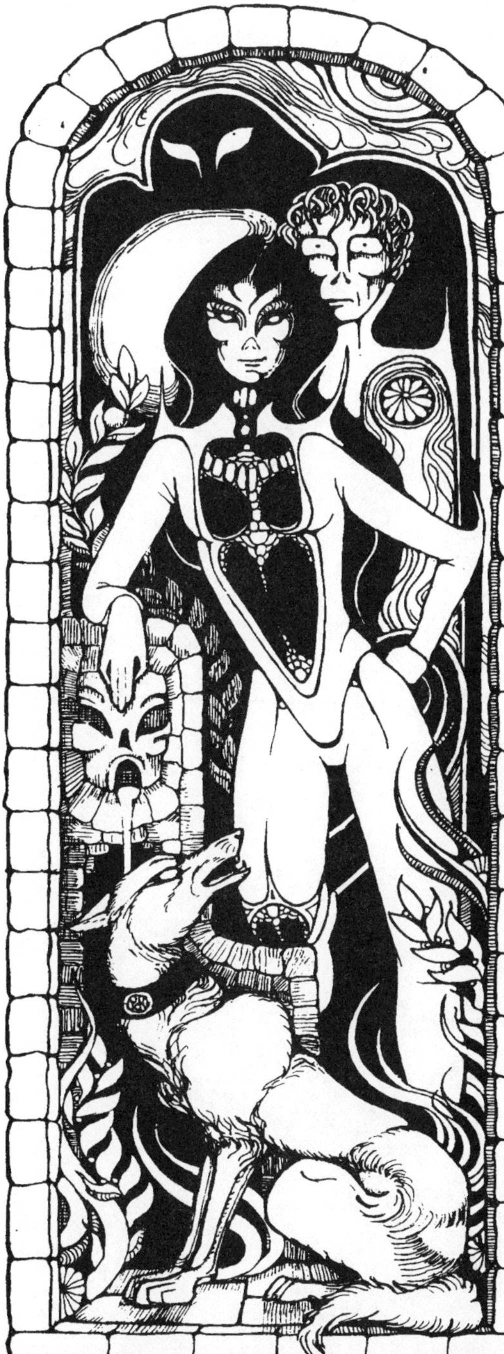
P.C. Hodgell

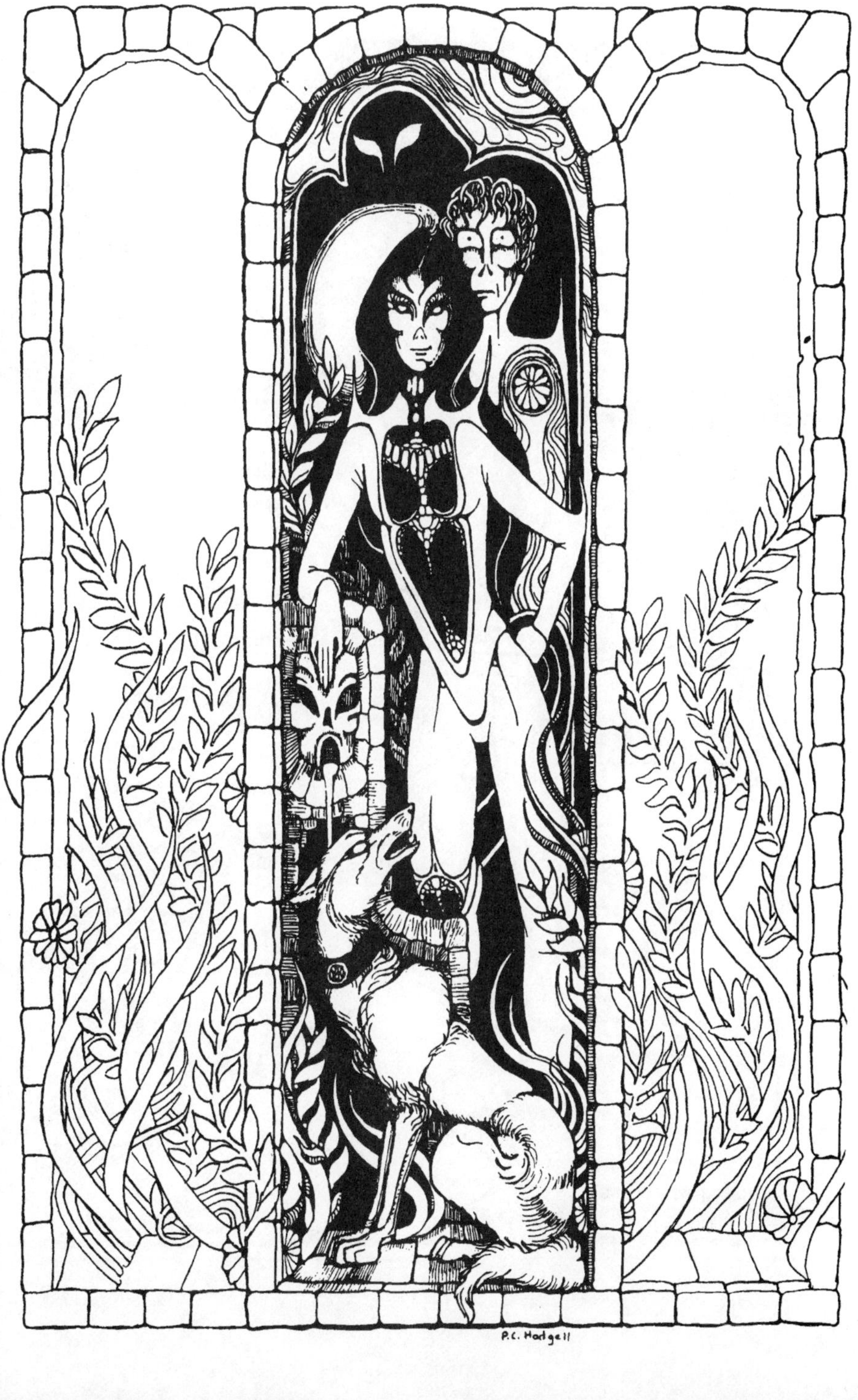
P.C. Hodgell

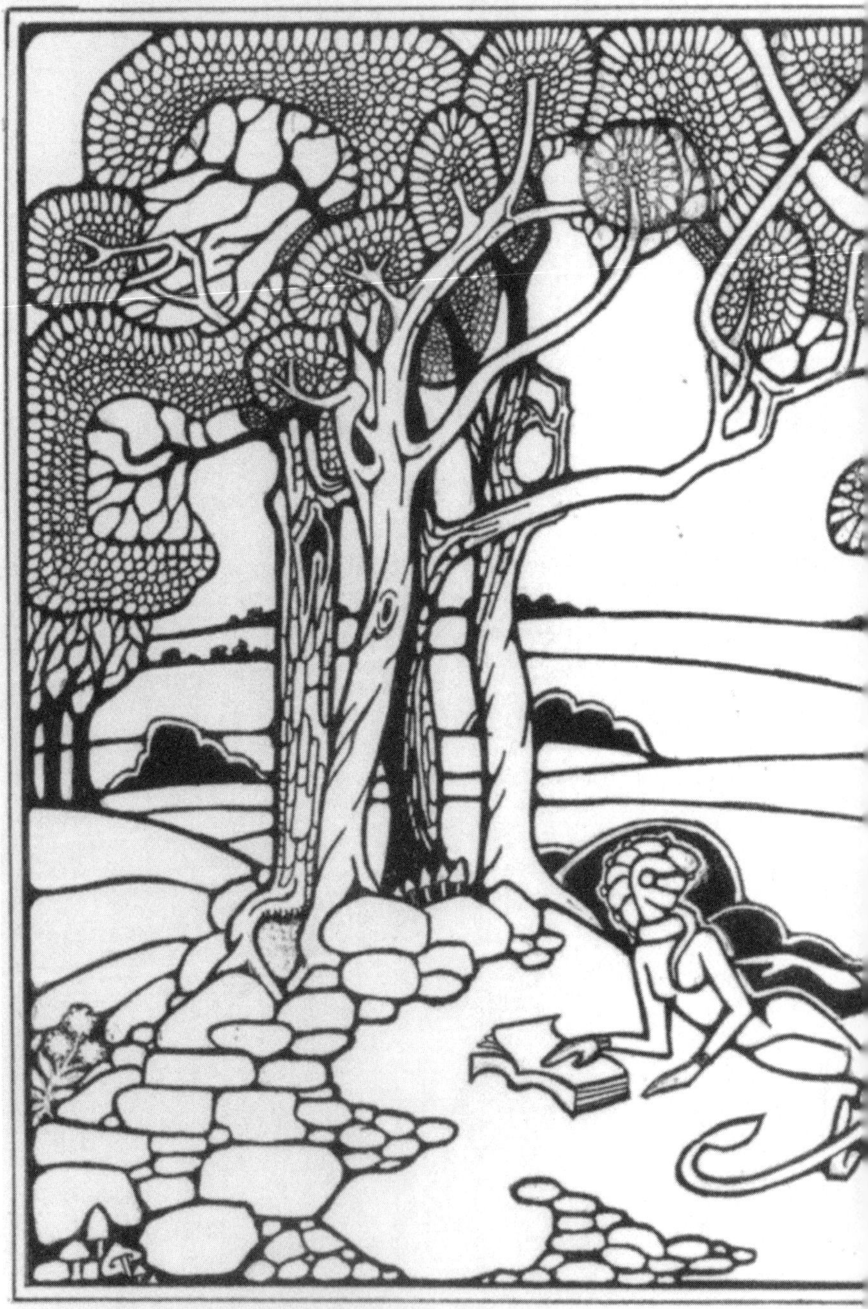

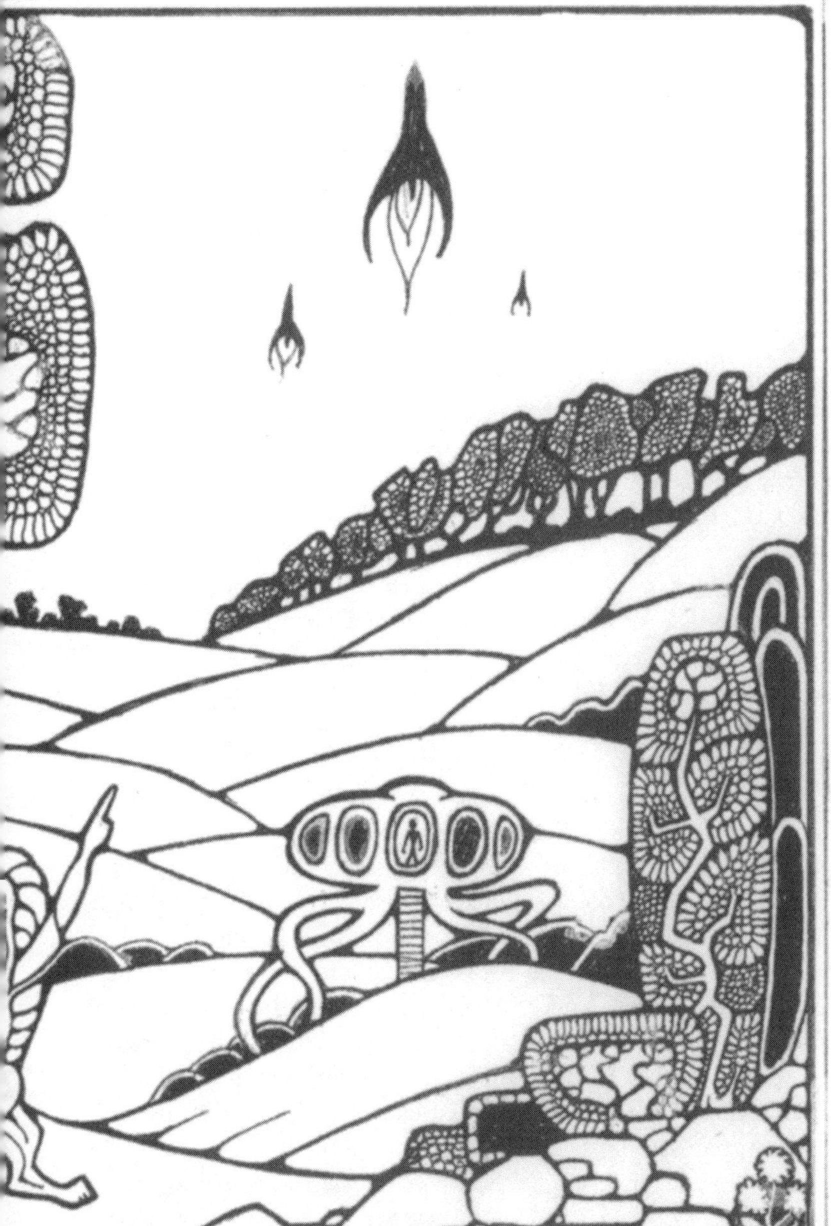

HODGELL/CHAPLIN--'85

An introduction to P. C. Hodgell

Pat Hodgell can't remember a time when she wasn't passionately interested in science fiction and fantasy. "*David Star Space Ranger* by Paul French was the first novel with which I fell in love, so much so that I started making my own copy of the library book, long-hand in a spiral notebook, complete with a carefully drawn facsimile of the frontispiece. Long afterward, I cam across a paperback reprint and learned that my beloved 'Paul French' was none other than the ubiquitous Issac Asimov."

Over the years, as her interest grew, Pat collected piles of paperback science fiction and fantasy novels and comic books. Soon, however, reading and collecting genre fiction wasn't enough for her and, after college, she began to write it as well.

"It would be nice to say that, after the long suppression of the writing impulse, the dam burst—but it didn't. Due to lack of practice, I simply didn't know how to put a story down on paper." Pat began to learn, however, and by the next summer she had several stories finished and an invitation to the Clarion Writer's Workshop. "There, for the first time, I found a whole community of people like me—storytellers, wordsmiths, an entire family I never knew I had," Pat says of the Clarion experience. "Even more wonderful, here suddenly were professionals like Harlan Ellison and Kate Wilhelm telling me that I could indeed write. I could hardly believe my luck." She made her first professional sale two years later. Since then, she's sold stories to such anthologies as *Berkley Showcase, Elsewhere III, Imaginary Lands*, and the *Last Dangerous Visions*. Pat has also published three novels: *God Stalk, Dark of the Moon*, (Reprinted together in the omnibus *Dark of the Gods*.) and *Seeker's Mask*, also a short story collection, *Blood and Ivory: A Tapestry*, all part of an on-going fantasy saga concerned not only with high adventure, but also with questions of personal identity, religion, politics, honor, and arboreal drift. She is currently working on her forth Jame novel.

Both of Pat's parents are professional artists. Other reputed ancestors include a decapitated French Huguenot, a sheep thief tried by Chaucer, and a "parcel of New York Millerites who in 1843 sold their possessions, put on white nightgowns, and sat on the chicken coop waiting for the world to end. When it didn't they moved to Wisconsin out of sheer embarrassment."

Pat earned her Master's in English Literature from the University of Minnesota, her doctorate at the University of Minnesota with a dissertation on sir Walter Scott's Ivanhoe, and is a graduate of both the Clarion and the Milford Writer's Workshops. In addition to her work with WDS, she is a lecturer at the University of Wisconsin-Oshkosh in modern British literature and composition, and teaches an audio-cassette-based course on science fiction and fantasy for the University of Minnesota.

Pat lives in Wisconsin, in a nineteenth-century wood-framed house, which has been in her family for generations. In addition to writing and teaching, she attends science fiction conventions, collects yarn, knits, embroiders, and makes her own Christmas cards.

Dark of the Gods
by
P. C. Hodgell

(Omnibus reprint of *God Stalk* and *Dark of the Moon*)

1-892065-26-6
$20.00

Whether you are meeting the Kencyr Jame
for the first time
or reawakening an old friendship,
Dark of the Gods is the place to start.

Jame is a Kencyrath, the chosen people of the Three-Faced God, who fight the demonic entity called Perimal Darkling. At the same time she fights an internal battle for her honor because 3000 years ago the leader of the Kencyrath betrayed his people to the Darkness for his own immortality.

She also must find her ten year older brother Tori and return to him the sword and ring of their father. If that is not enough she has to stand before the rathorns, wear the cloak of living snakes, visit the council room ablaze with stained glass, kill a god, resurrect a god.

Seeker's Mask
by
P. C. Hodgell

1-892065-34-7
$18.00

"If you remember, the last time we saw Jame, she had finally tracked down her twin brother Tori and now had to find a place for herself among the Kencyrs, those warrior-magicians she'd been searching for throughout the previous books. *Seeker's Mask* opens with the unruly Jame trying to fit into the constricting life found within the Women's Halls at Gothregor. Knowing Jame as we do, we also know it's a lost cause and in no time at all, she has set the quiet Women's Halls topsy-turvy, though it's not entirely her fault."

"True, she finds it difficult to fit in, but she does try. Only what can you do when Shadow Guild assassins come hunting you, not to mention old ghosts from her days in Tai-tastigon, the city of a thousand gods? It doesn't help, either, that no one in the Women's Halls seems willing to help her, or that her brother will have nothing to do with her. So in no time at all she and Jorin, the blind, cat-like ounce with whom she has bonded, are off and away once more, barely one step ahead of a multitude of dangers."

"Stated so simply as I have above, the bare bones of the plot undoubtedly sound like that of any one of the literally dozens of derivative fantasy novels that clog the shelves of our bookstores, but that's far from the case here. Like Guy Gavriel Kay and Patricia A. McKillip, like Jane Yolen and Midori Snyder and a very few other talented fantasists, Pat works with the archetypes of myth and high fantasy and uses them as a means of confronting and dealing with the real world, rather than as simple escapism."

Come check out our web site for details on these Meisha Merlin authors!

Kevin J. Anderson
Robert Asprin
Robin Wayne Bailey
Edo van Belkom
Janet Berliner
Storm Constantine
John F. Conn
Diane Duane

Sylvia Engdahl
Rain Graves
Jim Grimsley
George Guthridge

Keith Hartman
Beth Hilgartner
P. C. Hodgell
Tanya Huff
Janet Kagan
Caitlin R. Kiernan
Lee Killough

George R. R. Martin
Lee Martindale
Jack McDevitt
Mark McLaughlin
Sharon Lee & Steve Miller
James A. Moore
John Morressy
Adam Niswander
Andre Norton
Jody Lynn Nye
Selina Rosen
Kristine Kathryn Rusch
Pamela Sargent
Michael Scott
William Mark Simmons
S. P. Somtow
Allen Steele
Mark Tiedeman
Freda Warrington
David Niall Wilson

www.MeishaMerlin.com